A GUN TO PLAY WITH

When a series of brutal murders are committed in Sussex, Toby Vanne, an American airman on leave in Brighton, finds the dead body of a girl in a field near Lewes. She's been shot in the back with the type of revolver that was used to murder a shopkeeper in Forest Row nearby. The police call in Scotland Yard, but Toby begins his own investigation, taking into his confidence a young widow who is staying at the same hotel.

J. F. STRAKER

A GUN TO PLAY WITH

Complete and Unabridged

LINFORD
Leicester

First published in Great Britain

First Linford Edition
published 2008

British Library CIP Data

Straker, J. F. (John Foster)
A gun to play with.—Large print ed.—
Linford mystery library
1. Murder—Investigation—Fiction
2. Detective and mystery stories
3. Large type books
I. Title
823.9'14 [F]

ISBN 978–1–84782–411–0

Published by
F. A. Thorpe (Publishing)
Anstey, Leicestershire

Set by Words & Graphics Ltd.
Anstey, Leicestershire
Printed and bound in Great Britain by
T. J. International Ltd., Padstow, Cornwall

This book is printed on acid-free paper

Preface

A Gun To Play With is a work of fiction, and all the characters and events portrayed in it are fictional too. But in order to give the story a sense of reality the scene has been set in Sussex, and in Sussex towns and villages. Wherever possible, actual streets and buildings have been named; and the descriptions of these are, as far as I know, accurate. But in some instances I have, for obvious reasons, varied this rule. There is no Coniston Hotel in Hove. Nor is there a Cardiff Street or Smith Street in Brighton, a Union Street in Eastbourne, or a Havelock Drive in Haywards Heath. These, together with the 'Dayanite' Café near Golden Cross, exist only in my imagination.

J.F.S.

1

Sarah Caseman lay in bed and listened to the noises that ought not to have been. She was a light sleeper; it was the tinkle of falling glass that had awakened her. But now there were other noises: soft footfalls on naked boards, the squeaking protest of an unoiled hinge (the counter flap, she thought, her heart bumping wildly), the faint screech of metal against metal.

Terror gripped her, paralysing her limbs. Body trembling, teeth chattering, she lay unable to move. Then, with a supreme effort, she clutched at her sleeping husband's warm, pyjama-clad thigh.

The nervous fingers bit deep into his flesh. 'What the devil — ' he began, brushing her hand roughly away, aware only of the pain and the rude awakening.

'Listen! There's some one in the shop!'

It was an old, ever-recurring scare of Sarah's, but one that never failed to bring him to full consciousness. John Caseman

1

raised himself on his elbows, head off the pillow, listening. From below came a muffled thud, and then another. With an oath he pushed the bedclothes from him and swung his feet to the floor.

'What are you going to do?' she whispered.

'Do? I'm going down, of course.'

He was over sixty and not a big man, but he did not lack courage. He padded softly across the carpet to the bedroom door, struggling into his dressing-gown as he went.

'John, wait! They may be dangerous. They may . . .'

Her voice trailed into silence. He was gone. But in her it was fear, not courage, that produced the will-power necessary to force her trembling body out of bed. She would not stay alone in the dark, waiting for danger to come to her. In imagination she could already hear the creak of stealthy footsteps ascending the stairs, the muttered oaths as hands fumbled at the door-handle. Better to follow John and face in his company whatever threatened.

It took her some time to find and don

slippers and dressing-gown, to grope on her dressing-table for the torch. She had reached the small landing that overlooked the main road when she heard her husband's angry cry. There was the sound of a scuffle, of men swearing. Sarah hesitated. Then, loud and terrifying, came the sharp report of a gun . . . another . . . the thud of a falling body. The torch slipped from her fingers as she clutched at the sill for support. Running feet echoed clearly along the road; automatically, unconscious of the movement of her head, she glanced out of the window, catching a quick glimpse of two dark figures before they were swallowed by the night.

As she left the window to stumble blindly down the narrow stairs she heard faintly the hum of a car gathering speed.

★ ★ ★

The telephone rang in East Grinstead police station. Sergeant Pollock grimaced and reached for the receiver. It was one of those nights, he told himself cheerfully, when the darned thing never stopped ringing. Well, better that than monotonous silence. At least it helped to pass one's spell of night duty the quicker.

'East Grinstead police station,' he said crisply into the mouthpiece.

The voice that answered him was sharp and hurried. The Sergeant scented trouble.

'Dr Carrick here. Is that Sergeant Pollock?'

'Yes, sir.'

'Good. I'm speaking from the Casemans' shop in Forest Row. You know it?'

'Yes. On the Tunbridge Wells road.'

'That's right. Well, about half an hour ago two men broke into the place and shot the old man; he heard them, you see, and went down to investigate. They got him twice — neck and stomach. The ambulance is on its way, but I don't think there is much anyone can do for him now, poor chap.'

Sergeant Pollock drew in his breath, looked at the clock, wrote '01.34 hours' on his pad, and said, his voice briskly efficient, 'Any further information you

4

can give me, sir?'

'Not much, I'm afraid. Mrs Caseman rang me — she didn't think of the police, only of getting help for her husband. I came round right away; luckily I hadn't gone to bed, I was playing bridge. It's difficult to get anything out of her at present — she's not very coherent, poor thing — but I gather she was on the landing when the shots were fired, and saw two men running down the road a few moments later.'

'Can she describe the men?'

'I doubt it. She says she saw the back of one of them — he was short, she says, and wearing a dark jersey and trousers. Nothing about the other. But I haven't questioned her very closely. You may get more out of her later.'

'Did they have a car?'

'She didn't see it, but she says she heard one. Went off towards the village, she thought.' The voice spoke a few soothing words away from the mouthpiece, and then returned to it. 'Hurry, man, will you? The ambulance should be here at any moment, and I'll have to go with it to the hospital. I'll take Mrs Caseman with me. Can't leave her here.'

'I'll have some one there right away, sir,' the Sergeant promised. 'When you've finished at the hospital could you call in here on your way back to Forest Row?'

He replaced the receiver, wrote busily for a few moments, and then reached for it once more. He had known it was one of those nights, he thought grimly. But he hadn't bargained on murder.

★   ★   ★

Geoff Taylor gloomily surveyed that small stretch of the Eastbourne road visible from behind the counter of the 'Dayanite' Café. It wasn't that he minded the solitude (it didn't do a chap any harm to be on his own occasionally), it was the lack of custom that worried him. He needed the money, and he didn't like having to admit that Charlie Ellis had been right. Charlie had been all against staying open so late. 'Nothing doing after midnight,' Charlie had said. 'Of course, if you like sitting on your bum till all hours of the morning, go ahead. It's your bum. But don't expect me to do the same when I take over the night shift. It ain't economic, for one thing; and, for another, I like my bed.' And Geoff had retorted that at least they ought to give it a fair trial; they weren't known yet, he said, they'd only been going a few months. 'You wait till the summer,' he told Charlie. 'We'll do better then. It's only eleven miles to Eastbourne. Chaps'll bring their girls out for a snack and a cuppa after they've been dancing or what-have-you. Makes a nice run before bed. Maybe from Lewes and other places too.' But lately his optimism had begun to wane. The summer was nearly over, and the customers hadn't been rolling up the way he'd expected. That night, for instance — a fine, warm night — he hadn't taken a penny since just after midnight, and now it was nearly a quarter to two. You couldn't call *that* economic. Charlie certainly wouldn't. 'You've got a smashing wife,' Charlie would say, with that suggestion of a leer that always appeared on his face whenever he referred to Claire. 'Why don't you knock off and go home to bed, old man?'

Geoff had an answer to that, only he couldn't explain it to Charlie. Certainly he wanted to be home with Claire — but he also wanted more money. He wanted it so that Claire wouldn't have to work any more. He didn't approve of her working, he didn't like her earning more than he did, and he didn't like the man she worked for. He didn't trust him, either. Mike Watson was one of those flashy, free-and-easy types — a damned sight too free and easy with Claire, thought Geoff — and he wanted watching. The sooner Claire finished with him the better.

On the dark surface of the road a faint glow grew gradually into a dancing white beam, heralding the approach of a car from the north. Geoff Taylor listened intently. The road was straight, and from much practice he had learned to distinguish early between a motor that was slowing down and one that was going past. But this one had him at fault. He had already slumped despondently back on his stool when, with a shrill protest from screeching tyres as the brakes were suddenly applied, a black saloon swept past the range of his vision and came to a halt farther down the road.

Geoff heard it back towards the 'Dayanite' and stop short of it. He pumped expectantly at the Primus. He had noticed two people in the front of the car, but there might be others in the back. He hoped they were hungry. *And* sociable. He could do with a little cheerful conversation. Thinking of Mike Watson had depressed him.

But the man who appeared round the side wall of the café — they called it a café, but in reality it was no more than a coffee-stall — did not look a promising customer. He wore a blue suit, with highly polished brown shoes and dirty chamois gloves; his hair, sleeked and darkened with dressing, was in sharp contrast to the pale, bushy eyebrows. He answered Geoff's friendly greeting with a curt demand for two teas and two hot-dogs, and then walked to the edge of the pool of light and stood looking back up the road towards Uckfield.

Geoff poured tea from the urn, split the sausages, and placed them between thick slices of bread. 'Fine night,' he said, when the man returned to the counter. 'Just right for a spin, eh?'

The other grunted. He removed a glove, took a large, untidy bite at one of the hot-dogs, and then picked up the other hot-dog and a cup of tea and disappeared in the direction of the car. when he returned Geoff said hopefully, 'Your friend might like one of those cakes. They're quite fresh, tell her.'

The man stared at him, a cup of tea half-way to his lips. It was then that Geoff noticed the middle finger of his right hand was missing.

'No, thanks,' said the man. The stare wavered, and he turned to look over his shoulder. 'You get a lot of traffic on this road?'

'Not at this time of night, worse luck. You're the first customer I've had for over an hour and a half. Gets a bit monotonous. Come far?'

The other shook his head, finished his tea in one noisy gulp, put down the cup

— not very surely, so that it rattled in the saucer before settling — and once more walked away to peer intently up the road. Geoff began to feel uneasy. I don't like this bird, he told himself; he's got the wind up good and proper, or I'm a Dutchman. Giving me the jitters too; a chap doesn't act that way this time of night unless he's been up to something he shouldn't have. I'll be glad when he gets a move on.

The man came back and finished his hot-dog. Neither of them spoke. When the stranger suddenly put his hand to his pocket Geoff ducked instinctively, half expecting a gun. But it was only a crumpled ten-shilling note that was slapped on the counter. Geoff reddened, hoping the other hadn't noticed.

A car door slammed. Both men started. Keyed up as they were, any sudden action or noise was frightening.

'Quick, Joe! A car!'

The voice, low and with a metallic timbre, was as urgent as the words. The man in the blue suit did not wait for his change. In a flash he was gone. The door slammed again, an engine sprang to life, and the car moved away fast, its gears being changed in rapid succession.

Geoff Taylor came out from under the shelter of the 'Dayanite' and watched the red tail-light vanish in the direction of Eastbourne. Had that been a man's or a woman's voice, he wondered. Despite its urgency, there had been no fear in it, but rather a suggestion of pleasurable excitement; as though its owner were enjoying the chase — if chase there were. Yet Blue Suit himself had been scared stiff; no doubt about that. Geoff had seen his face when the voice had called.

He became aware of a glow on the road behind him, and turned to see the headlights of another car approaching. So that was what had caused them to skip! Maybe this was the police in pursuit.

He stood to watch the second car speed past — a cream-and-green Ford Zephyr, its driver the only occupant. Not the police, then, he realized, with a slight feeling of disappointment. Perhaps they weren't crooks. Perhaps Blue Suit had eloped with the boss's daughter, and that was her old man after them. And yet — well, in that case, why should the man be scared? Anxious, yes. But not scared, surely?

The man had left his glove on the counter, along with the ten-bob note. There was no name in the glove, either maker's or owner's. Geoff remembered the cup and saucer and plate that had gone with the car; well, the ten bob would cover that and the grub: he wasn't out of pocket. And he'd had a bit of excitement into the bargain. And that was that.

But it wasn't that. He could not put the incident out of his mind. He continued to puzzle over it on the way back to the small villa in Polegate that he and Claire had bought on mortgage two years before. He was still puzzling over it when he went upstairs to bed.

Claire was asleep, but she awoke as soon as he opened the bedroom door. She always did. He felt guilty sometimes, spoiling her night's rest. But Claire said it wasn't his fault; she was a light sleeper. And she never complained.

He went across to the bed and kissed

her, happily aware of the warm body under the lacy nightdress. 'You look good,' he said. 'Smell good, too.'

'You make me sound like the Sunday joint.' Her voice was lazy with sleep. 'How's business? Any better?'

He shook his head.

'No. Charlie's right, there isn't enough traffic on the road after midnight to make it worth while.' Her nearness, the scent and beauty of her, made the mere acquisition of money seem an unimportant thing. 'Might as well pack it in at eleven, and have a decent night's sleep for a change.'

She laughed at him gently. 'I wish I had a pound for every time you've come home and said that. I'd be almost rich by now.'

'I know. But this time I think I mean it. I'm fed up. Charlie doesn't stay after eleven when *he's* doing nights, so why should *I* be the mug? No. I'll give it one more week-end, and then finish. You'll see.'

Now thoroughly awake, the girl lifted herself on her elbows to look at him more

14

closely. She decided that he did indeed mean it.

'That's silly, Geoff. You're not giving it a fair trial. You said yourself it would take time to work up a decent trade, and now you talk of throwing in your hand after — what is it? — less than six months. That's not long enough, surely? I should say you ought to give it a year at least.'

He was disappointed. He had expected her to welcome the suggestion, to delight in the thought of having him home earlier. Of course, what she said made sense. But he was thirty-two, and Claire was five years younger, and when you were young and in love and had been married only two years it wasn't natural always to be practical. There were other and more important things than money.

He shrugged his shoulders non-committally. Because he didn't want to argue the point he told her about the man in the blue suit. 'I was thinking of going to the police,' he said.

'What on earth for?'

'I think he's a crook, that's why. The

car was probably stolen. A chap like him didn't look right in a Daimler, somehow.'

'Why not? All sorts of people have expensive cars these days.'

'I know. But he just wasn't the Daimler type. And it can't do any harm to let the police know.'

'If you're right — if this car *was* stolen — you don't want to get mixed up in it,' Claire said earnestly. 'Men like that can be dangerous. And if you're wrong you — well, you'd just look silly.' She yawned. 'You stay away from the police, darling. And come to bed now. I have to get up in the morning and go to work.'

He was tired too, and eager to do as she suggested. But when he came downstairs at eleven o'clock the next morning the incident still troubled him. He turned it over in his mind as he cooked his breakfast — Claire had been gone some hours — but it was not until he was eating his cereal that he thought to look at the daily paper.

It was on the front page; a small paragraph half-way down one of the middle columns:

16

SHOPKEEPER WOUNDED BY THIEVES

Shortly before one o'clock this morning two thieves broke into a small grocer's shop near Forest Row, Sussex. Mr John Caseman, the proprietor, who lives with his wife in a flat above the shop, was shot at and seriously wounded while tackling the intruders, who are believed to have got away in a car.

And then, in the Stop Press:

SHOP CRIME

John Caseman died shortly after being admitted to hospital.

His breakfast forgotten, Geoff sat pondering his problem. It did not take him long. Claire had said not to go to the police, not to get involved. But Claire hadn't known then about the shooting at Forest Row. That was murder. And if Blue Suit and his pal were responsible for that — as Geoff was convinced they were (why else the gloves, the nervousness, the sudden dash when pursuit seemed to threaten?) — Claire would be all in favour of his going to the police.

At the Sergeant's house the woman told him that both her husband and the constable were out. Would he leave a message, or call back? Geoff said he would do neither. He had shopping to do in Hailsham, he would see the police there.

The inside of Hailsham police station was unfamiliar to him. As he stated his business to the station sergeant excitement was tinged with disappointment. An ordinary front door, a passage with coat-pegs on the wall, and an outer office that might have been the gateway to any man of business had it not been for the uniforms of its two occupants. There were no steel grilles, no long and sinister passages leading to the cells. His ego felt deflated by this apparent ordinariness.

But Inspector Bostrell helped to revive it. He seemed impressed by Geoff's story. 'You were quite right to come to us, Mr Taylor,' he said. 'It may turn out to be a red herring, but we can put up with a few red herrings if we hook a real fish now and again. I'd like you to repeat your story to the detective-sergeant.'

He led the way out into the passage and through a door marked 'Court Room.' Geoff followed. This at least was more like the real thing, he decided, his imagination peopling the wooden benches with dangerous criminals and nervous witnesses, and the daïs with stern-faced magistrates. They went out into the open and across a courtyard; and then they were in a bare, white-washed office in which a broad-shouldered man in grey flannels and sports jacket sat writing at a table. The Inspector introduced him as Detective-Sergeant Greenley.

'What did this chap look like?' asked the Sergeant, after the story had been repeated and he had examined the glove.

Geoff told him. He was naturally observant, and he had had time enough in which to study the man in the blue suit closely.

The Sergeant nodded approvingly.

'Good. We should be able to recognize him from that. You say the car was a black Daimler saloon. Did you get the registration number?'

No, said Geoff. The man had not given him a chance, he had cleared off too quickly.

'What about the other occupant of the car? Did you catch a glimpse of him?'

'No. He — '

Geoff stopped, puzzled. They seemed to take it for granted that the other was a man. And one paper had described the thieves as two men. Yet he was sure that was wrong. He could not say why, but instinctively he knew that there had been a woman in the car.

'What's up?' asked the Sergeant. 'Remembered something?'

'I think the other person was a woman,' Geoff said slowly. 'Don't ask me why — I didn't see her, I just got that impression. And it wasn't because of her voice when she called out; it wasn't any shriller than a man's might have been if he were excited.' He grinned sheepishly. 'You probably think I'm daft, eh? But I bet it *was* a woman.'

The Sergeant considered this.

'It wouldn't be because this other person stayed in the car?' he asked. 'You are probably accustomed to couples pulling up at night, and the woman staying in the car while the man takes the grub out to her. It often happens like that, doesn't it? So maybe that was why you got the idea last night.'

Geoff goggled at him.

'Yes. Yes, of course. Two men in a car, and they both get out. But if only one gets out, nine times out of ten the other's a woman. Or a child. And this wasn't a child's voice.' He felt aggrieved that the other should have rooted out so easily the cause of his conviction — a conviction he had not been able to fathom for himself. Yet realization of the cause discredited the effect. It might have been fear of recognition, not sex, that had made Blue Suit's companion stay in the car. 'He might even have wanted to make me *think* he was a woman,' Geoff said, explaining the drift of his thoughts.

'He might,' the Sergeant agreed.

'It said in the papers that the Forest Row crime was committed by two men.' The detective's eyebrows lifted, and Geoff added hastily, 'I was thinking, you see, that that's who they were.'

'That is outside our province at the moment, Mr Taylor. Speculation will get us nowhere. What we have to do is to pass your information to those who can make the best use of it.'

When the Inspector returned after escorting Geoff Taylor from the premises Greenley was studying the map. 'That chap was probably right,' he said. 'He — ' The phone rang, and he picked up the receiver. 'For you.'

For a few moments Bostrell listened attentively. Then he began to give instructions, occasionally glancing at the Sergeant for confirmation. As he replaced the receiver, 'That was Mr Renwick, from Jevington,' he said. 'He's found the Daimler. It was parked on his land some time before six o'clock this morning, and it's still there. As you heard, I told him to keep an eye on it until we get there.'

'They could have been making for Eastbourne,' Greenley said. 'Probably left the main road at Dicker, ditched the car, and did the rest of the journey on foot. However, this is too big for us to handle.

I'll spread the glad tidings around, and then fetch the Daimler in here for safe keeping.' He laughed. 'In a few hours from now this place will be swarming with the Yard boys, I shouldn't wonder. The whole bag of tricks.'

★   ★   ★

When Detective-Sergeant Scott, attached to the local division of the Metropolitan Police, reported back to Croydon police station at six-fifteen that same evening he was met with the information that a certain Joseph Landor was wanted in connexion with the theft of a Daimler saloon car during the preceding night. Scotland Yard had reason to believe the car might have been used in the raid on a grocer's shop in Forest Row, in which the proprietor was shot and killed.

'Some one's pulled a boner,' was Scott's immediate comment. 'Landor may have pinched the car — that's right up his street — but he never did that Forest Row job. I know him. He's no killer, and he doesn't carry a gun.'

'The Yard think otherwise. You find the blighter and get him to talk.'

Joe Landor was not at his lodgings. He had gone out at nine o'clock the previous evening, said his landlady, and had not been back since. She seemed neither surprised not perturbed at her lodger's absence. Scott thought he knew why. But he himself was surprised. Car-stealing and breaking and entering were quite in line with Joe's record. But not violence or murder. Was it coincidence that Joe had been absent from home the previous night, or had he slipped a few rungs lower on the ladder of crime?

'You may find him at Dick's,' the woman volunteered. 'He goes there most evenings.'

Scott knew Dick's well. It lay just off the High Street, a mean and dingy café where food and drink were cheap and served without frills. Not essentially a rendezvous for the shadier characters of the district, it numbered a fair proportion of them among its customers. Dick Roberts, the proprietor, was an American negro from the Southern States; a big man over-burdened with fat, and with the fat man's proverbial good humour. Scott numbered him among his contacts with the underworld — contacts on which, in common with all detectives, he relied largely for information.

'''Evening, Mr Scott,' Dick rumbled, his voice sounding like the echo of an eruption in his enormous stomach. 'Ah haven't seen you around lately.'

'No. Some one in authority blundered. I was given a spot of leave. Cup of tea, please.'

There were four men in the narrow café, all of them strangers to the Sergeant. Three sat at a table, talking together in low voices. The fourth, a dark-haired, sallow-faced man with a hare-lip and a crooked nose, lounged at the counter. Scott wished him farther away. Dick would talk more freely if they were unlikely to be overheard.

But the man pushed his cup forward to be refilled, and did not look like moving. Scott decided to risk a harmless question.

'Has Joe Landor been in this evening, Dick?' he asked.

The grin froze on the negro's face as he turned to look at the man with the hare-lip. Scott, following his gaze, was startled. The man's sallow face was contorted into an even more ugly expression than that with which nature had endowed him. He glared at Scott, the thin lower lip pulled down to reveal uneven, blackened teeth. Then he slapped his cup down in the saucer and stalked out of the café.

The detective watched him go. Puzzled, he turned to the negro.

'What's biting him?' he asked. 'Was it something I said? Or did you forget to put the sugar in his tea?'

The other did not smile. 'It's his sister,' he said, removing the cup and saucer and mopping up the spilt tea. 'She's been missing since last night. He thinks she's gone with Joe Landor. Ah reckon it was your mentioning Joe that upset him, Mr Scott.'

The Sergeant leaned forward, his interest thoroughly aroused.

'What's her name?'

'Cathie. Cathie Wilkes.' Dick nodded

towards the door. 'He's Nat Wilkes.'

'And he thinks she's keen on Joe?'

'No. He says she ain't. That's what puzzles him, he says. Why should she run off with a man she don't even like?'

'Why indeed. How old is the girl?'

'Twenty-two, twenty-three.'

'Pretty?'

'Nat says so. Ah ain't never seen her.'

'Not much family resemblance, then,' Scott said. 'He's an ugly devil. What makes him think his sister's with Landor?'

The negro shrugged his shoulders.

'He didn't say. Nat Wilkes don't talk much. But he's looking for him, and I wouldn't like to be Joe if Nat finds him. Nat's crazy 'bout his sister, Mr Scott. A bit wild, he says she is; but seems like he don't mind that.'

The message from the Yard had mentioned the possibility of a woman having been in the Daimler with Landor. It seemed more than a possibility now, thought Scott. It also seemed that he had been wrong about Landor. No doubt Landor had persuaded the girl to spend a few days at the seaside with him, and had broken into the Forest Row shop for money with which to finance the jaunt. But why the gun? Why take it, let alone use it?

'What is Mr Wilkes's line of business?' he asked. 'I haven't run across him before.'

The negro glanced nervously at the three seated men. 'There's others been asking that,' he said, his voice low. 'Ah don't 'zactly know the answer, Mr Scott, but between you and me Ah don't think it's legitimate. Ah don't know as he's ever been in trouble with the police,' he added hastily. 'But there's talk.'

The Sergeant nodded. It occurred to him that, even if Wilkes did earn his living on the wrong side of the law, he might at least be prepared to co-operate with the police in finding his sister. Dick had said he was greatly attached to her.

'Where does Wilkes hang out?' he asked.

The negro shook his head.

'Don't ask me that, Mr Scott,' he pleaded. 'Ah don't know for sure, and even if Ah did Ah dursent tell you. Ah ain't 'zactly feared of Nat. But things happen to folk as talk about him. Ah don't want nothink to happen to me.'

Scott knew what he meant. The underworld had its own methods of retaliating on those who opened their mouths too wide. A tip-off to the police when something was cooking; an unfortunate accident; the beating up of the squealer or his dependants.

'Okay, Dick,' he said cheerfully. 'We'll find him without dragging your name into it.'

Again the negro shook his head, his fat cheeks swinging.

'That ain't no comfort, Mr Scott. Nat saw us together, he heard you asking about Joe. If you pick him up he'll still think it was me told you where to look for him.'

★ ★ ★

Geoff Taylor came home earlier than usual the next morning. He took the stairs two at a time. If Claire didn't wake of her own accord he'd wake her himself.

She had not returned from the office before he left for the 'Dayanite.' She might have been working late (she practically ran the Eastbourne business, he knew that), or she might have gone to the flicks; but whatever the reason the result was the same — he hadn't seen her for nearly twenty-four hours. That was no way for a married couple to live. Charlie was right; he was acting daft working so late. He'd see Charlie at the week-end and fix new hours.

The bedroom was in darkness, and for a moment he hesitated in the doorway; Claire usually left the small standard lamp burning for him. Then he felt for the light-switch and snapped it down.

The bed was empty!

He stared at it, unbelieving. It was not until he had searched the house for her and come back to the bedroom that he saw the note on the pillow.

Sorry, darling, but Mike Watson came over from Brighton and asked me to go to Birmingham for him this evening. He ran me home to pack a few things and to say good-bye, but you had already left for the café. I suppose we were late.

Must dash now. Mike's waiting to take me to the station, and there isn't much time. I'll be away about three days — back Monday morning, I hope.

Be seeing you. Look after yourself.

Love,
CLAIRE

He sat down heavily on the carefully smoothed coverlet and rumpled his hair with his fingers. God damn and blast it! he swore savagely. Married two years — and when did we last spend more than a few hours together? This is the second time she's run out on me without warning. She swore she'd never do it again, that she'd tell Watson to go jump in the sea if he asked her. But did she? Did she bloody hell!

He brooded darkly on Watson. Watson was a son-of-a-bitch, a no-good crook; he'd made money too fast to be on the level. A ruddy great mansion out at Hove, holidays in the South of France, a brand-new car last year and another this. Maybe he had treated Claire well; financially, anyway. But Geoff knew the reason for that. Splash enough money around and you got what you wanted. Anything — even Claire. That was Watson's motto. Only he hadn't got Claire, and he never would. Claire was too smart to be taken in by a smooth devil like Watson; she'd take what he offered, but she wouldn't give anything away. Geoff was sure of that. If he hadn't been sure he'd have put his foot down long ago. As he ought to have done, anyway. As he damned well would do as soon as Claire got back.

He went down to the kitchen and made a pot of tea, and sat at the wooden table telling himself what he would say to Claire, to Watson, even to Charlie, the next time he saw them. Dawn was breaking when he climbed, tired and angry and frustrated, into bed.

2

Lieutenant Toby Vanne, of the United States Air Force in Britain, jerked himself upright and twisted the steering-wheel sharply to keep the Riley away from the verge. The sun was hot, and leaden weights seemed to be dragging his eyelids down. He began to regret his visit to the pub in Alfriston; it had been stupid to put away four pints of beer in the middle of the day, with no lunch in his stomach to act as blotting-paper. In fact, it had been mighty stupid to drink beer at all. He didn't really go for the warm British variety, though custom had inured him to it.

He wondered idly what had happened to his appetite; although it was past one o'clock he had no desire to eat. All he wanted was to close his eyes, to relax against the warm, comfortable leather, and doze. He gripped the wheel more firmly, finding the impulse almost irresistible. The best thing you can do, fellow, he told himself sternly, is to find a nice, quiet spot in which to park, and have a nice, quiet snooze. You'll end up in the ditch, else.

The road bent sharply to the right, but straight ahead a rutted, grass-grown track led to what in the distance appeared to be a disused barn. With relief he accepted his own advice and, changing down, bumped slowly along it. The barn was still in service, he saw, with bales of hay stacked at one end; but behind it a field of corn had encroached on to the paths and among the crumbling walls. It was quiet and peaceful and solitary. Toby stopped the car, slid into the passenger seat, and was almost instantly asleep.

He awoke with a stiff neck, a mouth like an ash-can, and a realization that he would have to do something about that half-gallon of beer. Rubbing his eyes in the strong sunlight, he walked round to the back of the barn, the corn swishing against his legs. He had slept, he discovered with surprise, for little over half an hour.

Low brick walls criss-crossed the area,

and, nature assuaged, he was tempted to explore. But he did not get far. As he peered round the first wall he found that he was not alone. A trouser-clad figure lay there on its stomach, arms outflung, its head almost hidden by the corn. Toby hesitated, wondering if the stranger were asleep. It was an odd and uncomfortable spot to choose for an afternoon nap. An uncomfortable position, too; on a slope, with the head well below the level of the feet. He crept a little nearer, and stopped. A shiver rippled down his spine. The corn was red about the recumbent figure, an ugly purple stain disfigured the blue jersey. And in the centre of the stain a neat round hole spoke eloquently of death.

Toby was twenty-five; an easygoing, friendly young man, broad-shouldered and of medium height. Life for him had been easy and pleasurable, a cheerful journey unhampered by financial worries or ill-health. He had never been confronted with a dead body, had not even come close to an ailing one. It is doubtful whether even in the air he had given death more than a passing thought. But now, when the shiver had passed, and with it the momentary impulse to turn away, he went forward and knelt beside the body. He was surprised to find that it was that of a woman. He touched her cold cheek softly with his fingers, and then, very gently, he turned her over. The body felt stiff and the limbs were set, but he felt no revulsion. Only anger, and a deep pity.

He sat back on his heels to study her.

She was young and, even in death, very beautiful. Her eyes were closed, the jet-black hair framing the pallor of her face. There was an aura of peace about her, he thought — and felt relieved that death need not, after all, be horrible to look on. Certainly it was not so with her.

He began to consider what he must do. The police would have to be notified — but how? Should he telephone them from one of the houses down the road? That meant publicity; and for a reason he did not try to analyse he disliked the thought of strangers gaping at the dead girl. Her pathetic loveliness, which alive he might perhaps have passed unnoticing, had touched a chord in his heart. All her defences were down now, he told himself. He alone could protect her.

There would be a police station in Lewes. He would go there.

As he turned to leave he noticed a small piece of paper among the beaten corn. He had an intense dislike of litter, and mechanically he retrieved it and stuffed it into a trouser-pocket. He fetched his rug from the car and laid it gently over her. Then, with a prayer that she might remain undiscovered until he could return, he set off for Lewes.

The journey was short and he drove fast, his eyes fixed on the road ahead and his mind on the girl. It seemed inconceivable that any man (instinctively Toby assumed that the killer had been a man) could take life from so lovely a creature. If he could be given the chance to avenge her . . .

He gripped the wheel fiercely, and swore.

Lewes police station stands at the junction of several narrow streets, but

Toby was in no mood to bother about possible parking regulations. He pulled up squarely in front of the building and made for the door indicated by the familiar blue lamp. At the counter (rather like the reception desk at an hotel, he thought) a short, square-looking man was talking to the elderly constable.

'I was on my way home from Eastbourne,' the square man was saying. 'I parked the car outside the Crown at about one-fifteen and went in to lunch. When I came out a few minutes ago the damned thing had gone.'

'One moment, sir.' The constable came round the side of the counter and opened the door of a room opposite. 'Would you mind waiting in here, please?' he said to Toby. 'I won't keep you long. Or is your business urgent?'

Toby hesitated. No doubt the police would say it was extremely urgent. They would want to go dashing off to take finger-prints and photographs, to hunt for clues among the corn, to send out terse radio messages to other policemen and issue carefully worded statements to the

Press. But what was to be gained by all that? It might give the murderer a few more minutes of unhappy freedom, but it would not bring the dead girl back to life.

'No,' he said slowly. 'No, it isn't urgent, I guess.'

The constable eyed him speculatively and then went out, closing the door behind him. Toby knew that his argument was ill-founded, that he was being foolish and selfish. He was greedily hugging his secret when he should have been confiding in the police. He began to wish that he had answered differently.

How tough could a British policeman get?

'Name and address, please?' he heard the constable say, and noticed that the door of the waiting-room was ajar. The latch must be defective, he thought. Then came the square man's voice. 'Waide. George Waide. No. 15 Havelock Drive, Haywards Heath. I'm the Southern Area representative for Gay and Wyatt, the soap people.'

'And the number and make of the car, Mr Waide?'

'XYKC 71. A black Austin A40.'

'Were the doors locked?'

'No. Silly of me, I know. But I forgot.'

'One moment, please.'

Toby heard the constable repeating the details over the telephone, and his thoughts drifted back to the dead girl. He was not interested in the square man's missing car. Who was she, where had she come from? She would be about his own age, he thought, or perhaps a little younger. He had seen no ring on her left hand. There would be no husband or fiancé to mourn her.

He found himself wishing he could have seen her eyes.

'We will inform you as soon as the car is found, Mr Waide,' the constable was saying. 'Are you returning to Haywards Heath now?'

'Yes. I'll be there for the next fortnight. Just starting my holidays — and with no car, damn it! The wife will be furious.'

Toby was suddenly impatient, and a little fearful. He had been a fool to delay his report. No doubt the police would take a pretty bum view of his behaviour.

They might even suspect him of the murder.

This last thought was so alarming that he immediately opened the waiting-room door and went into the passage. The square man was just turning away from the counter. He had a round, tanned face, with a snub nose and little sunken eyes. His grey hair was beautifully waved. Toby thought it odd that a middle-aged man with a bulging waistline and no good looks should go to such trouble over his hair.

He waited until Waide had gone before he said, with some diffidence, 'I've found a body. A girl.'

The constable looked shocked and reproachful.

'We should call that urgent here, sir,' he said. 'You are sure she is dead?'

'Quite sure. She's been shot in the back. Must have been dead for at least some hours, I guess.'

The constable asked a few pertinent questions, and then said, 'You had better see the Divisional Detective-Inspector, sir. Come this way, please.'

41

They went along corridors and up a flight of steps into a small, bright room containing a table and two chairs. There the constable left him. 'Detective-Inspector Kane will be with you shortly,' were his parting words. Toby, now fully conscious of his guilt, wondered whether they constituted a threat or a promise.

But there was nothing threatening in Inspector Kane's appearance. He was a pleasant-spoken, spruce-looking man in a well-fitting grey suit, with matching tie and handkerchief. Toby thought him something of a dandy, but was relieved at his apparent mildness.

'You seem to have been rather dilatory in reporting this, Lieutenant,' Kane said, not unkindly. 'The telephone would have been quicker.'

'I know. But I figured secrecy was more important than time,' Toby defended himself.

'Not much secrecy about murder. Where is she?'

'I don't know. I mean I know, but I can't pinpoint the exact location. About four miles from here on the Polegate road.'

He went on to describe the lane and the barn, and the Inspector nodded. 'I know the place,' he said. 'We'll go out there. Excuse me while I put through a telephone call first.'

Left alone, Toby began to wonder about his lunch. Would they still be keeping it for him at the hotel? It seemed unlikely that he would ever eat it, unless Mrs Buell dished it up again for dinner.

The Inspector did not keep him waiting long. They drove down the steep High Street, past the lights and over the river, and at the bottom turned right along South Street. Once out of the traffic the car speeded up.

Toby found himself being questioned about his own movements that day. Where had he come from, where had he stopped *en route*, at what time had he left the pub in Alfriston? 'You can't identify the girl, I suppose?' asked Kane. 'Never seen her before?'

No, said Toby, he had never seen her before. I wish I had, he thought sadly, his mind enriching itself once more with a vision of her beauty. He was wrapped in a romantic dream, so that the veiled suspicion in the other's words were lost on him. Inspector Kane looked at him pensively. Seems a nice young chap, he thought, and probably on the level. But his wits seem temporarily to have deserted him. No doubt corpses are scarce in his life, and that's how they take him. And Americans — well, one never knew quite how tough or how sentimental they could be. An odd mixture.

'Been over here long, Lieutenant?' he asked.

'Nearly two years,' Toby said.

'Like it?'

'Uh-huh.' Normally he was enthusiastic about England, but now the conversation barely touched the fringe of his mind.

Since polite conversation seemed likely to be one-sided, the Inspector returned to the job in hand. 'How is the girl dressed?' he asked. Soon he would see for himself, but it did no harm to test the young man's powers of observation.

Toby told him.

For a moment there was silence in the car. Then Kane said, his voice taut, 'Say that again, will you?'

'Dark blue sweater and dark blue corduroy pants,' Toby repeated obediently, surprised at the interest shown in such a trivial point. What did it matter how the girl was dressed? She was dead; that was what mattered.

'And her hair? How about that?'

'Dark, and cut short. Kind of brushed forward, the way a lot of girls do it nowadays. I wouldn't know for sure what they call it. I'm not well up in hair-styles.'

'Poodle cut,' suggested the other, who thought he was. He leaned forward and told the observer to contact Control on the radio. Then he scribbled a message on a pad and gave it to the man to put through.

'This is it,' Toby said.

As they moved slowly down the track the observer was transmitting, giving a map reference and describing the way in which the girl was dressed. Toby heard a reference to Scotland Yard, but he was not greatly interested. He wondered if he would see the girl again before they took her away. He wasn't even sure that he wanted to. Not in that company.

He did not see her again. From behind the wall he pointed to where she lay, and then returned to wait by the cars. Men from the second car began erecting canvas screens round the body; a woman and three children, attracted by the unusual activity, appeared to gape. A policeman brought him his rug.

Other cars continued to arrive; with more policemen, he supposed, although only a few of the men were in uniform. There were photographers and a doctor. Sick at heart, he watched them all disappear behind the barn; in unhappy imagination he saw them mauling her about, prying and probing and searching. To them she was not just a beautiful girl lying quietly among the Sussex corn; to them she was a corpse, a body to be identified, the victim of a crime which it was their duty to investigate. She was, in fact, only another job. There would be little pity in their hearts, no romance in their souls.

A van came slowly down the track, turned, and backed close to the wall. Two men lifted from it what looked like a coffin, and Toby shuddered and turned away.

'I'm sending you back to Lewes now, Lieutenant,' said Inspector Kane, appearing suddenly from behind. 'You will have to wait at the station for us, I'm afraid. We haven't quite finished with you yet.'

He was glad to go. He did not want to see them take her away — he wanted to remember her as he had last seen her. But back in the familiar waiting-room at the police station he began to analyse his emotions, to chide himself for his foolishness in seeking romance in such an episode. The girl is dead, he told himself; she may be beautiful, but she's dead. You can't get het up over a girl who's dead — who, as far as you are concerned, was never even alive.

Dead! Dead! Dead! He hammered the word into his brain, hoping thus to cure his sickness.

He had to wait some time. When Inspector Kane returned he had with him a companion whom he introduced to Toby as Detective-Superintendent

47

Herrod of Scotland Yard. Toby looked at the newcomer with interest. Back in the States he had read plenty about Scotland Yard.

Maurice Herrod was forty-six; an inch or so under six feet, of medium build and inclining to stoutness. His dark hair was flecked with grey, there were creases at the corners of his startlingly blue eyes. He had a hawk-like nose, large protruding ears, an almost walnut complexion, and the slightly impatient air of a man who is always in a hurry. Apart from the walnut complexion, he reminded Toby of an American business friend of his father's.

'An unfortunate start to your leave, Lieutenant,' Herrod said. His voice was low-pitched, sympathetic. He reached for a chair and sat astride it, his arms resting on the tall back. 'Well, we won't keep you much longer. Just a few routine questions.'

If they were routine they were certainly probing, Toby thought. He felt quite exhausted when at last they were done, and he was out in the open again with Inspector Kane. As he climbed into the

Riley he said, 'I hope you are satisfied, Inspector. I don't want to spend the next two weeks dodging in and out of police stations. Hadn't you best check the car for finger-prints, just to know for sure that I didn't kill her?'

Inspector Kane grinned at him.

'That, sir, has already been taken care of,' he said cheerfully.

★   ★   ★

Superintendent Herrod held a conference that evening in the office hastily prepared for him at divisional headquarters. At the Chief Constable's request he had been deputed by Scotland Yard to assist the county police in dealing with the Forest Row murder. Now, with the discovery of the second murder, he had moved south to Lewes. 'It would seem that the two crimes are connected, sir,' he had told the Chief Constable. 'In which case I'll be better placed here than at East Grinstead. There's not much more to be learned at that end, I fancy.'

There were a large number of police

officers in the room: Baker, the County Detective-Superintendent; the Superintendents and Detective-Inspectors of the Lewes and Uckfield divisions; Inspector Bostrell and Detective-Sergeant Greenley from Hailsham; Detective-Sergeant Wood, of Scotland Yard, Herrod's assistant; and several less senior officers. Both Herrod and the Chief Constable believed in keeping every one fully informed. Nor were they alike only in this. Although dissimilar in appearance — the Chief Constable was tall and slim and, although older than the detective, looked considerably younger — both men were impatient of delay or incompetence, and expected of those under them the keenness which they themselves displayed. And, because they were of the type who inspire others, they usually got what they wanted.

'Landor seems to be our man,' Herrod was saying. 'His prints are on the Daimler (not on the wheel, but there is a good set upside down on the off-side door — made when he closed it, no doubt), and his description tallies with that of the man seen by Taylor at the 'Dayanite'

Café. John Caseman was shot at approximately one o'clock on the morning of the 12th; and three-quarters of an hour later Landor pulled up at the 'Dayanite,' twenty-five miles away. And Landor, remember, has been missing from his lodgings since the evening of the 11th.' He picked up a photograph and handed it to the Chief Constable. 'That's him, sir. I'm having it circulated. It ought not to be long before we pick him up.'

'I hope not. Brighton and Eastbourne are on the look-out for him. So are West Sussex.'

'Were the girl's prints on the car?' asked Baker.

'No.'

'Then there's little to connect her with Landor, is there? Nor with the Forest Row job?'

'Not specifically. But she answers the admittedly vague description of the 'man' seen by Mrs Caseman; short, wearing dark trousers and jersey. Five foot six is short for a man, though not for a woman. And both she and Caseman were killed by bullets fired from a .25 automatic. We haven't had the ballistics report yet, but no doubt we shall find that they were fired from the same gun.'

'Had the girl been interfered with in any way?' asked the Chief Constable. 'I'm trying to get at motive.'

'No, sir. And no sign of a struggle. When the gun was fired it could have been only a few inches from her back. It's my opinion they quarrelled over the money stolen from Caseman's shop.'

'Or perhaps Landor couldn't trust her to keep her mouth shut,' Inspector Kane suggested. 'If, as the Croydon report suggests, she was Catherine Wilkes, she had no criminal record and she was not infatuated with Landor. So maybe she boggled at murder.'

Herrod nodded approvingly.

'Good man. Yes, that's very likely. No quarrel, then — just a bullet when she had her back turned.' He frowned. 'Of course, she may not be Catherine Wilkes; and if she is it may prove difficult to identify her. The Croydon police cannot find anyone who admits to knowing the girl by sight, and Wilkes himself seems to have vanished from the district.'

'They don't sound like pillars of respectability,' was the Chief Constable's comment. 'But, crook or no crook, Wilkes may come forward when he reads her description in the evening papers. If he connects Landor with her disappearance the news of her murder should make him as anxious as we are to lay Landor by the heels.'

'One of the most puzzling aspects, to my mind, is Landor's use of the gun,' Herrod said. 'He has never been known to carry one before (or so say C.R.O.), and at his age he should have worked himself into a groove. A crook is as liable as any of us to commit murder, given sufficient incentive; particularly when a woman is involved. I grant you that. But what can have prompted him to take a gun with him on this expedition? Neither Caseman's nor the girl's death can have been premeditated, surely?'

The telephone rang. He picked up the receiver, and after listening for a moment handed it to the Divisional Superintendent.

'For you.'

The Superintendent dealt with the call. 'The Brighton police have picked up that Austin,' he said, when he had finished. 'The one that was stolen from outside the Crown early this afternoon. It was found abandoned in a side-street.'

'About that gun,' Herrod said, annoyed at the interruption, and trying to pick up his train of thought where he had left it. 'According to Landor's record, he doesn't appear to have been very successful at his chosen profession. He's had four previous convictions, and two of them after being caught red-handed. Yet on neither of these two occasions did he show any fight. So why the gun now?' And, having made his point, he asked, 'What's this about a stolen car? Anything in it for me?'

'There could be,' the Chief Constable said, and told him about Waide.

Herrod was enthusiastic.

'You're right, sir. It fits in very tidily. They abandoned the Daimler at Jevington at some time between 2 and 6 A.M. yesterday. We thought they were making for Eastbourne. Well, that may have been their original intention, but they seem to have changed their plans. Perhaps they guessed we'd look for them there, and came this way instead. The girl was killed at around two o'clock this morning — which means they had at least twenty hours to get from Jevington to where Vanne found the body. How far would that be?'

'Under ten miles, anyway. And there is a track over the Downs which would take them most of the way.' The Chief Constable leaned across to indicate a route on the map spread out on the table. 'It's a lonely bit of country; ideal from their point of view.'

'And you think Landor came on to Lewes this morning and pinched the Austin?' said Baker.

'I do,' Herrod said firmly. 'If we don't find his prints on it I'll eat my hat. Yours too, if you like.'

The Chief Constable laughed.

'I hope you don't suffer from indigestion, Mr Herrod,' he said. 'Superintendent Baker takes an outsize in hats.'

3

Coniston was a small private hotel run on the lines of a guesthouse. Toby Vanne, both as a boy and as a young man, knew it well. His father, as fervid an Anglophile as was his son, had lived for some years in England. Toby had gone to school in Sussex, and had often spent the summer holidays at Coniston with his parents. 'I like going back to the same hotel,' Mrs Vanne used to say. 'It's so nice to be welcomed as a *friend*. And there's no denying Mrs Buell is an excellent cook.' And on his return to England with the Air Force it had seemed natural to Toby that he should spend an occasional leave at Coniston.

Mrs Buell was the proprietress as well as the cook. She was a faded little woman, with faded eyes and faded hair and tired-looking skin. But she had tremendous energy, and never seemed to stop working. And she was always cheerful.

She welcomed Toby literally with open arms. 'I was worried something had happened,' she said, hugging him. She adored the young American; he was the son she had never had. 'You said you would be here in time for lunch.'

Since he knew she expected it, he kissed her heartily. 'I was detained,' he told her. 'Has Dave Parrot arrived yet?'

Mrs Buell stared at him.

'But didn't you know? He's not coming; his mother is ill. I had a letter from him the day before yesterday.'

Hell! he thought bitterly. First I go get myself involved in a murder, and then Dave has to walk out on me. What the heck is the good of a fortnight here on my own? Might as well pack it in right now. No, I can't even do that. Got to stick around for the inquest, the Inspector said.

He had a small table to himself at dinner. The other guests were mostly elderly couples or families with young children, and he could envisage no pleasant companion from among them. There was a dark-haired girl who sat by herself near the window. She was pretty enough, and at any other time his spirits would have soared at the sight of her. But he was not in a mood for girls, he told himself, thinking of that other.

Nevertheless, he looked at her more than once during the meal. There was something about her that reminded him of the dead girl. He even asked Mrs Buell about her later.

'That's Mrs Tait,' she told him. 'She came this morning. A widow, poor thing — and so young.' A sparkle came into her watery blue eyes. 'I'll introduce you in the morning. It will be nice for both of you to have some one your own age to talk to.' He protested that he was not interested, that that had not been the reason for his query. But she only laughed at him and bustled away.

He went up to his room to finish unpacking, his mind reviewing the day's events. Life seemed depressingly flat at that moment. The dead girl's beauty had stirred the romance which was never far from his soul (he was an impressionable young man); the brush with the police had stimulated his mind. Now there was nothing. And, what was worse, there was nothing to look forward to. Not for fourteen blessed days, if he could stick it that long.

He was picturing the girl again when he recalled something which had puzzled him at the time and had then been swamped by subsequent events. Why had Inspector Kane showed such interest when he had learned how the girl was dressed? And there was something else. Superintendent Herrod, they had told him, was from Scotland Yard. Yet he had appeared on the scene far too quickly to have come down from London. He must have been in Sussex already — yes, and in touch with the local police, or they would not have known where to find him. But what was he doing there? Had there been a previous crime which . . .

He fished out the morning paper; as yet he had had no time to do more than glance at the headlines. Perhaps there was something there which would explain the Superintendent's presence.

It was on the front page. He was surprised that he had failed to see it before.

* * *

The Chief Constable of East Sussex has enlisted the aid of Scotland Yard in investigating the murder of John Caseman, who was shot and fatally wounded when thieves broke into his shop at Forest Row, Sussex, early yesterday morning. Detective-Superintendent Herrod, who was responsible for bringing William Greensmith to trial for the murder of Naomi Cope, the Kensington model, has been assigned to the case.

The thieves, one of whom was described by the murdered man's wife as being short and slight and wearing dark trousers and jersey, are known to have got away with over £100 in cash. A stolen car, later found abandoned near Eastbourne, is believed to have been used in the raid.

* * *

Slight . . . and wearing dark trousers and jersey . . .

'No!' Toby said vehemently, aloud. 'I

don't believe it.' A girl with a face as serenely beautiful as hers couldn't have been a crook — possibly a killer, at that. Either the police or the newspapers had got it wrong.

He looked down at the paper again. There was more.

* * *

The police are anxious to interview a man named Joseph Landor, who they hope may be able to help them in their inquiries. Landor, who lives in Croydon, is aged thirty-eight, is about 5 feet 10 inches in height, and of medium build. He wears his brown hair brushed straight back, and the middle finger of his right hand is missing. When last seen he was wearing a navy blue suit and brown shoes.

Anyone having knowledge of his whereabouts is asked to communicate with the Chief Constable of East Sussex, telephone number Lewes 1111, or with any police station.

* * *

For a while Toby sat on the edge of the bed, thinking about the girl. And Landor. Landor, he presumed, was the man the police held responsible for the shooting at Forest Row. The appeal had been carefully worded, but one did not have to be particularly smart to deduce that.

And Landor had presumably killed the girl as well.

There might be more news in the evening papers. Since the Coniston had no licence he decided to go out for a drink. There was nothing to do in the hotel; he might as well sit in a bar and read the papers over a whisky. It was too early to go to bed.

He had changed before dinner, but he had not transferred all the contents of his pockets. As he fished in his trousers for the loose change he brought out with the money a folded piece of paper. An address was written on it — 17 Cardiff Street, Brighton. It had no significance for him, and he frowned at it, wondering how it had come into his possession.

Then he remembered. He had picked it up near the dead girl.

He felt a twinge of fear. This could be dangerous. The police would never believe the truth — that he had forgotten it, that he had not until now even read what was on it. Already they were suspicious of his behaviour; now they could accuse him of concealing vital evidence, of deliberately impeding the course of justice. What was the penalty for that?

He re-examined the paper. On the reverse side was a roughly drawn map which it did not take him long to recognize as of part of Brighton. The station was marked on it, and the Clock Tower. So too was Cardiff Street, with a heavily inked cross near one end. That, he supposed, indicated No. 17.

How important was it, he wondered. What would the police be able to learn from it? In addition to the address itself, probably the writing and even the paper would provide information for the experts. On the other hand, it might be quite unconnected with the girl. It could have been dropped by some one before the murder was committed; it might have lain there for days. It might be a red herring which would only confuse and mislead.

Toby sighed. That was an argument which did not even convince himself; he knew that he was merely seeking an excuse for not handing the paper over to the police. But at least he need not make an immediate decision. First he would see what the evening papers had to say.

They were all much the same, he found; probably the information had been handed out by the police in the form of a statement. It amounted to no more than he already knew. The body of a young woman had been found by a passing motorist (thank goodness none of them mentioned his name; at least he was unlikely to be pestered by reporters) in a barn near Lewes. And, apart from her description, that was all. Apparently she had not yet been identified.

By the end of his second whisky he was still undecided. He wished he had some one — Dave, or one of his brother officers — whom he might consult. As it was he had to play it alone. Well, there was one thing he *could* do; he could have a look at

No. 17 Cardiff Street. Maybe he would get a lead from there.

It was dark when he left the pub and climbed into the Riley. He did not know the back streets of Brighton well, but he had the map to guide him, and he found Cardiff Street without much difficulty. It was not an attractive thoroughfare; narrow and ill-lit, and flanked mainly by what appeared to be warehouses and small factories. If Brighton had any association with the crime, he thought, Cardiff Street could be the right place in which to look for it.

He drove the length of the street. It seemed deserted, and he turned and came back, stopping the car round the corner to avoid attracting attention. Then, torch in hand, he went in search of No. 17.

Unlike most of the buildings, No. 17 was numbered. It consisted of what appeared to be a double-fronted garage, with a small door at the side leading to a workshop above. By the light of his torch he could see that the upper windows were cracked and dirty; one of them was boarded up. Tiles were missing from the roof, and the general impression was of neglect and disuse. But not so the lower half of the building. There was plenty of rust and little paint, but the big padlocks were bright and had recently been oiled; the two small frosted windows in each of the doors were clean and uncracked.

He tugged at one of the doors, hoping to move it sufficiently to enable him to shine his torch through the resulting gap. But the door did not budge. There was nothing to be learned that way.

He was moving across to the small door at the side when behind him a car door slammed. Toby jumped and turned swiftly. He had not heard the car approach.

'Looking for something?'

The man's voice was smooth but uncultured. He stood by the car, one hand in his jacket pocket. In that dim light Toby could not see his face under the narrow-brimmed trilby. He wondered uneasily if the hidden hand held a gun. In that setting, and with murder fresh in his mind, a gun seemed natural enough.

'I was looking for some place to garage my car,' he said, hoping his voice sounded natural. 'I was told I might strike lucky round here.'

A torch shone suddenly, the beam moving slowly from his feet to his face. Toby blinked and shaded his eyes. The beam left him, moved to the padlocked doors behind, and went out.

'Nothing here,' said the man, his voice more genial. 'You on holiday? Yank, aren't you?'

'American.' And then, deciding it was his turn to ask a question, 'Does this place belong to you?'

'Sort of. Where are you staying? We don't usually get holiday-makers in this part of the town.'

'That's my business,' said Toby, feigning irritation. He would need to know more about his questioner before supplying that piece of information.

To his surprise the man laughed.

'Sure it is. And those locks you were fiddling with are *my* business, see? And there's no garage to let in Cardiff Street. Get me?'

'Sure.'

A match spluttered and went out. Another match — and Toby saw, as the man shielded it to light a cigarette, that his right hand was heavily bandaged. He caught a glimpse of the upper part of the man's face before the match was thrown down.

'Well, I'll be getting along,' Toby said.

'Yes, do that.' The stranger opened the door of the car, and Toby noticed for the first time that there was another man in the driver's seat. 'Enjoy your holiday. But keep down by the sea. It's not supposed to be so healthy up here.'

The door slammed. Toby waited for the car to move. But it remained stationary, and he guessed that they were waiting for him to leave first. He strolled leisurely across the road, passing behind the car and noting the number. It was a Sunbeam Talbot.

As he turned the corner out of Cardiff Street the car still had not moved. Whatever the man's business there, he apparently had no intention of conducting it while there were strangers around.

Back in his room Toby undressed and got into bed, and then lay thinking. It had been a queer incident. A disturbing one, too. The man had seemed pleasant enough, had offered no violence; but he had made it perfectly clear that Toby was not welcome in Cardiff Street. Why? Did No. 17 house something or some one that it would be unwise to allow others to see? That it would be dangerous to allow the police to see? Did it, for instance, house Landor?

That, thought Toby, is jumping too far. Even if there is something crooked going on it doesn't have to be connected with the dead girl. That piece of paper . . .

He wriggled uncomfortably. Stop trying to excuse your behaviour, you damned hypocrite, said his conscience; of course the two are connected. Either the girl or her murderer dropped that address; it would be stretching coincidence too far to suppose otherwise. So the alternatives are obvious. Either you compound a felony by hanging on to that piece of paper and saying nothing to the police, or you hand it over and take what's coming to you.

69

And that will probably be plenty.

The alternatives may be obvious, he answered back, but that doesn't help me to choose. I'm not all that worried about compounding a felony. Not in general, and certainly not with my own neck in danger. I would cheerfully destroy that damned piece of paper and forget all about it. Except for one thing — and that is, that by doing so I may be helping Landor, or whoever murdered the girl, to get away with it. And I'd hate like hell for that to happen. I would rather incriminate myself than feel that I'd betrayed her.

For some time he tossed and turned in the bed, unable to reach a decision. And then, like driftwood to a drowning man, the third alternative occurred to him.

He would catch the murderer himself!

Why not? He knew as much as the police. More — for he alone knew about Cardiff Street. All their resources — their records, their laboratories, their underworld contacts — could not compensate for that piece of knowledge. Landor must be in Brighton (and that was something else they didn't know), and with one finger missing he should be easy to recognize. If that address had any significance — and if it had not he was completely justified in keeping it to himself — he had only to haunt Cardiff Street, and sooner or later Landor must show himself.

It was as simple as that.

He was drifting happily off to sleep when a new and disturbing thought brought him back to full consciousness.

Landor! A finger missing from his right hand!

And the right hand of the man he had met in Cardiff Street had been covered by a bandage.

★ ★ ★

Mrs Buell did more than introduce them. She put them at the same table.

When Toby came down to breakfast the next morning and found the girl already there he could not decide whether to be annoyed or amused. It did not occur to him to be pleased. Now that he had committed himself to a man-hunt he would have preferred to give it his undivided attention. But since he knew she had had no part in the arrangement, that it was due to Mrs Buell's overdeveloped strain of romance, he could not blame the girl. Since she was there it behoved him to be polite, if nothing more.

'I hope you don't think *I* fixed this,' he apologized. 'It was Mrs Buell's idea, not mine.' He blushed, realizing that it would have sounded more gallant had he pretended otherwise. 'But it suits me fine,' he added limply.

Her large, dark eyes considered him. His ginger hair, tough and bristly, was cut very short. His nose was broad and flat, his skin freckled, his eyes grey and set well apart. There was a dimple in his chin; his grin, frequent and boyish, was infectious. And when he spoke his Middle West accent was interspersed, in odd contrast, with an occasional unconscious return to the precise phrasing of an English public schoolboy.

'I don't mind,' she said, her voice low.

He originated what little conversation

there was. But he found it heavy going. Mrs Buell had said she was a widow; since she was so young her husband's death must have been recent (although she was not in mourning, he noticed), and any probing into her past might cause distress. She did, indeed, impress him with an air of tragedy; her smiles were lukewarm, her voice had the ring of pathos in it. She looked thin, he thought — although later he was to revise this impression, for she was slim and beautifully proportioned. But she had obviously lost weight — perhaps through grief over her husband's death — for her frock was gathered at the waist, and a worn mark on the red leather belt showed that the buckle had not always been pulled so tight.

When he ran out of general conversation he began to tell her about himself. But since this to him was an unaccustomed topic the silences grew longer and more frequent.

'It's a grand morning,' he said for the third time, after a particularly long silence. And added as a variant, 'Thinking of going for a bathe?'

She shook her head.

'No. I'm not a good swimmer, and the water will be fairly rough in this breeze.'

'A deck-chair and a book, then?'

'I don't think so. I'll probably go for a walk along the front.'

There was no enthusiasm in her voice. Toby felt a sudden desire to cheer her up. He said impetuously, knowing it would upset his plans and accepting the delay, 'Would you care to come out with me in the car? She's sort of a relic, but she goes.'

The girl turned to him, leaning forward. The dark eyes shone, her lips were parted to show white, even teeth that would have done credit to a dentifrice advertisement.

'I'd love to.'

Toby decided that his sacrifice was amply rewarded.

They climbed the steep hill that leads to the Downs, and for a while sat gazing out to sea over the roof-tops of Brighton. Then down to Patcham and along the main road to Pyecombe, where they forked right to Clayton and Ditchling. At first the girl was silent; but soon she was talking gaily and freely (though not, he noticed, about herself), and he mentally congratulated himself on having drawn her out of her shell. The treatment, he decided, must be continued. A few more doses and she would be a different person.

When they reached the long, straight road that crosses Ditchling Common he said, 'Would you care to take over for a while?'

She accepted with alacrity. She leaned slightly forward as she drove, her body rocking gently, seeming to urge the car on. Toby eyed the mounting speedometer needle with some dismay; she obviously had a mania for speed. But she handled the car well, and he had not the heart to check her enjoyment.

'I love driving,' she said. 'To me everything about a car is exciting.'

'Even the works?'

'Of course. I'm quite an experienced mechanic, and I don't mind how dirty I get.' She took her eyes off the road for a moment to smile at him. 'What made you buy an English car? I thought all Americans went in for Cadillacs and suchlike.'

He grinned. 'The Riley suits me, I guess. I'm an unpretentious guy.'

Some distance ahead of them a cat strolled leisurely across the road, pausing midway to stretch and shake a hind-leg. Then, as they neared it, it suddenly turned and ran back. Involuntarily Toby arched his back, pressing with both feet against the floorboards. But there was no check to the Riley's progress, no hurried tug at the steering-wheel. The speedometer needle barely quivered.

He looked back to where the cat lay dead on the road, and then sideways at the girl. She was gazing straight ahead, intent on her driving. He was beginning to wonder whether she had even seen the animal — until she said, her voice cool and composed, 'No sense in trying to avoid a cat. Not at speed. It might lead to a serious accident.'

She was right, of course; although put like that it sounded callous. He knew that had he been driving he would instinctively have tried to avoid the animal; but that might, as she said, have endangered human life. The girl took no such risk. With her it was first things first. She'd be grand in a tight corner, he thought, with grudging admiration. Grudging — because, however unreasonable the thought, she seemed temporarily to have shed some of her femininity.

On Chailey Common they parked the car and went for a walk. The breeze had dropped, the sun was hot; when they came presently to an invitingly green slope she sat down with a sigh of content. 'I don't know why I chose the sea for a holiday,' she said. 'This is far nicer.'

He stretched himself at her side, propped on one elbow, and watched her covertly as she sat, her arms wrapped round her knees, staring fixedly at the distant Downs. Was he fickle, he wondered, in being glad of her companionship? Yesterday he had mooned over a dead girl; was he now falling for a live one? It wouldn't do, he told himself. He was a man with a purpose, a man dedicated;

until his purpose had been achieved he could not afford diversions. Not even such an attractive diversion as Mrs Tait. If he was set on cheering her up he must be careful not to overdo it.

'What's your first name?' he asked. 'If we are to be friends I can't go on calling you Mrs Tait. Much too formal.'

'Crossetta.'

'Come again?'

She laughed. 'Crossetta.'

'Say! That's kind of unusual, isn't it? I've never heard it before. Does it have any particular meaning?'

'Only to my parents. I think they invented it. Mother said my father had longed for a son, and when I was born she thought he would be terribly disappointed. When he was allowed to see her she said, 'It's a girl, dear. Are you cross?' And he smiled and said, 'No, of course not. Or perhaps — well, just a little cross.' So they christened me Crossetta. But shorten it to Etta if you wish. Most people do.'

'I don't know. I reckon Crossetta might kind of grow on me.'

'I hope it does,' she said softly. He looked up sharply at that, but her face was turned away from him. 'I know *your* name,' she told him. 'Mrs Buell practically gave me your life-history yesterday afternoon. She seems very fond of you; she got terribly worried when you didn't turn up at the expected hour. Why were you so late?'

He did not answer. He was remembering the cat, and the way in which she had handled the Riley. Yesterday he had longed for some one in whom he might confide. And now . . .

'Was it a girl?' she asked, turning to smile at him.

Toby plunged. 'Yes, it was,' he said soberly. 'Only she was dead, and I found her.'

The smile left her face. 'Oh!' she breathed. And then, 'Where?'

'Near Lewes. She had been shot in the back. I told the police, of course. Only unfortunately I forgot something, and now that something looks like being mighty important.' He sat up. 'I'd like to tell you about it if you reckon you won't be bored. May I?'

She shook her head, her eyes intent on his face.

'Of course,' she said. 'It won't bore me, I promise you that.'

★ ★ ★

'Well?' Superintendent Herrod demanded. 'What luck?'

Sergeant Wood shrugged. He was not given to words where words were unnecessary. A long, spare man, almost bald at thirty, he was a great favourite with the Superintendent. Herrod valued his tenacity, his refusal to admit defeat. When Herrod looked ahead Wood looked back, in general refusing even to consider a theory until he was certain of his facts. But he did not lack imagination. Occasionally he surprised both himself and his associates by indulging in a wild flight of fancy. It was as if his imagination had rebelled from being kept constantly in check, and had burst uncontrollably through the barrier erected against it.

'Depends on how you look at it,' he

said now. 'Landor's prints weren't on the Austin. Plenty of others, but not his.'

Herrod swore softly. Superintendent Baker smiled, and pushed his hat gently across the table. 'You might care to make a start on that,' he said. 'Save yours for dessert.'

The other grunted. 'Some other time. I'm not hungry now.' He looked at the Sergeant, and his eyes narrowed. 'Come on, my lad, out with it. I know you. What have you got up your sleeve?'

Wood grinned.

'The dead girl's prints, sir. They were on the Austin.'

The two Superintendents stared at him.

'But that's impossible!' Baker exclaimed. 'According to the doctor, she was killed around two o'clock yesterday morning. That is, twelve hours before the car was stolen.'

'Before the car was *reported* as stolen,' Herrod said.

There was silence. Then Baker said, 'Yes. Yes, I see what you're getting at. If the owner of the car lied about the time and place of the theft — if it was stolen *before* 2 A.M. — then Landor could have driven the girl in it to where we found her, killed her, and then gone on to Brighton.' He frowned. 'It's odd about those prints, though. Landor didn't bother to wipe them off the Daimler; why should he do so on the Austin? How could he, anyway, without removing the girl's as well?'

'Her's were on the steering-wheel,' Wood said. 'She must have been driving.'

'Were they, though! Clear?'

'No. Smudged, as though gloved hands had gripped the wheel after her. But clear enough to identify them.'

'Landor had only one glove,' Herrod said. 'Unless he pinched the girl's; she didn't have them when we found her. But I would like to know why the owner — what's his name, by the way?'

'Waide, sir. George Waide.' Wood had prepared himself for that question. The Superintendent had a good memory for faces, but he was a little weak on names.

'Why should Waide lie if that's the way it happened? He couldn't know his car had been used by a murderer. Personally,

I think we're on the wrong track. It seems to me far more likely that Waide killed the girl. That *would* necessitate a lie. Landor and the girl could have made for Eastbourne and then separated, and Waide might have picked her up later. In the evening, say. Perhaps they went for a spin, and he made a pass at her — and then, when she refused to play ball, he shot her.'

'A bit drastic, don't you think?' Baker suggested. 'And, in that case, who stole the Austin? Some one must have done so, or Waide wouldn't have been fool enough to draw attention to himself by reporting it.'

'And there's the gun, sir,' Wood objected. 'The same gun was used to kill Caseman and the girl. How could Waide have got hold of it?'

'I know, I know!' Herrod sounded impatient. 'I can play that game too. If the girl was just an evening pick-up, what are her prints doing on the steering-wheel? She wouldn't be driving, would she?' He sighed. 'Where does this chap Waide hang out?'

'Haywards Heath.'

'We'll pay him a visit after lunch.' He turned to Baker. 'You might warn the local police. I'd like them to keep an eye on the house until — ' The telephone rang, and he picked up the receiver. 'Who? Oh, yes. Yes, show him up right away, will you?'

There was a pause.

'We've got a visitor,' Herrod said, his voice a purr of satisfaction. 'There's a gent downstairs thinks the dead girl may be his sister. And his name, believe it or not, is Nathaniel Wilkes.'

4

Nat Wilkes's ugliness shook them, as it shook most people when first confronted with it. But he was neatly and unobtrusively dressed and spoke with a cultured accent. Public-school man gone wrong, thought Herrod. Well, with a pan like that he must have found it more than difficult to lead a normal life, poor chap. He'd be something of a liability in office or showroom, and I certainly can't imagine him having fun with the girls.

He began to understand why Wilkes had been so elusive. Why, too, he had been so attached to his dead sister. Hers would be the only feminine beauty Wilkes was ever likely to bask in at close quarters or at all permanently.

I hope he doesn't take it too badly, Herrod thought.

The mortuary adjoined the fire station and was only a few hundred yards from the police station. A uniformed sergeant unlocked the door and stood aside for them to precede him into the bare outer room. The walls were lined with white tiles. To the right two coffin shells rested on brackets, and through the gap they could see the shrouded figure of the dead girl lying on the white pedestal slab in the far room. The air was sweetly heavy with disinfectant.

The sergeant partially withdrew the sheet, and for nearly a minute Wilkes stood motionless, gazing down at the girl's white face. Herrod watched his hands. Hands, to his mind, were often as expressive as faces. But Wilkes's hands did not clench angrily into fists, or nervously twiddle the fingers, or clutch emotionally at their owner's trousers. They remained still.

Wilkes turned, his face as uninformative as his hands. 'Yes,' he said, 'that's Cathie,' and walked with short, jerky steps out into the sunshine.

Back at the police station Herrod asked him about the girl. Wilkes was polite, but obviously unwilling to disclose more than he considered necessary. He had returned to their flat late on the Thursday evening, he said, to find his sister missing. She had left a note to say that she would be away for a few days, and a neighbour had seen her go out earlier, wearing jersey and trousers and carrying a small suitcase. He had no idea what had become of her from then on until he read the description in the newspapers.

'You didn't know she was with Landor?' asked the Superintendent.

'I thought it was a possibility,' Wilkes said guardedly, scowling.

'Why? Was he a friend of your sister's?'

'No. She knew him only slightly. But she had told me the previous evening that he had asked her to go away with him. I told her not to be a fool; Landor was no good, I said. I thought that was the end of it.'

Herrod tried to probe further, seeking background. But Wilkes, having told the essentials, was saying no more. His attitude seemed to be that they knew who the girl was, and it was up to them to find Landor. He had done his part.

'That's all very well, Mr Wilkes. But it

would simplify our task if we knew a little more about them both,' Herrod said. It was unpleasant to have to talk sharply to a man whose sister had just been murdered, but he could not understand the other's attitude. 'You are sure in your own mind that it was Landor?'

Wilkes shrugged. 'Who else?' he asked, gazing out of the window.

The man was too calm, too indifferent. Was it a pose, or had the Croydon police been mistaken in stressing his devotion to his sister? Even the mention of Landor's name appeared to arouse in him no antipathy. Could it be —

'Will you be staying in the neighbourhood, Mr Wilkes?' he asked.

'I don't know. I haven't thought about it.'

'There will be the inquest to attend,' the Superintendent pointed out. 'And no doubt you will wish to make arrangements for your sister's funeral.'

'Yes. Yes, of course.'

But it was clear that the thought had not occurred to him.

'The local police will put you wise,'

Herrod said. 'I'll take you along to the Chief Inspector.'

When he returned to his office he stood for some time staring, as Wilkes had done, out of the window. But his brain registered nothing of what he saw; it was alive with fancies.

Presently he shrugged, tugged impatiently at his tie, and went out to lunch.

* * *

'What do you intend to do?' asked Crossetta, as they walked back to the car.

'Nothing until this evening,' Toby said. 'I'll have to run over to Eastbourne this afternoon. A guy I know is in hospital there. I said I'd look him up.'

He felt immensely cheerful. The girl had been wonderfully understanding, eager to help in a campaign which she had agreed was wrong and had then unhesitatingly accepted. He blessed Mrs Buell for having brought them together. By withholding evidence from the police he considered that he had made the pursuit of Landor his duty. The advent of

Crossetta Tait as an ally made it almost a pleasure.

'And this evening?'

'Cardiff Street,' he said promptly. 'The guy with the bandage — he wouldn't live there, I reckon, but he must live somewhere. If he turns up to-night I'm going to follow him.'

'Do you think he is Landor?'

'Could be. If not, then I guess he knows where the fellow is hiding.'

'May I come with you?' she asked. 'To Cardiff Street, I mean.'

He grinned. 'Sure. Glad to have you. But keep out of the way while the bandage is around. I'd say he's a mean guy.'

They drove back to Brighton through Plumpton and Falmer. On the way Toby said, 'I wonder what goes on at No. 17? It's some sort of a garage or workshop, I reckon — in which case there would be men working there during the day.' He frowned. 'A pity I have to go to Eastbourne. I can't ditch this guy, but I'd sure like to take a look at Cardiff Street this afternoon.'

'I could do that,' Crossetta said eagerly. 'I'd love to.'

The possibility had already occurred to him. But now that she had volunteered he hesitated to accept.

'We don't know what these fellows are up to,' he said doubtfully. 'If they're hooked up with Landor they're probably dynamite. I'll not have you taking risks.'

'Risks are fun. They're what make life worth living.' She turned to him, her eyes sparkling. 'Not that there would be any risks this afternoon. Not in broad daylight.'

'No, I guess not,' he said, pleased at her eagerness. They would be on surer ground that evening if one of them at least had spied it out beforehand. 'Okay. But for the Lord's sake be careful.'

'I find that easier than being good,' she said demurely.

* * *

Toby avoided the police station as he drove through Lewes that afternoon. He had no wish for a further meeting with Superintendent Herrod. But as he approached the corner near where he had found the girl he slowed. Then, acting on impulse, he swung the car on to the track leading to the barn.

Too late he realized that others were there before him. Two cars, one a big grey Buick saloon, the other a police car, were parked at the far end of the track. A uniformed constable was standing near them. But there was no space in which to turn, and he drove slowly on.

Detective-Inspector Kane came from behind the barn with another man, recognized the Riley, and walked over to speak to Toby. He will now be either wittily sarcastic at my expense, the American decided, or damned inquisitive.

But Inspector Kane was neither.

'This is Mr Wilkes, Lieutenant,' he said. 'It was his sister, Miss Catherine Wilkes, whose body you found yesterday.'

Toby gave a quick look at Wilkes's face and shuddered inwardly.

'I — I'm terribly sorry,' he mumbled, knowing it was inadequate.

Wilkes nodded, saying nothing. He

bade the Inspector good-bye, climbed into the Buick, and bumped off down the track.

Toby stared after him.

'He sure is an ugly-looking devil,' he exclaimed. 'I'm sorry for him, naturally, but — well, did you ever see such a face?'

'He certainly hasn't got his sister's looks,' Kane agreed.

Toby sighed. The dead girl's image was not so clear now. It was becoming inextricably merged in his mind with that of Crossetta.

'Not very forthcoming, was he?' he said.

'What did you expect? What *does* a chap say to the man who found his sister's body — 'Thanks very much' or 'Pleased to meet you'? Neither of them sounds right to me.' The detective settled his trilby hat more firmly on his head. 'Well, I'm off. Wilkes wanted to see where she was murdered. Morbid — but reasonable, I suppose. What brought *you* out here again, sir?'

'I was just passing,' Toby said. 'Then I saw the two cars, and wondered what was going on.'

When the police car had disappeared round the corner towards Lewes he decided to leave also. He would not carry out his original intention, which had been to take one final look at the fatal spot. It was, as the Inspector had said, a morbid fancy. Better let it ride; he would learn nothing new.

He spent the afternoon at the hospital, ate a large tea, and then headed back for Brighton. Once in the car again his spirits soared. He told himself it was because he was anxious to get started on his self-appointed task, to hear what information Crossetta had been able to glean. But he had a guilty feeling that it might also be because of Crossetta herself.

He had intended to return along the coast, via Seaford and Newhaven; but he mistook the turning out of Eastbourne, and found himself once more on the Lewes road. As he passed the now familiar track he glanced down it — and braked sharply.

A car was standing by the barn.

He got out of the Riley and walked back to peer up the track. He recognized the car; it was the grey Buick in which Wilkes had driven away a few hours earlier. Puzzled, Toby stood watching. But there was no sign of Wilkes himself, and presently he walked slowly back to the Riley. He did not want the man to think he was spying on him. Only — well, why should Wilkes have returned, and without the police? What could he hope to discover there that he or the police did not know already?

Well, it's none of my business, he thought. But it sure is odd.

He did not see Crossetta immediately on his return to the hotel, but when she came down to dinner she was wearing trousers and a tight-fitting green jersey. Toby winced. Mrs Buell would not approve of such attire, he thought. Neither did he. It reminded him too acutely of Catherine Wilkes.

The girl noticed his disapproving look, and laughed. 'No good your turning up your nose at me,' she said. 'I bought this outfit this afternoon. I can't help it if you don't like it.'

She was slim, and moderately tall. He

thought trousers suited her better than they suited most girls. 'I guess I'm old-fashioned,' he told her. 'I prefer women in skirts.'

'So do I. But I don't intend to explore dirty, cobwebby old buildings in a summer frock.'

'What old buildings?'

She would not tell him at once, tantalizing him. She was all excitement, and he marvelled at the change wrought in her since that morning. He would have liked to think it was due to him, but he knew it was not. The thrill of adventure was upon her.

Eventually she said, her voice conspiratorially low, 'There was some one there this afternoon. I didn't see them, but I heard them working behind those big doors. I thought I might catch them when they left, but they foxed me. They went the back way.'

Toby whistled. 'I didn't know there was a back way.'

'Well, there is. In Smith Street. It runs parallel to Cardiff Street. At the back of No. 17 there's a big yard; it's enclosed by a high wall, but the gate wasn't locked, so I went in and had a look round. There are one or two empty sheds, and a lot of junk. And there is a wooden staircase that leads to the top floor, and' — here her voice sank even lower — 'the door at the top is broken. It won't shut properly.'

'Say! That's great.' And then, alarmed, 'You didn't attempt to explore, did you?'

'No. I wanted to — I even went up a few stairs. Then I realized that once I got above the height of the wall I could be seen from the street, so I came down. Besides, I hadn't got this outfit then, and I knew it would be pretty mucky up there. But I'm certain about the door, Toby. Can we have a look round tonight?'

He nodded dubiously, not wishing to commit himself.

'Do you think anyone saw you?' he asked.

'One or two men went past as I was waiting,' she admitted. 'But I don't think they had any connexion with No. 17. They just glanced at me casually and walked on.'

'They must have had bad eyesight, I

guess,' Toby said gallantly.

But he was worried about the proposed expedition. It could be highly dangerous. The man who had spoken to him in Cardiff Street the previous evening had uttered a fairly blunt warning that it would be safer to stay away from there. And he did not fancy embroiling Crossetta in a possible rough-house.

'What did you do with yourself this afternoon?' she asked.

He told her. Some of the gaiety left her after that, and they finished the meal in silence. When they were drinking their coffee in the lounge he said, 'What's wrong? You've closed down on me.'

'I know. It — well, it was all such fun before. But knowing the girl's name — that makes it more real, somehow. It was just a game — and now it's murder. And then there's her brother, poor thing. Was he terribly upset?'

'Difficult to say. It wasn't easy to watch his face. But he seemed the phlegmatic type. I figured he was more preoccupied than upset.'

'Preoccupied with what?'

'His sister's death, I guess.'

Crossetta shuddered. 'How dreadful for him!'

But she soon recovered her spirits. They decided to wait in a pub until it was dark, bolstering their courage with alcohol. Not that Crossetta's courage needed bolstering, he thought. If either of them had the wind up it was he. Not on his own account, but on hers. He was beginning to doubt the wisdom of allowing her to accompany him.

She went up to her room to get ready. When she came down she was carrying a large white suede handbag on which the initials C.T. were embossed in gilt.

Toby laughed.

'What's the matter?' she demanded. 'What's funny about me?'

'That handbag. I guess it's not quite what the well-dressed burglar is wearing this season.'

She looked at the offending bag and smiled. 'I suppose it is rather conspicuous,' she admitted. 'All right, I'll leave it behind. I'd forgotten I was wearing trousers. I can stuff the essentials in the pockets.'

After a couple of double whiskies Toby felt fine. He noticed that Crossetta drank little; she made one small gin and tonic last the hour and a half they had to wait. But she was as gay as he when they set off for Cardiff Street in the Riley.

It was a dark night, with plenty of cloud and no moon. They parked the car just before the entrance to Smith Street, and the girl led the way into the yard. Toby switched on his torch, and saw that it was much as she had described it. 'Don't shine it up the stairs,' she whispered. 'Some one might see it. Come on, let's go up and have a look round.'

'No,' he said firmly. 'I'm going alone.'

'But I — '

'No,' he said again. And then, with sudden inspiration, 'Always guard your exit; that's an essential. You stay by the gate and warn me if anyone comes. I'll feel safer that way.'

He climbed the stairs gingerly, feeling his way, not daring to use his torch. At the top a railed balcony ran the length of the building, and at the far end of this was the door. Toby reached it, and felt with his fingers for the gap. Yes, it was there. He put his shoulder against the door and shoved carefully, fearful of making a noise. A moment later he was inside.

'Crossetta,' he hissed.

'Yes?'

'I'm in. Keep your eyes skinned. I shan't be long.'

He moved cautiously into the building, leaving the door ajar, and switched on his torch. He was in a large room which, he judged, completely covered the top of No. 17. At one end were piled empty wooden crates and packing-cases, and under the front windows stood several work-benches. Apart from these the room was empty.

No wonder they don't bother to lock the darned place up, he thought, disappointed.

But he did not leave at once. Stepping gingerly on the rotting boards, he searched the floor for a possible trap-door to the garage below. When that failed he remembered the small side-door that opened on to Cardiff Street. The stairs were in the far corner; they creaked and sagged under his weight, but he went down them and along the short passage at the bottom. There were no bolts on the door, but it was securely locked. Examining it by the light of his torch, he doubted if a key had turned in the lock for many months past.

He went back up the rickety stairs, across the dusty floor, and through the far door. He was half-way along the balcony when Crossetta cried out.

'Look out, Toby! There's some one in the yard!'

Her voice came from the gate, but he could not see her. He could not see anyone. For a moment he hesitated, afraid of the danger that might be lurking in the darkness below. Then a gun barked at the foot of the stairs, and a bullet sang upward and past him, burying itself in the projecting roof. He flattened himself against the wall, heart pounding, eyes closed, waiting for the second bullet and the tearing pain that it would bring with it.

But the gun was silent. There was no sound, save from the city outside the yard. And suddenly his fear was gone, and he knew what he had to do. He could not use the stairs, with the gunman lurking at the bottom; and to retreat into the building would be suicidal. In there he would be completely at the man's mercy, for there was no other way out.

Nor could he desert Crossetta.

He edged slowly along the balcony, away from the stairs and towards the door he had just left, thankful for each step that did not bring a bullet. It seemed an interminable age before he had reached the far end and could sink back into the recess of the half-open door. For a moment he waited, listening. Then, galvanizing himself into sudden and violent action, he grasped the balcony rail and, flinging himself up and over, landed with a crash on the corrugated iron roof of the shed below.

Pain shot through his left wrist; his whole body was jarred by the fall. But even had he wished he could not pause. The roof sloped steeply, and he found himself slithering helplessly down it. Then he was at the edge, and had dropped with a thud to the concrete below.

Crossetta was outside the gate. He caught her hand, and together they raced for the Riley.

'Phew!' he breathed, as the car swung away from the kerb and gathered speed. 'That was plenty close. It's the first time I've ever been shot at, and I hope it's the last. It's not an experience I can recommend.' She made no comment, and he asked anxiously, 'Are you okay, Crossetta?'

'Yes, of course.' Her voice was harsh, intense. 'Are you?'

'Yes. I sprained my wrist when I landed on the roof, and there's a damp, sticky feeling to my knees which indicates a loss of skin in those parts. But I'm all in one piece, and with no holes drilled in me.'

He felt exhilarated. He wanted to laugh and to sing, to put his foot down hard on the throttle and feel the Riley move. It had been his first experience of acute personal danger, and he knew that he had acquitted himself well. From now on, he thought elatedly, life can be all bullets and bruises and I shan't care. I can cope, damn them!

'You ought not to have waited,' he said.

'You ought to have cleared off as soon as you'd warned me. The fellow might have taken a shot at you as well.'

Crossetta was silent. Taking a quick glance at her, he saw that her eyes were wet. He pulled in to the kerb, stopped the Riley, and, leaning across, put an arm round her shoulder.

He felt her stiffen and shrink away from him.

'Sorry,' he said, removing the offending limb. 'I wasn't trying to get fresh. I don't like to see you upset, that's all.'

She turned to him then, putting one hand on his arm. Her moist eyes glittered in the lamplight from across the street.

'You don't understand,' she said fiercely. 'I'm not upset because I was scared, but because I let you down. It was all my fault.'

'Nonsense.' Cheerfulness, he decided, was the best cure for what he diagnosed as an understandable attack of nerves. 'I'd have invaded the joint anyway, once I had discovered the way in. You don't want to blame yourself for that. But what I can't figure out is how that guy got into the yard without your seeing him.'

'That's just it, Toby,' she said. 'That's what I was trying to tell you. I didn't stay by the gate.'

'Oh. Where did you get to, then?'

'Up the stairs. After you'd disappeared inside I followed you. It didn't seem fair that you should have all the fun; after all, it was I who had found the way in. But when I got to the top I realized I was being selfish, that I was letting you down. So I went back.'

'And during that time, I suppose, he slipped in through the gate,' Toby said thoughtfully. 'What made you yell? Did you see him?'

'Not really. There was just a shadow that moved.' She shuddered. 'Do you think it was Landor?'

'Could be. Of course, if we were the police we'd find the bullet and check with the ones that killed Caseman and Miss Wilkes. That way we'd know for sure if it came from the same gun. But the way it is — well, we can't go back and search for the bullet, and even if we managed to find it we'd be no wiser. That's where we fall down, you and I, on a job like this.'

'Do you think we ought to tell the police about this evening?' she asked hesitantly.

'Sure we ought to. But I don't think we will. They would want to know what we were doing there, and I would have to tell them about the map. That would get them real mad at me. It's close on two days now since I found it.'

'But if some one heard the shooting this evening he'd report it, wouldn't he?'

'I guess so. But there's nothing to connect us with it, and no corpse. I'd say the police would have quite a job tracing it to us.'

They were in Hove when she asked, 'What do we do next?'

'We don't do anything,' he told her. 'From now on I'm tackling this on my own hook.'

'But you can't drop me like that, Toby,' she pleaded. 'I admit I wasn't much help this evening, but next time I'll do everything you say. I promise.'

'I'm not blaming you for what happened this evening,' he said, warmed by her pleading. 'It's just that I don't want you to get hurt. Anyway, from now on we're not raiding any more joints. That's out for keeps.'

★ ★ ★

Inspector Wittering stood smartly at attention as Herrod, followed by Sergeant Wood, bustled into his office at Haywards Heath police station.

'Nothing to report, sir,' he said, in answer to the Superintendent's inquiry. 'I've had two men out there since they phoned from Lewes. No one has left or entered the house.'

'Good. Let's get cracking, then.'

At the corner of Havelock Drive the car stopped, and Wittering spoke to the uniformed constable who came forward. Then they drove on to No. 15, an unpretentious semi-detached house with a garage at the side. A curtain twitched as they walked up the garden path.

Mrs Waide opened the door at their knock. She was a big, untidy woman, devoid of beauty and its aids. 'I'm afraid my husband is out,' she said, after Herrod had introduced himself. 'Is it about the car?'

Herrod said it was, and asked when her husband would be back.

'I really don't know.' A small girl wriggled her head between the door and her mother and gazed up at the visitors. Mrs Waide pushed the head back with a large, work-roughened hand. 'He went off this morning to watch cricket at Lord's. Or was it the Oval? No, I'm sure he said Lord's. And afterwards he's meeting a friend, so he'll probably be late.'

'How late?'

'I don't know,' she said again.

'H'm! A pity. Perhaps you would be kind enough to telephone me at the police station when he returns? I would prefer not to leave it until the morning.' He smiled, noting her worried expression. 'There are certain formalities, you know, before we can hand over the car.'

'Yes,' she said. 'Yes, of course.'

Back at the police station Herrod said, 'I'm going to the Oval. You might contact the Kennington police, Inspector, and ask them to warn the Surrey secretary that Sergeant Wood and I are on our way. And keep an eye on Havelock Drive. I'll phone you later.'

In the car Wood said, 'Why the Oval, sir? Mrs Waide seemed fairly certain that he had gone to Lord's.'

'Mrs Waide isn't a cricket fan. Neither are you, apparently. There's no cricket at Lord's to-day.'

The time was a quarter-past four when they entered the ground, and the players were leaving the field for the tea interval. The Superintendent, a keen cricketer, was disappointed. He had hoped to combine business with pleasure.

The secretary was expecting them. Five minutes later his voice boomed out over the public address system.

'Will Mr George Waide, of Haywards Heath, please come to the secretary's office?'

They waited for ten minutes, but Waide did not appear. 'Give him another call, will you?' Herrod said.

But the second appeal was no more successful than the first, and presently

Surridge emerged from the pavilion, and behind him the Surrey eleven. Herrod turned to the secretary.

'Who's batting?' he asked.

'Carr and Revill.'

'Oh. Well, we'll give him a few more minutes.'

But Laker and Lock were bowling with their accustomed accuracy, the Surrey fielding was tight, and run-getting was obviously going to be difficult. At five o'clock Herrod decided he had no reasonable excuse to stay longer, thanked the secretary, and made for Kennington police station. From there he phoned Wittering.

'No change, sir,' said the Inspector. 'He hasn't come back, and his wife hasn't left the house.'

'Right. I'll phone you again after I've been out for a meal.'

The second call had a more positive result. 'Mrs Waide has just rung, sir,' Wittering told him. 'Her husband had phoned to say he would be spending the night in Town. She explained about the car, and he said it would have to wait until the morning.'

'Where is Waide staying?'

'His wife didn't know.'

'That I can well believe,' Herrod said, replacing the receiver. And added under his breath, 'The dirty dog!'

5

George Waide arrived at Lewes on Sunday morning, after first reporting at Haywards Heath police station. He seemed surprised that the Austin was not to be handed over to him immediately, and still more surprised when he was taken upstairs and ushered into Superintendent Herrod's office.

'No trouble, I hope,' he said, panting a little. 'Found it in Brighton, I understand. Quick work. Any damage?'

Herrod looked him over, and was not impressed by what he saw. Vain, he thought — and mean eyes. And those podgy hands indicated the sensualist. I fancy I wasn't far wrong in assessing why he didn't go home last night. These fat men . . .

Here he remembered his own expanding waistline, and said hastily, 'We went to a lot of trouble to find you yesterday, Mr Waide. I even got the Surrey secretary to broadcast for you at the Oval.'

'Ah, yes. I'm sorry about that, Superintendent. My wife had got it wrong. I was at Lord's, not the Oval.'

Herrod's eyebrows shot up; his prominent ears wiggled slightly.

'Really? What were you doing there?'

Waide rushed headlong to disaster. 'Watching the cricket, of course. What else should I be doing?'

'There was no cricket at Lord's yesterday, Mr Waide.'

'Oh!' Waide's little eyes seemed to shrink still farther into their sockets. He lifted and stuck out his chin as though his collar had suddenly become too tight. 'Well, well! Fancy that!'

'Suppose you tell me where you *really* were?' Herrod suggested.

'No.' And then, becoming annoyed at the other's unwinking stare, 'Why the hell should I? What concern is it of yours how I choose to spend a Saturday afternoon?'

'None,' Herrod said.

He began to write. Occasionally he looked up, studied the round face opposite him intently, and then bent again to his writing. The only sounds in the room were the faint murmur of his pen and the laboured breathing of the uneasy Waide. Detective-Sergeant Wood sat impassively in the background.

The silence got on Waide's nerves. He began to wriggle on his seat. Eventually he burst out irritably, 'Some of you fellows seem to think you're God Almighty, the way you expect us to unburden ourselves at your slightest behest. But I suppose I may as well tell you. I wasn't breaking the law, damn it, I was meeting a girl friend.'

Herrod nodded, wondering what sort of a girl could stomach Waide.

'I gave the wife the usual reason,' the other went on, a self-satisfied smirk on his face. No doubt he was recalling the previous night. 'Cricket in the summer and football in the winter. But, to tell you the truth, Superintendent' — and he leaned forward in a confidential manner — 'I've never watched either since I was a kid. I'm not interested in sport.'

That I can well believe, thought Herrod. Not outdoor sports, anyway. He stifled a slight sensation of nausea and said, 'Thank you, sir. We shall, of course, respect your confidence.'

'I should damn' well hope so,' said Waide. 'Now, how about my car? Do I get it or don't I?'

Herrod watched him, toying with his pen.

'There's a slight hitch, I'm afraid. You are quite certain that the car was stolen from outside the Crown here between one-fifteen and two-fifteen on Friday afternoon?'

'That's what I said, didn't I? While I was at lunch.'

Again there was silence. Herrod wondered what thoughts, what fears, might be in the other's mind. 'A young woman was murdered near here early on Friday morning,' he said slowly.

'Yes, I know. I read about it in the papers. But how does that concern me?'

'That's what I hope to discover, Mr Waide,' Herrod said, never taking his eyes off the man's face. 'Impressions of her fingerprints were found on your car, you see.'

Waide's whole body seemed to sag, and he clutched the edges of his chair with both hands. 'But — but that's impossible!' His voice was hoarse and cracked, and he cleared his throat noisily. 'Unless, of course, she was in the car after it was stolen.'

The Superintendent shook his head.

'You forget, Mr Waide — or perhaps you didn't know — that she was murdered *before* your car was stolen. Twelve hours before.' He waited for the other to speak, but Waide said nothing. 'Would you care to reconsider your previous statement?'

Still Waide was silent. Eventually he said, 'I'd like to speak to my solicitor first. Can that be arranged? He has an office in Lewes. I could phone him.'

His solicitor was an elegant, rather superior young man by the name of Quigley. 'I have advised Mr Waide to give you the full facts, Superintendent,' he said, after consultation with his client. 'He has behaved foolishly, perhaps, but not criminally. He has nothing to fear from the truth.'

The truth — if it was the truth — made a sordid tale. As Herrod listened to it he realized, with some satisfaction, that his judgment of the man had been accurate enough.

He had intended spending Thursday night in Folkestone, Waide said, calling on customers in the coastal towns on his way home the next day; but, finding himself ahead of schedule, he had pushed on, hoping to reach home late on the Thursday. By half-past six that evening he had completed his business, and was having a drink in the Queen's at Eastbourne before setting off for Haywards Heath, when he was accosted by an old friend. They had a few drinks together, then moved on to the Albion, and from there the meeting developed into a pub-crawl. At about ten o'clock he found himself alone in a pub — whether his friend had passed out or gone home he didn't know — and was picked up by two women. At closing-time the elder of the women suggested he was in no state to drive to Haywards Heath, and that he had better spend the night with her. The

118

three of them got into the Austin, drove some distance from the centre of the town, and he then parked the car on some waste land and spent the night in the woman's flat.

'What about the other woman?' asked Herrod. 'What happened to her?'

'I don't know. I think she cleared off after we parked the car, but it's all rather hazy. I was pretty full, you know.'

'She didn't go to the flat?'

'No. I didn't see her there, anyway.'

'All right. Go on,' Herrod said.

'Well, at about seven o'clock the next morning I woke up, feeling like nothing on earth, and wondering where I was and what the devil I'd been up to. Then I saw the woman and remembered. I couldn't face her at that hour, so I got up and dressed without waking her, and cleared off. I'd be home to a late breakfast, I thought. And then I found that the car had gone.'

'You're sure you went to the right place?'

'I thought so. But to make quite certain I wandered round the district for a while.

After that, having had no luck with the car, I decided to go back to the woman's flat and get her to help me. Then I realized that I didn't know the name of the street or the number of her house. I didn't even know her name — except that she was called Anna. I was properly stumped.'

'Why didn't you go to the police?'

Waide shook his head.

'You're not a married man, Superintendent, or you wouldn't ask a question like that. I'd have had to give details, you see. And if the car was recovered and the thief caught all those details would have come out in court. I couldn't face that. My wife would have found out what I'd been up to, and our marriage would have been finished. Mrs Waide is a very jealous woman.'

From his opinion of the man Herrod would not have expected a broken marriage to upset George Waide. But he knew that often the most promiscuous of husbands hold their homes dear.

He refrained from comment.

'After a lot of thought I decided my

best plan would be to alter the time and place of the theft when I reported it,' Waide said. 'And that's what I did. I had breakfast, caught a train to Lewes, filled in a bit of time, and went to the Crown for lunch. And then I came round here.' He leaned as far forward as his stomach would permit. 'And that's the gospel truth, Superintendent. I know absolutely nothing about the girl or her murder.'

'You will, of course, wish to verify the truth of my client's statement,' said Quigley. 'There should be no difficulty about that. He tells me he can supply you with the name and address of the friend he met at the Queen's, and he thinks he could find the café where he had breakfast. They might remember him there. So might the booking clerk at Eastbourne Station. Or, for that matter, the ticket collector at Lewes.'

Herrod shook his head.

'You're a lawyer, Mr Quigley, so I don't have to tell you that what Mr Waide needs is an alibi for the time of the murder. What he did the previous evening or the next morning is by the way. Can he

121

produce the woman he calls Anna? She seems to be the essential witness.'

It was Waide who answered.

'You know I can't.' He was almost tearful. 'I told you, I don't know her name and I don't know where she lives. How *can* I produce her? Even 'Anna' may be wrong. It's what she told me to call her, but it may not be her real name.'

'If she's a regular she may be known to the Eastbourne police,' Quigley suggested.

The Superintendent nodded. 'She may. Would you recognize her if you saw her again, Mr Waide?'

'I might. I'm not sure.'

'Well, let's concentrate on the little you *can* tell us. What about the pub where you met these women? Any help there?'

Waide shook his head. He looked a chastened and unhappy man. A frightened man, too. All the bounce had long since disappeared.

'I might be able to find it,' he said. 'It all depends.'

'H'm. Well, how about the women? You say you were tight when you met them;

but you weren't tight the next morning, and presumably you had a look at this Anna before you left the flat. What does she look like?'

'She's in the early forties, I should say. Plump, short — about five foot two — and a natural blonde. At least, I remember thinking it was natural.'

'How was she dressed the previous evening?'

'Oh, Lord!' Waide struggled desperately with his memory. 'A blouse and skirt, I think, with a thin, dark blue coat over it.'

'And the other girl?'

There were beads of perspiration on Waide's face. He pulled out his handkerchief with a shaking hand and wiped them away.

'It's no good,' he said miserably. 'I don't remember. She was younger than Anna, and dark. Good-looking, too. But I don't know what she was wearing, or anything else about her. I didn't sit next to her; I didn't talk to her. She was just a rather shadowy figure in the background.'

'The girl who was murdered was young and pretty and dark,' Herrod said. 'I want you to have a look at her, Mr Waide.'

Waide grimaced. But he was obviously glad to be done with questions.

'It won't be any use,' he said, 'but I'll look if you want me to.'

The visit to the mortuary did not take long. Herrod watched Waide closely as he gazed down at the dead girl, but the man gave no sign of recognition. A sickly green pallor began to spread over his face, and the Superintendent, recognizing the symptoms, hurried him out of the building.

He was too late. Waide retched and was sick.

'Sorry,' he said after. 'My tummy hasn't been behaving itself lately. And all this excitement, and then . . . ' He gulped. 'Sorry.'

When he had recovered Herrod said, 'Well? Did you recognize her?'

'Not really,' said Waide. 'It might be her, and I'm not saying it isn't. But I told you, I didn't take much notice of her that evening. It was Anna sat next to me in the pub and did all the talking. And me being more or less blotto . . . '

He shrugged.

Herrod concealed his disappointment. 'Did you lock the car when you parked it?' he asked.

'I think so. No — Anna locked it for me. I remember her giving me back the keys.' He put a hand in his pocket. 'There they are.'

The Superintendent examined them. 'There's no ignition key here,' he said, handing them back.

'No. I usually leave that in the car.'

They were back in the police station now. Herrod said, 'You and I, Mr Waide, had better spend an afternoon by the sea. At Eastbourne.'

They drove down after lunch. Superintendent Farrar, of the Borough police, was an old acquaintance of Herrod's. They had worked together before, and the detective knew the other's value. But with so little to go on he was not hopeful of success.

Superintendent Farrar thought otherwise.

'We had a similar case only last month,' he said. 'The man, a visitor to the town,

125

picked up a woman when he was drunk and spent the night at her flat. And *his* car was missing the next morning. But he wasn't quite as drunk as your chap seems to have been. He was able to show us where he parked the car — and from what you tell me it could be the same place as where Waide left his. If that is so . . . '

He paused significantly.

'A racket, eh?' Herrod said. 'The woman picks up a drunk, sees that he parks his car in a prearranged spot, and takes him home for the night. That ensures her accomplice of at least eight hours clear before the theft is discovered. A handy start, eh?'

'Very. And it seems that in both cases the woman took the man's keys, ostensibly to lock the car for him. I've no doubt she took damned good care to leave it unlocked.'

'How about the woman, then?' Herrod asked. 'Did you find out anything about her?'

'No. She was never traced. It was just an isolated instance, and there was no reason to suspect her. She certainly couldn't have pinched the car — which, incidentally, has not yet been recovered.'

'Let's have a look at this parking lot, then,' Herrod said. 'If we can make a start from there it'll be something.'

'Right. I'll send Newman with you. He was in charge of the previous job.'

Waide recognized the parking place at once. 'Yes, this is it,' he cried delightedly, rubbing his podgy hands together. 'I left the car over there, and we walked . . . ' His face clouded as he gazed in turn down the four streets. 'I think we went that way and turned off somewhere. But I can't swear to it, I'm afraid.'

'Can you say roughly how far you walked?' asked Detective-Inspector Newman.

No, he could not. They drove slowly down the streets he indicated, hoping he might recognize the house. But Waide was lost. 'They all look alike, don't they?' he said, perplexed. 'And when I left in the morning it never occurred to me to take note of where I was. My one idea was to pick up the car and get cracking.' He looked coyly at the Superintendent. 'I don't make a habit of that sort of thing, you know. First time it's happened in years. Wouldn't have happened then if I hadn't been plastered.'

Herrod nodded, disbelieving but unconcerned. The man's morals were not his business. 'Let's try the pubs,' he said to Newman. 'Even if he was too drunk to recognize the barman, the barman may recognize him.'

They made for the centre of the town first, since Waide was certain that after leaving the Albion he and his friend had gone on to the Clifton, and that he had not returned to the front. And here they were more fortunate. At the third pub they stopped at Waide nodded eagerly. Yes, he said, that was it. He was almost sure that was it.

It was. The bar was closed, but the barman was the licensee's nephew and lived on the premises. As soon as Herrod had explained their business and the man had taken a good look at Waide he grinned.

'Sure I recognize him,' he said. 'Proper plastered he was. But no trouble.' He turned to Waide. 'Let me see now. Wednesday — no, Thursday night, wasn't it? You went off with them two floozies, didn't you?'

Waide was about to speak, but Herrod stopped him. 'Do you know the women?' he asked the man.

'Me?' The barman stared at him wide-eyed. 'No fear. The blonde's been in once or twice before, but I never seen the other.'

'Would you recognize the other if you saw her again?'

'I might,' he said doubtfully. 'But they sat over in that corner, and it was blondie come up for the drinks. I never had a proper squint at her friend.'

Herrod had had a photograph taken of the dead girl. When he showed it to the man the latter's eyes nearly popped out of his head. ''Struth! A stiff, eh?' He glanced over his shoulder at Waide, and lowered his voice to a whisper. 'Was it him done her in?'

'I'm trying to find out who killed her,' Herrod said. 'That's why I'm here. Is that the girl who was with the blonde?'

'Could be,' the other said. 'It's like her. But — well, a stiff's a stiff and a girl's a girl, if you get me. They don't look the same, see? But — ' He took another look at the photograph. 'Yes, it could be her.'

'But you're not certain, eh?'

'No. A stiff — '

'All right.' Herrod didn't want to hear any more about stiffs. 'How often does the blonde come in?'

'Two or three times a week. But not reg'lar.'

'Was she in last night?'

'No. Nor Friday. Probably be in to-night, though.'

'We may as well see this through now we're here,' Herrod said, as they left the pub. 'If she doesn't turn up to-night we'll have to keep a watch on the place until she does. Looks like a nice job for some one.'

They returned to the police station. At half-past six Sergeant Wood and Inspector Newman left for their vigil at the pub, with instructions to persuade the woman to accompany them to the station for questioning. 'If she refuses we'll bring

Waide over,' Herrod said. 'But we don't want to do it that way if it can be helped.'

Again their luck was in. They had to wait some hours, but at eight-thirty the two detectives were back with the woman. 'The Inspector handled her a treat,' Wood said. 'I didn't think we'd budge her, but — well, she's here. A bit truculent, but I think that's for show. If you ask me I'd say she's scared.'

She was much as Waide had described her. Herrod greeted her politely, forestalling her protest. 'I'm sorry to inconvenience you, madam,' he said. 'We shan't keep you long, but we hope you may be able to identify some one for us. May I have your name, please?'

'Anna Kermode.' Her voice was shrill and brittle. 'And really, Inspector, I don't like — '

'Superintendent,' he murmured. 'Superintendent Herrod. And your address, Mrs Kermode? Or is it Miss?'

'Mrs,' she snapped. 'I'm a widow. And the address is 48 Union Street. And will you please tell me — '

She stopped. Herrod had nodded to

the Sergeant to admit Waide, and the latter, his fat face beaming, was gazing in happy recognition at the woman. But Mrs Kermode was far from happy. She backed away from him, fear writ large on her painted face, both hands twisting the strap of her large, shiny handbag.

'Do you know this gentleman, madam?' Herrod asked.

'No,' she said, after a moment's hesitation that was not lost on the detectives. And then, with more determination, 'I've never seen him before. Never.'

'But, Anna,' Waide protested. 'Don't you remember — '

Herrod silenced him, and signalled once more to the Sergeant. Waide, still protesting, was ushered from the room.

'Now, Mrs Kermode — '

'I tell you I don't know him,' she interrupted. 'That's plain enough, isn't it? What more do you want?'

'Sit down, please.' The Superintendent's voice was suddenly stern, and she obeyed reluctantly. 'A witness has stated that you and that gentleman left the pub together one evening last week in company with another woman. So some one, you see, is lying.'

'Not me,' she said. 'We may have left at the same time, but that doesn't mean I know him, does it?'

'You were seen drinking and talking with him before you left,' Herrod told her. The woman made no answer, and he went on, 'I'll be frank with you, Mrs Kermode. Mr Waide — that's the gentleman who was in here just now — is under suspicion of having committed a serious crime. He says he has an alibi — that he spent the night in question at your flat. So you see how important it is that — well, that you should not be mistaken.'

Watching her, he experienced surprise and some doubt. Why was she no longer afraid? What had he said to dispel the fear that had certainly been there before?

'What is he supposed to have done?' she asked curiously, her voice quieter, more composed.

'We won't go into that now. But have you or have you not met Mr Waide before?'

'Yes,' she said sullenly.

'Did he spend a night at your flat?'

'Yes.'

'When?'

'Thursday night,' she said, after consideration.

And that seems to dispose of Waide, thought Herrod.

'Why did you at first — er — fail to recognize him?' he asked quietly.

He thought he knew what her answer would be, and was surprised that it was so long in coming. 'You know how it is. One doesn't like to discuss one's personal affairs with Tom, Dick, and Harry,' she said eventually. 'People jump to conclusions — and one's got one's pride, Inspector.' ('Superintendent,' he murmured again.) 'I did it as a favour to Mr Waide — he was in no condition to drive home. And when I saw him here to-night I thought, well, he's a nice one, he is, telling tales about me. That's no way to return a kindness, I thought. But, of course, when you explained . . . '

Yes, he thought, that's what I expected her to say. But she isn't convincing. That

134

ought to be the reason — but it isn't, I'm sure it isn't. Yet how . . .

'Who was the girl who was with you in the pub that evening?' he asked suddenly — and knew he had struck at the vulnerable point. The fear had come back to her eyes; her dignity was gone. So it was the girl she had been worried about, not Waide. That was why . . .

'I don't know,' she said. 'We just got talking in the pub. I don't know her name.'

'But the three of you left in Waide's car?'

'Did we? Oh, yes, so we did. She lived out my way. Mr Waide offered to give her a lift.'

I bet it wasn't Waide who offered, Herrod thought. Not if he was as tight as he makes out. He was about to produce the dead girl's photograph for the woman's inspection, then changed his mind. If she were lying, if she in fact knew the girl, she might still deny the photograph. But the corpse itself might shock her into the truth.

'I would like you to come to Lewes

tomorrow, Mrs Kermode,' he said. 'There's some one else I want you to see.'

'Who?' She was still nervous. And then, when he shook his head, 'Well, I can't. Not tomorrow. I'll be at my sister's all day, looking after the kids while she visits her mother-in-law. The old lady's sick.'

'When will your sister be back?'

'I don't know. Seven, maybe.'

'This is urgent,' Herrod said. 'Give me your sister's address, and I'll have a car there at seven-thirty to take you to Lewes.'

She hesitated. 'Make it half-past eight,' she said reluctantly. 'I'll want my supper first.'

They brought Waide back when the woman had gone. 'She's lying, Superintendent,' he said desperately, his eyes searching the room. 'That *was* Anna. Why have you let her go?'

She's lying, Herrod thought, but not about you. 'It's all right, sir,' he said soothingly. 'Mrs Kermode has corroborated your statement.'

'She has? Oh, thank God for that!' Relieved, Waide flopped into a chair.

136

'Does that mean I'm in the clear, Superintendent? You won't want me any more?'

'That's about it, sir. But I'd like to hang on to your car for a day or two. I don't want to inconvenience you, but it may have more to tell us. I'll try — '

'My dear fellow, don't give it another thought. Keep it as long as you wish.' He was bubbling over with bonhomie and good humour. 'I'm so damned glad to be out of this mess I wouldn't care if I never set eyes on the car again.'

He laughed, and licked his lips. 'This calls for a celebration, you know. Besides, I'm damned dry. I suppose you wouldn't care — '

'No, thank you, sir. Not at the moment. But don't let that stop you. If you want to go off for a quick one the Sergeant and I can pick you up at the pub when we're ready.'

Waide went — glad, no doubt, to be rid of policemen.

Before they left Herrod had a word with Superintendent Farrar.

'This Anna Kermode,' he said. 'I don't

know what she is or what she does, but I could bear to find out. I fancy she's more than just a casual pick-up who took a man back to her flat. Can you keep an eye on her? Or shall I get the Yard to send a man down?'

'Better let us handle it,' Farrar said. 'Our chaps are familiar with the district, and they may know some of the good lady's associates. But what are we looking for?'

'Damned if I know. I can't believe that she's tied up with Landor, but it *could* have been the Wilkes girl who was with her that evening. I may be better informed on that by to-morrow night. And Landor and the girl could have pinched Waide's car after he and Anna had left it.'

'That still doesn't make Anna more than a casual pick-up,' Farrar said.

'I know. Unless it was a put-up job between her and Catherine Wilkes. Only in that case — well, keep an eye on her, anyway. It may be a waste of time, but at least we're playing safe.'

On their way to collect Waide Sergeant

Wood said, 'When you were questioning Waide this morning, sir, and he wouldn't come clean about yesterday afternoon, what was it you were writing? It had me puzzled.'

'Eh?' Herrod was also puzzled. Then he grinned. 'Oh, yes, I remember. Just a dodge of mine, Wood. Some energetic scribbling interspersed with the occasional piercing glance at the suspect — it gets 'em rattled. They think you're writing their dossier, or a 'wanted' ad.'

'Yes, sir. But what did you write?'

'Nothing important. I'll show you when we get back. No — wait a minute.' He fumbled in his pockets, and presently produced a crumpled sheet of paper. 'I remember now — I picked it up. It wouldn't have done to leave it on my desk, revealing the idle thoughts of the great detective to all and sundry. Here, read it!'

The Sergeant read it.

A fat little bounder named Waide
Had been most inexpertly made.
He had eyes like a pig,

And his tum was too big,
And his soul was completely mislaid.

'All my own work,' the Superintendent said modestly. 'Not bad, eh?'

6

It had been a pretty good day, Toby thought contentedly, as he sipped a whisky and ginger ale after dinner. They had bathed and lazed and bathed again, and walked on the pier, and tried most of the side-shows; and after tea they had sat in deckchairs on the beach and talked. There had been one little black cloud when the constable had asked to see him at lunch-time, and they had both panicked, expecting his immediate arrest; but the man had only brought a formal summons to attend the inquest at Lewes on the morrow, and the cloud had passed. To-morrow was to-morrow; it could not spoil to-day.

'Time we were off' he said, putting down his glass. 'Ready?'

She nodded eagerly. 'I couldn't be readier.'

She's sure got guts, Toby thought admiringly, as he followed her from the hotel. I'm in this because I can't help myself; and, Catherine Wilkes apart, it's also a personal matter for me now. A guy tried to bump me off last night, and nobody's going to throw lead at Toby Vanne without a comeback. But Crossetta, she's tagging along just for the fun of it. Seems like she gets a real kick out of it, too.

They had kept away from Cardiff Street during the day; apparently No. 17 functioned only after dark. Toby felt a thrill of excitement as they parked the car (out of sight, but within easy distance in case they had to run for it) and he and the girl walked quickly past the entrance to Cardiff Street and turned into Smith Street.

The yard was deserted. No sound came from it, no light, no sign of life. Toby probed its depths with the beam from his torch, keeping the girl behind him.

'Okay,' he said. 'Let's go round the front.'

The front too was in darkness. So, apart from an occasional street lamp, was Cardiff Street. Looking down its gloomy length, Crossetta wondered if any but themselves and their quarry ever sought it willingly.

'First on the field, apparently,' Toby said. 'That's fine. We will now take up battle stations.'

They crossed the street and parked themselves in the shadows of a narrow alley between two tall buildings. At the far end of the alley was the Riley.

'Lines of retreat properly secured,' Toby said. 'Now we just wait.'

'For how long?'

'Until some one turns up, I guess. Or until we get bored.'

He thought it unlikely that he would get that way himself. She was close beside him; the scent of her hair was in his nostrils. He would have preferred to have his arm around her waist, her head on his shoulder. But he had learnt from experience that Crossetta was curiously averse to physical contact, and he did not want to overplay his hand.

Yet once the thought had occurred to him he could not will it to cease. It kept nagging at his mind, so that presently he grew fidgety and edged away from her.

'What's the matter?' she asked.

'Cramp,' he lied. And then, filled with a sudden brain-wave, 'Crossetta, if some one spots us — a policeman, say, or — or anyone — I'm going to put my arms round you and pretend I'm kissing you. They won't bother about us if they think we're canoodling. You don't mind, do you?'

'No,' she said, after a pause. But he knew that she did mind, and it bothered him. Didn't she like him enough? Or was she still in love with her dead husband?

He wished he knew.

They did not talk much. The noises of Brighton were all about them, yet distant, so that they felt strangely isolated. The sound of a car approaching caused them to tense expectantly, only to relax as it went past the end of the street. Once hurried footsteps along the pavement off which they waited made Toby raise his arms hopefully. But the footsteps crossed the road, and the man passed by on the opposite pavement without noticing them.

And then, some ten minutes later, their

patience was rewarded. They heard the hum of an approaching car, and crept farther into the shadows. This time the car did not pass. It swung round into Cardiff Street and pulled up outside No. 17.

'Here we go!' Toby whispered.

The small parking lights on the car, and the general gloom of the street, did not make observation easy. They crept forward a little. A man got out of the car, a door slammed. The man appeared to be fumbling with the lock on one of the big doors, and presently it opened and he disappeared into the farther darkness.

They heard the door close. A light was switched on inside the building. 'I wish we could see,' Crossetta whispered. 'I want to know what he's doing. Couldn't we sneak round to the back?'

'Not this time,' said Toby. 'No more bullets for me.'

They had not long to wait. Ten minutes later the lights went out and the man reappeared, locking the door behind him. As he climbed into the car Toby gripped the girl's arm.

'Come on. Time we were leaving.'

The car moved quietly off down the street, and they turned and ran down the alley towards the Riley, tumbling into the seats as they reached it. 'It's the Sunbeam again,' Toby said, pressing the starter. 'I got the number. This time we'll track it to its lair.'

They saw it pass the end of the street, and went after it. It seemed unlikely that the man could know he was being followed, but they kept well behind, taking no chances.

The man in front seemed to be in no hurry. They came to the Old Shoreham road, and headed west. Past the football ground, and then right, past the big stadium and into a part of the town that was foreign to Toby. The traffic grew less, and he dropped farther behind, anxious not to arouse suspicion. Presently the Sunbeam slowed, turned down a tree-lined avenue, and then into a private drive. Toby drove past it without pausing, took the first turning that offered, and stopped.

They looked at each other.

'Now what?' asked Crossetta.

He thought quickly. He wanted a closer look at the house, at the man — or men — in the Sunbeam. But if the man with the bandaged hand should see or recognize him . . .

'Care for a walk?' he asked. 'Just to the gate, to see what gives? I don't want — '

She was out of the Riley and running down the road before he could finish the sentence. Toby stared after her uneasily. Was he playing fair? Wasn't it rather ungallant, not to say cowardly, to take advantage of her disregard for personal safety in this way? No harm could come to her unless she went looking for it; the men did not know her by sight, they would have no reason to suppose she was spying on them. But Crossetta was impetuous. She might not be content merely to observe. She might . . .

If she's not back mighty smart, he told himself, I'm going after her.

Crossetta ran silently, her rubber-soled sandals making a swishing sound on the pavement. She slowed to a walk as she reached the drive; there was a street lamp almost directly opposite, but she did not hesitate. Keeping to the shadows, she slipped past the open gates and on to the large grass semicircle that lay beyond the trees. From there she had a better view of the house.

Despite its imposing entrance it was no mansion, but a pleasant two-storied building; double-fronted, and with a projecting portico flanked by slender stone pillars. Light glowed behind drawn curtains in one of the ground-floor rooms; the rest of the house was in darkness. The Sunbeam was parked on a paved court to the right of the building.

On the far side of the lawn Crossetta paused; but all was still and quiet, and she tip-toed across the gravel drive to the narrow strip of grass that bordered the wide rose-beds along the front of the house. Again she paused, excitement mounting in her. The lighted window was slightly raised; there was a gap in the curtains, widened occasionally by the faint breeze that stirred them. If she could get closer . . .

With a swift glance to right and left she

pushed her way through the rose-bushes and pressed her slim body against the wall. There were two men in that part of the room visible to her. They lounged in deep armchairs — one facing, one with his back to her. All she could see of the latter was his dark, well-greased hair and the upper part of his blue-clad left arm. The other man she judged to be tall, although his sprawling pose obscured his height. He too had dark hair, and was dressed in dark grey flannels and a light sports jacket. His bandaged right hand dangled over the side of the armchair, his left hand held a half-empty glass which he idly rocked backward and forward on the wide chair-arm, his eyes fixed on it in scowling meditation.

For fully a minute she watched, while neither man spoke. Then the one she could not see burst out with, 'We've got to do *something*, surely?'

'Such as what? Put an advertisement in the papers?' asked the other, his eyes still fixed on the rocking glass.

'How should I know? That's your job, not mine. You're the boss. All I say is, you can't just let it slide.'

The bandaged hand was raised to the chair-arm; the man pulled himself a little more upright.

'Why not? There's nothing to connect us with the job, is there? You're too easily scared, my lad. I'm not saying it's a hundred per cent safe; but who expects to be safe in this racket? We came into it to make money, and by God we've made it. No need to start beefing just because we trip up once in a while. The job's gone wrong — okay. So what? We may lose a few quid over it, but there's no real danger. Not what *I* call danger.'

'How do you know that? If the police — '

Behind the girl a voice said evenly, 'Mind the roses, lady.'

Crossetta dropped her arms and swung round. On the drive a man stood watching her, a cigarette glowing between his lips. As he drew on it she saw his face — white and puffy, with a weak, receding chin. She pushed her way through the bushes and stood, hands in pockets, staring back at him.

'Well?' she asked defiantly. 'What now?'

The man seemed taken aback by her aplomb. He removed the cigarette from his mouth and threw it away. It made a glowing arc in the darkness. 'You'd better come inside,' he said. 'The guv'nor wouldn't like it if I was to keep you standing out here. We're hospitable, we are.'

Something moved in the shadows behind him. It approached silently, and a moment later a dark figure stood on the edge of the lawn, faintly outlined by the light from the window. Crossetta smiled, and moved nearer to the man.

'I'm not dressed for a social call,' she said lightly. 'We'll make it another day, shall we?'

But he had finished with badinage. 'You come on in,' he said, and stepped forward to grasp her arm. As he did so the dark figure leapt across the gravel, a fist shot out and landed with a crack on the side of his jaw, and the man went down.

Crossetta laughed delightedly. She stepped up to the recumbent figure, kicked him delicately on the posterior, and as delicately stepped over him.

'Lovely, Toby,' she said. 'You ought to be a boxer.'

'And you ought to be spanked,' he said. 'Come on — let's get out of here before his pals interfere.'

Hand in hand they ran down the drive. As they neared the gates a window was raised noisily and a voice roared, 'Hey! What's going on out there?' Toby wondered whether a bullet would follow the voice; but it did not, and then they were out in the comparative safety of the road. They slowed momentarily, listening. There were voices on the drive, but no pursuing footsteps. They hurried on to the car.

As they drove back to Coniston Crossetta told him what she had seen and heard. Toby wanted to scold her for acting so rashly, but he could not. She had so obviously enjoyed her adventure. He contented himself with saying, 'You'd have been in real trouble, my girl, if I hadn't decided to find out what you were up to.'

'I could have dealt with *him*,' she said.

It was a confident but not a boastful statement. Toby wondered how much right she had to be confident. She had courage; but courage alone might not have been sufficient, perhaps, against desperate men. He remembered the bullet that had missed him so narrowly at No. 17 the previous evening, and shivered.

'That guy with the bandaged hand — did he look like Landor?' he asked.

'No. At least, not like the description given in the papers. But the other man, the one I couldn't see — *he* could have been Landor. He was wearing a blue suit, and his hair was the right colour.'

Toby was puzzled. And worried. The affair was not developing the way he had anticipated. He had expected that Cardiff Street would lead him inevitably to the wanted Landor. Landor would be hiding there, perhaps; alone and desperate, or secretly succoured by one of his crook friends. A few days of patient watching and waiting until he was sure, a word to the police, and that would be that. He had not reckoned on gun battles and slugging matches, or that Landor's friends (if they *were* his friends) would live in a fine house and be so well organized. Was Landor concealed in the house they had just left? It seemed fairly certain now that he wasn't at No. 17.

'Who *are* all these guys?' he said irritably. 'The papers didn't mention a gang. There was just Landor and the girl — and she's dead.' Crossetta did not answer, and after due thought he added, 'Looks like we've bitten off more than we can chew.'

'You're not thinking of going to the police, are you?' she said quickly.

'I guess we ought to. It was different when Landor looked to be on his own. But with a bunch of hoodlums behind him — well, I'd say we'd be crazy to carry on alone.'

'They may be nothing to do with Landor.'

'You think not? Wasn't it that piece of paper I found by the girl that led us to Cardiff Street? How come these others are so interested in No. 17 if there's no

154

connexion with Landor?'

She made no comment on that. 'I bet the police take it out of you,' she said thoughtfully. 'You'll make a welcome scapegoat. What's the worst they can do to you? Put you in prison?'

'Cheerful, aren't you?' Toby said. 'Yes, I guess so. I'm not so hot on the law over here, but it'd mean gaol back home.'

They were in the hall, bidding each other good-night, when she said earnestly, 'Don't tell the police, Toby. It would be asking for trouble, and probably quite unnecessary. Sooner or later they'll pick him up, with or without our help. A man like that can't just disappear.'

'Folks do.'

'Yes, I know. But surely only when they've made all the necessary arrangements before-hand? Landor wouldn't have done that. He can't have known he was going to kill that shopkeeper.'

'No. But he may have provided for the possibility. And it looks as though he did. Why else is he still at liberty?'

'You haven't given us or the police much time to find him, have you? All things considered, I should say you and I haven't made too bad a start. Why not give us a chance to finish the job?'

'I'll sleep on it,' he promised.

As it happened he slept very little that night. He was too worried. And when he came down to breakfast the next morning he was still undecided.

Crossetta frowned at him. 'You look like death warmed up,' she said. 'Blood-shot eyes with bags under them. Not feeling nervous about the inquest, are you?'

'Good Lord, no! Why should I be?'

But he was. Not of the inquest itself, but of once more having to face the police. They would be there in force, he supposed, and Herrod would probably want to talk to him. He wondered if he would be able to answer them naturally, talk to them without arousing their suspicions.

'Are you coming with me?' he asked.

She shook her head vigorously. 'No, thank you. I'm on holiday, and inquests aren't my idea of fun. Will you be back to lunch?'

'I hope so.'

The inquest was held in Lewes Town Hall. Dr Eaves, the deputy coroner, was a fair-haired man with a penetrating voice that played havoc with Toby's nerves. The audience was not large, consisting mainly of Pressmen on the look-out for something sensational.

In this they were to be disappointed.

Dr Eaves, seated at his table, explained to the jury the nature and extent of their duties, and then asked them if they wished to view the body. This seemed to take the jury by surprise. Uncertain and unhappy, they eventually decided that they did.

The coroner's officer led them from the court.

Toby was the first witness to be called on their return. His evidence, he knew, was only formal; all that was wanted from him was an account of the finding of the body. He was merely a curtain-raiser to the main proceedings. But because of his inward sense of guilt the taking of the oath and the subsequent questioning by the coroner gave him the unhappy sensation of being, not a witness, but a criminal in the dock.

As he sat down again he saw the keen eyes of Superintendent Herrod fixed on him contemplatively. Toby nodded, and after a pause Herrod nodded back before turning his attention to the next witness.

This was Nat Wilkes. A ripple of noise swept through the court at his appearance, and the coroner frowned. If I felt as though I were in the dock, Toby thought, he *looks* as though he ought to be. It must be mighty tough to go through life with a face so formidable.

Wilkes identified the corpse as that of his sister Catherine, and told under what circumstances he had last seen her. Toby listened to him with interest. Hitherto the girl had been first a body and then a name; now she was taking shape as a person. But not a very tangible person, for Wilkes was brief in his information and monosyllabic in his answers. The coroner became a trifle testy. While anxious not to be harsh on a bereaved brother, he had a duty to perform.

'It would appear, Mr Wilkes, that there

is no direct evidence that your sister left home in the company of this man Landor?' he said.

'No,' Wilkes agreed.

'Had she ever gone away with him before?'

'No.'

'And you can furnish us with no reason why she should have done so on this occasion?'

'No.'

The questions went on. Gradually a shadowy picture formed in Toby's mind — a picture of a wayward, spoilt young woman, a beautiful orphan who lived alone with her brother in lodgings and furnished flats, often on the move, with no close friends and little companionship. No wonder she ran away, Toby thought. She must have been bored to distraction.

The medical and police evidence that followed did not interest him greatly. It was all very scientific and formal, and much as he had expected; particulars of how the deceased had met her death, the nature of the wound, and what had caused it. He noticed that Superintendent

Herrod made no reference to Landor, or to the shooting at Forest Row; and Dr Eaves in his summing up was careful to point out to the jury that, apart from Nathaniel Wilkes's unsupported opinion, they had heard no evidence to show that the girl had been in the man's company. The jury retired for ten minutes, and came back to record — as the coroner had hinted that they should — a verdict of murder against some person or persons unknown.

Toby wondered whether he should speak to Wilkes. He was anxious to get back to Coniston and Crossetta, but it seemed heartless to ignore the man. Wilkes, however, showed every indication of wishing to be ignored. He walked purposefully from the hall, stopping to speak to no one. I shouldn't think he was an easy guy to live with, Toby decided, watching Wilkes's ugly but expressionless face. I wonder what his job is.

Superintendent Herrod was wondering much the same thing.

'I understand you are staying in Brighton, Mr Wilkes,' he said, planting his burly figure squarely in the doorway.

'Yes. They have my address at the police station.'

'Will you be there long? How about your job?'

'Until after the funeral.' Wilkes ignored the second question, and moved pointedly to one side. 'Excuse me.'

The Superintendent watched him go. Then he turned, nearly bumping into Toby.

'Ah, Lieutenant Vanne! Enjoying your leave?'

'Yes, thanks.' Toby was struggling with his conscience again. If he were ever to confess this should be the moment. He said, avoiding a decision, 'You wouldn't call Wilkes loquacious, would you? He gives very little away. Did you do any better with him than the coroner?'

'Not much.'

'I only met him once before,' Toby went on, still vacillating. By monopolizing the conversation he might keep the other at bay. 'That was on Saturday, when Inspector Kane was showing him where his sister was killed. But to-day he

161

completely ignored me.'

'Really?' The Superintendent's eyebrows lifted slightly. 'And what took you back to that unfortunate spot, sir?'

Toby coloured.

'Curiosity, I guess. I was on my way to Eastbourne, and a morbid instinct impelled me to have another look at it.'

'Not engaging in a little detection on your own?'

The young man forced a laugh. To his own ears it sounded hollow.

'Say, don't worry about competition from me, Superintendent,' he said; 'I'm no sleuth' — and realized that he had now burnt his boats behind him. The way to confession was closed. Yet it was some relief to have reached a decision, even though it might be the wrong one.

But the detective was still there, still regarding him with a somewhat quizzical look. In an attempt to lead Herrod's thoughts away from himself he said, 'Did you know that Wilkes went back again on his own later that same afternoon? It seemed kind of queer to me.'

'Back to the barn?'

'Yes. I saw him there on my way home after tea. At least, I saw his car. I suppose he was around.'

If the Superintendent made anything of this he was not giving it away. 'Mr Wilkes is a law unto himself, I fancy,' he said, and wondered how far that was true. 'You mustn't judge him by your own standards. Going back to Brighton now, Lieutenant?'

'Yes. After I've made some inquiries about the funeral and ordered some flowers. I guess there won't be many, poor girl.'

He was glad to get away. Despite the Superintendent's apparent friendliness, one never knew where one was with those fellows. They could be pleasant as what-have-you one moment, he suspected, and snapping handcuffs on your wrists the next. Bluff was part of their stock-in-trade.

Did detectives make good poker-players? He wouldn't care to risk sitting in at a school with them, anyway.

But as he got out on to the open road his relief evaporated, and conscience

163

began to nag him once more. He was not behaving like a good neighbour. The police were striving to bring a murderer to book, and he was doing his best to thwart them by withholding what might prove to be vital evidence. That might please Crossetta, but it wouldn't please the police, and he wasn't sure that it pleased him. And if he had not been such a darned coward he would now be on his way home with a clear conscience.

Or would he? He might well be in gaol.

He scowled at the windscreen and trod on the accelerator. The Riley was running well. The exhilaration of speed gradually possessed him, scattering his troublesome conscience with the wind. Perhaps Crossetta was right in believing that Landor was bound to be caught. And at least he was now certain of a few more days of close companionship with her. Maybe in that time their intimacy would ripen, so that it would not die with the end of the adventure that at present sustained it.

The traffic lights were against him as he approached Palace Pier, and he sat admiring the flowers and idly watching the holiday-makers, singling out the prettiest girls and mentally comparing them with Crossetta. Most of them came off second best, he decided.

And then, directly ahead of him, he saw the Sunbeam.

7

It came from Marine Parade and followed the one-way stream of traffic up Old Steine. As the lights changed to green Toby went after it. He had not recognized the driver — a shortish man in a cap — but he thought it was probably the fellow he had knocked down outside the house the previous evening. He was of about the same build. But it was the car, not the man, that was important. As the dead girl had led him to Cardiff Street, and Cardiff Street to the Sunbeam, so the Sunbeam might lead him to Landor. And Landor was the one man who could redeem him in his own mind. His conscience had been temporarily dormant, but it had not died. Only Landor's capture — and through his own endeavours, at that — could eliminate the stigma of moral cowardice that haunted him.

The Sunbeam carried on past the Pavilion, up York Place, and along the London

Road. Toby had no difficulty in keeping it in sight, for the driver appeared to be in no hurry. But once past Patcham and out on the wide arterial road the Sunbeam began to draw away from him. If we're off on a trip to London, thought Toby, urging the Riley on, I'll lose him before long.

But just over a mile past Patcham the Sunbeam forked left along the Horsham road. It was not travelling so fast now; and when it turned into the lane leading to Poynings Toby was afraid, as he rounded each bend, that he might find himself too close to it. At the road junction in the village it had disappeared; he turned right and was lucky — it was still ahead of him. They went through Fulking and along the dusty lane towards Edburton, with open fields beyond the low walls and hedges, and the South Downs towering away to the left. And then, as the Riley crested a rise, he saw the Sunbeam, some two hundred yards ahead, turn off to the left down a rough track that led to what appeared to be a large barn.

Toby pulled up sharply. There was no cover, either for himself or for the car. The road was straight and level, the hedge almost non-existent. If the man ahead was making for the barn he could not fail to see the stationary Riley when he got out of the car.

Toby did not want to alarm him, to let him so much as suspect that he had been followed. He waited until the Sunbeam stopped in front of the barn and then drove slowly on. As he passed the entrance to the track he saw the man leave the car and, after watching the Riley until it was well down the road, disappear behind the barn. Toby wondered whether the barn was indeed his objective, or whether he was making for the distant farmhouse that he could see beyond it, half hidden in a fold of the Downs.

He drove thoughtfully back to Hove.

Lunch at Coniston was nearly over. Crossetta, who was finishing the remains of a large helping of raspberry tart and cream — she had a healthy appetite — greeted him with undisguised relief. 'I thought you were never coming,' she said.

'I had visions of you eating bread and marge in Lewes Gaol. Is everything all right?' He nodded, and was about to tell her his news when she added, 'You didn't tell, did you? About Cardiff Street?'

'No. But I — '

'Good for you.' There was joyous warmth in her voice. 'It would have ruined everything if you had.' She waited impatiently while the maid placed cold ham and salad in front of him, and then leaned forward, her eyes dancing. 'I've been busy, Toby. I've discovered who your friend with the bandaged hand is!'

'You have?' It was obvious that she was too full of her own news to listen to his. That must wait. He said, displaying the approval he knew she expected — and which he honestly felt — 'Say, that's great! How did you manage it? Who is he?'

'His name is Michael Watson. He owns the house we went to last night, and he's quite a rich man. He has two cars, and a motor-cruiser which he keeps at Newhaven.'

'Ready for a trip across the Channel if necessary, eh?' said Toby. 'Well, I bet he didn't come by all that honestly. Where did you dig this up?'

'From various people. I asked the postman first, after I'd managed to locate the house — that took me some time, as I only had a vague idea where it was. All I got from him was the name — but that was a good start. So then I went shopping.' She laughed. 'There are more shops in that part of the town than you'd think. I had to buy an awful lot of things I didn't need, but I got what I wanted.'

'And what was that?'

'Information, silly. About Mr Watson. It only needed a little judicious gossip.'

Plus sex appeal, thought Toby. 'Did you discover what his racket is?' he asked. 'How does he make the money?'

She frowned. 'No one round there seems to know. The greengrocer said he was in business; something to do with exports and imports, he thought. But that's rather vague, isn't it?' The frown vanished, to be replaced by a dimpling smile. 'The chemist said Watson throws lots of parties, and has a weakness for pretty girls. He hinted fairly broadly that

170

I'd be right up Watson's street. Nice of him, wasn't it?'

'Sure.' But he did not return the smile. Noting the look on her face, he said sharply, 'You're not figuring on making Watson's acquaintance, are you? Socially, I mean. Because if you are — '

'Of course not.' She stretched delicately. 'Though you must admit it would have advantages. Fun, too.'

'That depends on what you call fun. I'd say it sounds more like suicide.'

She laughed. 'For you, perhaps. I don't think there'd be much danger in it for me. Now tell me about the inquest.'

The dining-room was empty but for themselves and the maid, who was hovering at the far end of the room waiting for Toby to finish. He pushed away the sweet and stood up.

'Not here. In the car. I'm taking you for a drive.'

'Thank you. Are we going anywhere in particular?'

'You'll see.'

He drove along the front to Shoreham and then went north, turning right at

Upper Beeding and right again on to the Edburton road. He told her about the inquest, and when he had finished she was silent for a while. Then she said, 'What would happen if the police never found Landor?'

'Nothing, I guess. What could happen? Presumably there can't be a trial without a prisoner.' Recalling the inquest had reawakened his conscience, and he said, 'They *must* find him. Soon, too. If they don't it means I'll have to tell them about Cardiff Street. I funked it to-day, but I can't go on funking it.'

'Perhaps we'll strike lucky this afternoon. Or this evening.'

'I sure hope so. The thought of what that Superintendent will have to say when I tell him gives me the shivers. Yet I can't let a murderer escape just to avoid an unpleasant interview with the police.'

'There'll be more in it than an unpleasant interview,' she reminded him.

He slowed down as the barn came into sight. 'Take a good look at it,' he said, pointing it out. 'That's our objective.'

'What — now?'

'Yes. But not in the car. On foot.'

They parked the car in Fulking, and he told her how he had followed the Sunbeam that morning. Crossetta was delighted. 'But wouldn't it be wiser to explore it after dark?' she objected. 'It's so open. If there's anyone there they'd be bound to see us coming.'

'I know. But if we were caught there after dark we'd be caught with our pants down — if you'll pardon the expression. What reason could we give for being there? They'd know for sure we were snooping. If there's something fishy going on and they thought we'd got wise to it they'd have us in their pockets. They could do as they liked with us. But not in broad daylight, with men working in the fields and within earshot. Besides, they won't necessarily be suspicious — I hope! If we walk from here across the fields to the foot of the Downs, make our way along to the farmhouse and approach the barn from that direction, there'd be no reason to suppose we are other than ordinary hikers.'

'If they recognized you there would be.

And your red hair is visible from quite a distance, Toby.'

'Uh-huh. But only Watson knows me by sight, and he's unlikely to be there. All the same, it might be wiser if I went alone. You could keep an eye on events from the road, and warn the police if anything goes wrong.'

She was out of the car before he had finished speaking.

'Oh, no, you don't,' she said firmly. 'Not again. I'm not much of a pedestrian, but I'm coming with you. This might turn out to be fun.'

It was farther than they thought. The ground was hard and the sun warm, and by the time they had reached the farmhouse Toby was perspiring freely. Even Crossetta, in her thin summer frock, looked hot and tired. But when he suggested a rest she would not have it.

'I'd rather go on,' she said. 'We can rest later.'

They saw no one at the farmhouse, although there was evidence that it was inhabited. Washing hung on the line to dry; a bicycle stood propped against a wall. But no livestock, no squawking chickens. No dog ran out to bark at them.

A queer sort of farm, Toby thought. He began to feel uneasy. He had spoken optimistically of the workers in the fields who would be their safeguard, but now there was none in sight. If trouble lay ahead they would have to cope with it unaided.

As they plodded down the dusty, uneven track to the barn they saw that it was built solidly of brick, with a wooden loft above. Two enormous wooden doors, heavily studded with iron, filled the southern end of the building. A ladder left in position led to an opening in the loft.

'Try to talk and act naturally,' Toby said, aware that he was doing neither. 'Some one may be watching us.'

Crossetta laughed. It was a laugh full of infectious gaiety, and he grinned at her, heartened by it. 'You're a marvel,' he said. 'Remind me some time to tell you how much I like you. But what's funny?'

'You,' she said. 'I've never heard a more conspiratorial whisper.'

She began to chatter cheerfully. As they

neared the barn she said, in a loud, plaintive voice, 'I must sit down for a few minutes, Toby. I'm hot and thirsty, and my feet ache. There wouldn't be any water to drink here, would there?'

She spoke so naturally that at first he did not realize she was putting on an act, and looked at her in commiseration. Then, noting the sparkle in her eyes, he said, 'I shouldn't think so. But I'll have a look.'

He walked slowly round the building. The only entrance was by the large wooden doors, and these were securely locked. When he came back to Crossetta she had taken off her shoes and was massaging her feet.

'I can't get in,' he told her.

'What about the loft? There might be a tank up there. I don't suppose the water would be fit to drink, but at least I could bathe my face.' She laughed. '*And* my feet.'

He climbed the ladder gingerly. The opening loomed dark above him, and it occurred to him that it was in just such a spot that Landor might be hiding. And

Landor would be invisible in the gloom — whereas he, Toby, would be silhouetted against the light, a sitting target.

He stopped. The strength ebbed from his legs; the clamminess of his hands was not entirely due to the sun. He leaned forward, resting his body against the ladder.

Hell! he thought, surprised. I'm scared.

Crossetta was watching him. 'What's the matter?' she called. 'Giddy?'

Fear was nothing to be ashamed of; he had experienced it before, and would, no doubt, experience it again. It was in the giving way to fear that a man became a coward. And no one had ever called him that.

Had Crossetta ever known fear, he wondered. Or did she lack the necessary imagination?

'No, cramp,' he lied. 'In my leg. I'll be okay in a moment.'

It did not make it easier to realize that, if Landor were up there and had not known that some one was on the ladder, he would certainly know it now. But he forced himself to go on. Slowly, each movement of arm or leg a mental and physical torment achieved only by tremendous effort, he climbed nearer to the dark void above. It was not the *man* who frightened him — at that moment he would have welcomed the physical relief of a scrap — it was the terrible finality of the gun that seemed to paralyse his limbs. There was no defence, just as there would be no warning. There would be a sharp instant of pain — and then, perhaps, oblivion.

But he went on. He remembered the bullet that had missed him so nearly at No. 17, and the excitement that had filled him later. He had thought then that he could face anything.

Well, he was facing it now. There could never be a worse moment than this.

His chin was level with the floorboards, and he paused again, prepared to duck at the least sound, letting his eyes become accustomed to the gloom. Now he could see the rafters, and presently the far end of the loft. It was not so dark as he had anticipated; there were narrow slits of light in the roof. Gaining courage, he mounted higher and stepped off the ladder. A few loose bricks littered the floor, and he picked one up. It would provide no protection against a bullet, but the feel of it in his hands was good.

The loft was empty. He leant against a rafter, letting the relief flood over him, regaining normality, furious with himself at having panicked to no purpose. Then he dropped the brick and hurried down the ladder.

'Well?' asked Crossetta.

'Nothing.' His voice was a croak. He swallowed and tried again. 'Nothing. It's empty. There's no one there.'

'I heard a crash. What was that?'

'Only me dropping a brick.' It sounded funny, and he laughed and felt better. 'I'd picked it up, just in case Landor might be waiting for me.'

'Oh.' She looked at him pensively. Toby wondered if traces of the fear that had possessed him still lingered on his face. 'What do we do now?'

'What can we do? If there is anything to see it's behind those damned doors.'

The girl scrambled to her feet and

confronted him, hands planted firmly on her slender hips.

'If you've made me walk all those miles for nothing I'm going to be angry,' she said unreasonably. 'There must be *some* way of finding out what goes on here. Why not try the doors again? And I'll go up to the loft. Maybe there's a crack or two in the floorboards that I can squint through.'

But the doors were as solid and opaque as they could be. Toby lay on the ground and tried to peer through the narrow gap at the bottom. Satisfied that he could do no more, he stood up, brushed his trousers, and was about to join Crossetta in the loft when a voice behind him said angrily, 'And what might you be a-doing of, mister? This here's private property.'

Toby wheeled sharply. The man was no taller or broader than himself, but he looked tough. A dark stubble adorned his chin; he wore an old khaki shirt, open at the neck, and his corduroy trousers were tied with string below the knee. Yet he did not look like a labourer. Neither his face nor the V of his neck was red or weather-beaten.

'Nothing in particular,' Toby said. 'We were out walking, and decided to have a look at the barn. No harm in that, is there?'

His tone was not conciliatory. Nor did he feel conciliatory. If the fellow wanted trouble that was okay by him.

'Yank, eh? Where's t'other on you?' the man demanded.

'In the loft. She'll be down in a minute.'

He spoke loudly, hoping the girl would hear him. He did not dare to look up. If the newcomer were one of Watson's friends there might be trouble brewing. Real trouble. And the man stood too close to risk taking his eyes off him.

'So it's a she, is it?' growled the other. 'Well, I'll ruddy soon get her out of that.'

He made a move towards the ladder, but Toby was quick to bar his way. 'No need to get excited,' he said. 'She won't do your damned barn any harm. If it *is* yours.'

The man thrust his unshaven face still closer. His breath was sour, and involuntarily Toby leant away.

'Listen, mister. This here barn's private, like I said. You're trespassing, see? And the guv'nor don't like Nosey Parkers any more than wot I do. So hop it, will yer? Nor you don't have to wait for your bint neither; I'll deal with her.' He flung out an arm to brush Toby aside. 'Go on, get cracking.'

Toby hit him. It was a foolish and unwarranted act of aggression, right out of line with his normal easygoing conduct. But those few nerve-racking moments on the ladder had left him with a burning desire to assert himself — forcefully, if possible — and the surly newcomer's out-thrust chin proved irresistible.

It was not a well-aimed blow. It caught the man high on the head, so that he reeled back. But he was not hurt. Fists clenched, his face suffused with wrath at the indignity he had suffered, he steadied himself and bore in to the attack. A rock-like fist landed on Toby's chest, making him gasp; a swinging right crashed into his ear, so that he stumbled sideways in a daze; and then, as he instinctively put out an arm to ward off the next dose of dynamite, something cracked against his forehead and he lost consciousness.

He opened his eyes to find the ground hard beneath his back and Crossetta bending over him. His head ached abominably. He put up a hand to shield his eyes from the sun, and discovered that some one had bound a handkerchief round his forehead.

'How do you feel, Toby?' asked Crossetta.

'Lousy.' He tried to sit up. She put an arm behind his back to steady him, and then took it away. 'Phew! That devil sure packed a solid punch. My nut feels like it had been hit with a brick.'

'So it was,' came the man's voice from behind him.

Startled, Toby tried to turn his head, but abandoned the effort in a fresh spasm of pain.

The man came to stand beside him.

'Your girl friend done it,' he said, grinning as he jerked a thumb at Crossetta. 'Heaved half a brick at you, she did. That's wot layed you out; it weren't me. Though I'd have done it meself, mind you, if she'd left me to it. Easy, you was. Dead easy.'

Toby swivelled his eyes to gaze in perplexity at the girl. She nodded guiltily.

'I'm terribly sorry, Toby. I didn't mean to hit you, you know that. But you were getting the worst of it, and I couldn't bear the thought of your being hurt. I had to do *something*. So I picked up one of the bricks on the floor and threw it at him.'

'And hit you,' said the man. 'Funny, ain't it?'

'Sure. Very funny.'

It wasn't easy to be coldly dignified in his present position, and slowly and cautiously he scrambled to his feet. That also, he knew, was a clumsy and undignified procedure.

As he straightened his back Crossetta started to giggle.

'I guess I must be lacking in humour,' he said. 'I seem to be the only one around here unable to raise a laugh.'

Crossetta laid a placating hand on his arm.

'Oh, Toby, don't be angry,' she pleaded.

'It was wicked of me to laugh after what I did to you. And of course it isn't funny really. It was just that — well, I — '

She dissolved into helpless laughter.

The man was as startled as Toby. He stared at her open-mouthed. Then he slowly shook his head.

'It weren't all *that* funny,' he said doubtfully.

Toby suddenly warmed to him. He ignored the laughing girl. 'I'm sorry I hit you,' he said. 'It was a crazy way to act.'

The man grinned.

'I bet you're sorry all right. You won't half have a sore head termorrer. But don't mind me, mister. I enjoyed it.'

'You certainly pack a wallop,' Toby told him. 'I'm not sure which hurt most, you or the brick.'

'You want to be more careful who you pick on next time,' the man said, obviously pleased at this compliment to his fists. 'I could see you'd been in the ring, but you was shaping like a novice. You hadn't a chance. I used to be middle-weight champion of the Navy — and I keeps in training. I don't think as how I've slowed up much.'

Toby said he didn't think so either. 'It was decent of you to stick around after,' he added.

'I thought I'd got a corpse on me hands. You was out cold.'

Crossetta had stopped giggling and was making up her face. His exchange of pleasantries with the man had put Toby in a better humour; he decided to forgive. He realized that her laughter might have been due to hysterics, caused first by the fear that she had killed him and then by the relief that she had not.

He smiled at her. 'I guess it had a funny side, at that,' he said. 'But it's a joke that shouldn't be repeated too often. My head wouldn't stand it.'

She smiled back at him.

'That's nice of you, Toby. I behaved like a pig, and I really am sorry. Your head must be terribly sore. Don't you think you ought to go back to the hotel and lie down for a while?'

'Maybe. I'll get the car.'

'No, I'll get it. You wait here. I won't be long.'

He did not argue; his head hurt too much. He leaned against the side of the barn and chatted desultorily with the man. Presently he asked, 'Why were you so annoyed at finding us here? We weren't doing any harm.'

The other frowned.

'Maybe not. But my guv'nor don't like trespassers, same as I said. I'm paid to keep 'em away, see? Maybe you're okay, and maybe you're not. But I'm taking no chances.'

'Fair enough,' Toby agreed.

'No hard feelings?' the man asked anxiously. He seemed to have taken a fancy to his late opponent.

Toby assured him that there was none. Now that they were on such an amicable footing he would have liked to ask further questions (who, for instance, was the 'guv'nor' — Watson?), but he knew that to do so would arouse the man's suspicions. He had had enough trouble for one day. But he did manage to lead the conversation on to crime in general, and from thence to the recent murders at Forest Row and Lewes. He even mentioned

Landor by name, watching his companion closely; but the man gave no sign that the name had any particular significance for him. Toby wondered how much he knew of his 'guv'nor's' activities. Very little, probably — though he might suspect more.

He was glad to see the car. Crossetta had been right, bed was the place for him. He was even more certain of it when, having said good-bye to the man, they jolted down the track. His head felt as though it might come apart at any moment.

'Take it easy,' he groaned when, out on the road, Crossetta began to accelerate. 'If you brake suddenly I'll probably pass out on you.'

But he felt better as the journey proceeded. The girl handled the car smoothly; the cool breeze soothed him. 'What's under the handkerchief?' he asked, probing gently with his fingers. 'I can feel an outsize in eggs, but there doesn't seem to be any gore.'

'Not much,' she agreed. 'It only grazed the skin. It didn't hit you squarely, thank goodness.'

'Squarely enough. Remind me to teach you how to aim properly before you come to my rescue again. I'm not likely to survive many more such rescues.'

He spoke jokingly, but Crossetta appeared to resent the remark. There were furrows in her pretty forehead, and for the rest of the journey she had little to say. Toby decided it had been a tactless remark, but could not rouse himself to jolly her out of her ill-humour.

When they reached the hotel she said, 'Shall I telephone for a doctor? Just to make sure you're going to live?'

He flushed. 'Cut that out, Crossetta. I'm not going to quarrel with you, and I don't need a doctor. Now go ahead and see if the coast is clear, will you? I don't want to be caught looking like something out of a casualty-clearing station.'

He reached his room unchallenged. Crossetta went with him, and took off the handkerchief (his own, he discovered), and bathed his forehead. There was an ugly bruise, and some of the skin was missing; but there was no deep cut.

'It might have been worse,' he said,

surveying the damage in a mirror. 'But I'm not as beautiful as I was. Maybe that's why you don't love me any more, eh?'

'Get into bed,' she said, unsmiling. 'I'll be back shortly.'

She returned with tea and a bandage. 'I told Mrs Buell you'd banged your head,' she said. 'She wanted to have a look at it, but I talked her out of that. I knew you wouldn't want her now.'

'I'll say not!'

He was aware that for no apparent reason her ill-humour had left her. She was as gay and as friendly as ever, and, for once, womanly in her attention. As he lay enjoying her nearness, delighting in the touch of her fingers on his forehead as she arranged the bandage, he began to wonder about her. What a creature of moods she was! And how swiftly her moods changed!

'You've blossomed out quite a lot since Friday,' he told her. 'When I first saw you you looked like you were a timid, sad little mouse that had ventured too far from its hole in the wall.'

'I'm not sure that I like being called a mouse.'

'Oh, but you're not. That was my mistake. I never guessed that you had such a talent for intrigue and mayhem. I know better now.'

'If I seem different it's because life has suddenly become exciting,' she said. 'I was bored before. And I can't stand boredom. Danger or death before dullness — that's my motto.'

She spoke lightly, but he guessed there was some truth behind the words. She was too vital a person to stagnate.

'It sounds kind of gruesome,' he said. And then, because it was the first occasion on which they had discussed personalities, he risked a question. 'Maybe I shouldn't ask this, but — what was your husband? I've wondered plenty about him.'

He could not see her face, but her voice sounded very far away as she said quietly, 'He was an airman. That was how he died.'

She sat with him while he had his tea. 'Now you must rest,' she said firmly, picking up the tray. 'I'll draw the curtains.

I'll pop in later to see how you are.'

'Not too much later. I shan't sleep; I never do in the afternoon. Right now I have every intention of coming down to dinner.'

'Well, we'll see.'

In a few moments she was back. 'I'm going to be bored without you, Toby,' she said. 'May I borrow the Riley?'

'Sure.'

But after she had gone he remembered her motto, and wondered if he had been wise to consent.

8

'If you want to talk things over,' said the Chief Constable, 'why not come and have dinner with me this evening? My wife is away on holiday with the kids, but the woman who 'does' for us isn't a bad cook. I'll ask Baker as well. How about Sergeant Wood?'

'He'll be busy, I'm afraid. But I'd like to come. And thank you.'

Herrod liked the Chief Constable, both as a man and as a policeman. He liked the pleasant but firm manner in which he handled the men under him, he admired his air of 'no nonsense.' His own efficiency was reflected in the efficiency of his force. Yet he might not go down well at Whitehall, Herrod reflected. 'Rules and regulations,' he had heard the Chief Constable say to a somewhat scandalized Inspector, 'are useful. But don't be hide-bound. Make them your servants, not your masters. Knowing when to forget is sometimes more useful than knowing when to remember.' Whitehall might not like that — it hinted at the unorthodox. Well, he can be as unorthodox as he likes, thought Herrod, as long as he plays ball with me. As he certainly has done so far.

The dinner was excellent. At first Herrod had studiously avoided talking shop, thinking that the other two might prefer to wait until after the meal. But the Chief Constable had other ideas.

'Something of a deadlock, isn't it?' he said, dissecting with skill the carcass of a plump young chicken. 'With Waide eliminated you're temporarily out of work, aren't you? Landor seems to be the only person who can fill in the few remaining gaps. All we can do now is sit tight and wait for him to be picked up. And I fancy that won't be done in Sussex. Right now he's probably back in London.'

'That's the way it looks,' Herrod agreed, watching his host with fascination. He knew his own limitations as a carver. 'But I'm troubled by a nasty, nagging doubt as to whether in fact

Catherine Wilkes *was* killed by Landor. Even with Waide out of it, I'm inclined to think she wasn't.'

Baker's jaws ceased masticating, the Chief Constable laid down his knife and fork. Both stared wide-eyed at Herrod.

'I've tried to put myself in Landor's place,' the latter went on. 'He's thirty-eight, and a man well set in his ways. He's a crook — not a clever crook, as witness his four previous convictions — who specializes in breaking and entering. Shops and warehouses, mostly. He has never shown fight when cornered, and he has never been known to carry a gun; Scott, who knows him fairly well, says he's a mild-mannered, friendly sort of chap. And, if one can believe Wilkes, he is — or was — in love with the girl Catherine. Agreed?'

They nodded.

'All right. Now, it seems fairly certain that he persuaded the girl to go away with him. Since he was usually broke, it is suggested that the Forest Row job was to supply the cash for this romantic interlude. That may be so, but we can't prove it. And Landor must have known that we couldn't. Apart from the fact that Caseman was shot, that the money was stolen, we know nothing. They left no finger-prints, no one saw either them or the car. (Mrs Caseman's evidence was too sketchy to be of real value.) Once they were away there was absolutely nothing to connect them with the crime. The very fact that a gun had been used was, in a way, in Landor's favour. It was outside his *modus operandi*. He would not appear on the short list suggested by Records.'

'Odd that he should take a gun with him on that particular occasion,' Baker said. 'It's not the sort of thing one usually packs when taking a girl to the seaside for a holiday. Not, of course, that I know much about that,' he added hastily.

Herrod grinned, and then was serious. 'I was coming to that later. But the point I want to make first is this. There can be no doubt that Landor stopped at the café near Golden Cross, and there is also no doubt that he was in something of a panic at the time. You have only to talk to the café proprietor to know that. And when he went he went in such a hurry that he left a glove on the counter. He would never have been so careless had he had his wits about him.'

'If he hadn't lost that glove he might not have left his print on the Daimler,' Baker said. 'But thank Heaven he did. Without that print he might never have been suspected.'

'Exactly. But — what *caused* him to panic? He was an old hand at the game. He must have known that he was clear away, that he had not left his trademark on the job. So — what was it?'

'The gun, I imagine,' the Chief Constable said. 'He knew that if he were caught it might mean curtains for him.'

'Perhaps. It makes sense, anyway — though I think there was a further reason. But can you explain why, if he was so very, very frightened' — Herrod spoke slowly, stressing each word — 'he should pause in his flight merely to eat a snack at a wayside café? Does *that* make sense?'

It was plain, from the look on their

faces, that it did not.

'Yes, that certainly takes some explaining,' the Chief Constable said thoughtfully. 'I suppose the obvious answer is that he was hungry. But under the circumstances that hardly seems reason enough.'

'Perhaps his girl-friend was hungry,' Baker said, smiling. 'That would carry more weight with him. It's wonderful what love can do, they say.'

But Herrod did not smile.

'Yes,' he said slowly. 'Yes, I think that *is* the answer. Though love, I fancy, had nothing at all to do with it.'

'But — you're not serious, are you? *I* wasn't.'

'I know. But I am.' He paused, guiltily enjoying their unconcealed bewilderment. 'You see, I don't believe it was Landor who shot Caseman. I think the girl did it.'

'Good Lord!'

'It makes sense, you know,' Herrod said eagerly. 'It explains much that otherwise seems inexplicable. Landor did *not* step out of his groove. He had planned a simple raid on a village shop, similar to others he had carried out with varied success. But he had no gun, and he didn't know the girl had one. When she suddenly produced it and shot the old man it must have given him the shock of his life. No wonder he was scared.'

The woman came in to remove the dishes and to carry the cheese and biscuits from the sideboard to the dining-table. At his host's recommendation Herrod helped himself to the Stilton.

'After all, what do we know about her?' he said, when the woman had gone. 'Damn all! Her brother was as close as an oyster. Well, perhaps he had good cause. Perhaps he guessed the truth.'

'It might be that,' said the Chief Constable. 'If he was devoted to her, and if he believes that Landor killed her, he might decide to let Landor take the blame for both murders. And if Landor, when caught, thinks otherwise — well, what then?'

'Who'd believe him — with the girl herself murdered? What proof could he bring? And it is just possible,' Herrod said, as a new thought occurred to him, 'that Wilkes may have decided that

Landor should *not* be caught.'

'You're not suggesting that he would shield the man who shot his sister, are you?'

'No. No, I'm not suggesting that.'

His answer was significant enough. They did not press him to explain further.

'We've wandered a little, haven't we?' Baker said presently. 'You still haven't told us why you think Landor stopped at the café.'

'Because, as you said, his girl-friend was hungry. She was made of sterner stuff than he — a murder couldn't spoil *her* appetite, apparently. And Landor, scared of the possible consequences of what had happened at Forest Row, was still more scared of the girl. Romance, I imagine, had departed from his mind. He had discovered, to his horror, that Catherine Wilkes was a killer. And when they came to the café and she told him to stop — he stopped. One doesn't argue with a killer.'

'You've got something there,' said the Chief Constable. 'All right. But if we accept your theory — how does it continue?'

200

'I'm not so clear about that,' Herrod confessed. 'In fact, it is what happened after they left the café that I wanted to discuss with you. We know they got as far as Jevington in the car; by side-roads, presumably, since they didn't pass through a checkpoint. But after that — well, it's a toss-up. Did they stick together, or did they separate? Did they make for Eastbourne or Lewes? Or Brighton, even? You can take your choice. I have my own theory, of course, but I won't say I'm sold on it. I'd like to hear yours.'

'Well, we know the girl was in Waide's car some time later that day,' Baker said. 'Or early the next morning, perhaps. And as the car was stolen in Eastbourne I'd say that's the way they went first. On foot, over the Downs.'

'Yes, I think so too. But what did they do when they reached the town? Stick together? Or separate?'

'I know what I'd do if I were Landor,' said the Chief Constable. 'I'd lose that young woman just as quick as I could, before she took it into her head to turn the gun on me.'

'And you, Mr Baker?'

'I don't know. I agree that she wouldn't be the ideal companion; but, on the other hand, I'd be rather unwilling to let her out of my sight. I'd like to know she wasn't flashing that gun of hers too freely, inviting the police to pick her up — I wouldn't trust her, you see, not to split on me. No. All things considered, I fancy I'd feel safer if I could keep an eye on her.'

'It may be that Landor wasn't given the choice,' said the Chief Constable. 'The girl had the gun, she was the dominant partner. What would *she* want to do?'

Herrod nodded eagerly.

'That's the way I look at it, sir. Landor is torn both ways — but not the girl. If Wilkes is right she had no love for the man. She knew he had a criminal record, that he had left his glove at the café and, probably, his fingerprints on the Daimler. Once the heat was on it would be Landor the police would look for; and Landor had a finger missing, something that the most casual passer-by would notice. If she stuck to Landor she hadn't a chance; alone, she might make it. Unless she's a nitwit,' he concluded, heaving himself out of his chair as his host stood up, 'I say she told Landor to buzz off. And he buzzed.'

'It's likely enough,' the Chief Constable agreed, leading the way to a small, comfortably furnished sitting-room, where coffee awaited them. 'Though she would be wrong on at least one of those premises. Despite his missing finger, Landor is proving a very elusive quarry. Black or white, Mr Herrod?'

'Black, please.' Herrod held the fragile china in one large hand, added sugar, and stirred thoughtfully. 'Yes, you're right there, unfortunately. He's been too clever for us so far. Yet I can't understand why he was so damned careless as to leave his prints on the Daimler. Most unprofessional. Why didn't he give it a rub before leaving it?'

'Too terrified of the girl, I dare say. Hadn't recovered his wits,' said Baker. 'Why do you suppose she went with him, though, if she wasn't in love with him?'

'Fed up with her brother, perhaps. Anything for a change. We don't know enough about her to guess.' Herrod sipped, and put down his cup. 'And now we come to the sixty-four-dollar question. Who killed Catherine Wilkes? And with her own gun? It need not have been Landor, you see; and it wasn't our fat friend Waide. Yet the girl was in Waide's car. Must have sat in the driving-seat, too, since her prints were on the steering-wheel.'

'Perhaps she stole it,' Baker suggested.

'Yes, I think she did. In fact, I think she was the dark girl who was with Anna Kermode that evening when Waide picked them up in the pub. I hope Mrs Kermode will confirm that when she sees the body.' He looked at his watch. 'That'll be at nine o'clock — I'll have to go soon, sir. But, even if I'm right, there must have been some one else in the car with her. Either they started off together from Eastbourne or they met on the way. And presumably that some one else killed her.'

'A mysterious Mr X, eh? How do you think he became involved? Accidentally — or on purpose?'

'At a guess, I'd say accidentally.'

'Why?'

'Simply because our very meagre information points that way. Wilkes insists that his sister knew no one in Eastbourne, had never even been there. That being so, it seems the more likely that, if she *did* pinch the Austin, she pinched it on her own. But I admit it's pretty thin.'

'It is, isn't it?' The Chief Constable smiled. 'It becomes even thinner when you follow it to its logical conclusion.'

'What's that?'

'That a girl, wanted for murder and escaping in a stolen car, took pity on a jerking thumb and stopped to give some one a lift.'

'Well, she might,' Herrod said doggedly, his face slightly flushed. 'I'm not saying she did — but she might. It depends on what was in her mind. She might have seen some way of making use of this other party.'

'Well, it's a nice line in theory,' Baker said. 'But there's not much we can do about it, is there?'

'I wouldn't say that.' Herrod stared fixedly at his empty cup. 'It's a long shot, of course, and it would take time. And men. I don't know how many houses there are between the barn and Polegate — I don't think we need try farther back than that, anyone wanting to thumb a lift would get out on to the right road before doing so — but — '

The Chief Constable laughed.

'So that's it, eh? Damn it, I believe you had this in mind all the evening. To prove something that you agree is a long shot, you want me to put my chaps on a house-to-house inquiry over a stretch of road that must be nearly ten miles long. That *is* what you're asking, isn't it?'

Herrod grinned, so widely that his ears appeared to move suddenly outward.

'I wasn't asking, sir. But since you've been kind enough to make the offer I'll accept it gladly. And thank you.'

★   ★   ★

Mrs Kermode was plainly nervous. On the pavement outside the mortuary she chattered shrilly, her hands playing with the strap of her bag as Herrod had seen her do at Eastbourne. Occasionally a hand was lifted to pat her hair or finger the imitation pearls round her throat.

'I don't like it,' she said again. 'I've never seen a corpse before. It — it's a horrible thing to ask of me, really it is. I wouldn't have come if I'd known, Inspector, and that's gospel truth.'

So I suspected, he thought, resigning himself to demotion. Mrs Kermode seemed unable to recognize the higher ranks. 'We none of us enjoy it,' he told her, 'but it will only take a moment. Now, if you're ready . . .'

She advanced fearfully into the outer room, wincing at the coffin shells against the wall. Then, as she caught sight of the shrouded figure in the far room, she paled and turned abruptly, clutching at the Superintendent's arm.

'I can't do it, Inspector,' she wailed. 'Not if you paid me a thousand pounds I couldn't do it.'

Herrod hesitated. Should he appeal, cajole, threaten? He signalled to Wood, and each of them caught hold of an arm, propelling her gently forward. She began to cry, but made no protest in words.

'Now, Mrs Kermode . . . '

A sergeant pulled the shroud away from the dead face.

Herrod felt the woman go rigid, saw her eyes widen. Then, with a loud shriek, her body went limp. She would have fallen had not he and Wood held her up.

They got her out into the open air, half carrying, half propelling. If she had fainted she recovered consciousness very quickly. But her face was grey, her eyes were shut. She moaned faintly, clutching the Superintendent tightly for support.

'Get her into the car,' he said. 'We'll run her up to the station and have some one take a look at her.'

But by the time they reached the police station Mrs Kermode had recovered sufficiently to walk, still clinging to Herrod's arm, to the waiting-room. She flopped limply on to a chair.

'I'm sorry,' she said weakly.

The Sergeant gave her her handbag. She began to fumble with the catch.

'I'm sorry too,' Herrod said. And meant it. 'But we had to know.'

She looked at him out of the corner of

her eyes. Then she turned again to her bag, produced from it a mirror and powder compact, and began to repair the damage she apparently considered her complexion had suffered. A lipstick followed, and she smeared it thickly over her lips, her mouth making strange pouting contortions as she did so. Watching her, Herrod found his own lips beginning to twitch in sympathy.

He rubbed them with the back of his hand. 'Feeling better?' he asked.

'Yes.' She peered into the mirror, moving it and her head from side to side, patting and pushing her hair with her free hand.

'Who was she, Mrs Kermode?'

She gave a final pat and prod, tucked away the mirror, and closed the bag with a snap. Then she turned her plump face to look at him squarely.

'I'm sure I don't know,' she said evenly.

'You've never seen her before?'

'Oh, yes. But I don't know who she is.'

He clucked impatiently. 'I don't want to badger you, madam, but I would like to remind you that the girl was murdered.

And it's my job to find out who murdered her. So will you please stop beating about the bush and tell us what you know of her?'

'But I told you yesterday, Inspector.' Herrod grimaced, Sergeant Wood grinned. 'At Eastbourne. She and I happened to be sitting at the same table, and we exchanged a few remarks. About the weather, you know, and things like that. Nothing personal or important. And then Mr — ' she groped in her mind for the name and failed to find it — 'then he joined me, and we had a few drinks together. And as we were leaving I said something about living in Union Street, and Miss — she said she lived out that way too, and could we give her a lift. And we did.'

'She didn't mention her name?'

'No.'

'Where did she get out of the car?'

'When the — when he parked it, I think.'

For a little while he gazed at her with unwinking blue eyes. He was trying to make up his mind. At first she returned the stare. Then her pale eyes flickered, and she looked away.

'Catherine Wilkes,' Herrod said, loudly and suddenly. 'Does that name mean anything to you, Mrs Kermode?'

She had started at the sudden break in the silence, and then turned to him again, her eyes wide in astonishment.

'Who?' The syllable was drawn out, running up a scale.

'Catherine Wilkes.'

'Never heard of her,' she said, with conviction and obvious satisfaction. 'Who is she?'

Herrod shook his head and stood up. 'We'll send you home now,' he said wearily. 'Thank you for coming.'

He stood under the blue lamp and watched her as she climbed, not very modestly, into the back of the police car. As it moved away from the kerb he saw with astonishment that she was actually waving to him. His own right hand lifted half-heartedly, and then dropped quickly.

'I need a drink,' he muttered. And made for the Crown.

9

Toby awoke at six o'clock, and was surprised to find that he had been asleep. Surprised, too, to find himself in bed. Then he remembered, and fingered the lump on his head. It was still there, and still painful. He wondered if Crossetta were back from wherever she had gone in the Riley, and if she had been in to have a look at him while he slept. She's not the anxious, solicitous type, he told himself, but she gave me this ruddy egg. She ought to be interested in watching it hatch out.

But it was Mrs Buell, not Crossetta, who visited him some ten minutes later. She insisted on removing the bandage — 'Young girls are so haphazard' — to satisfy herself that all was well, and exclaimed in sympathy at the sight of his forehead. She brought him a mirror that he might see for himself, and he agreed that it was quite a mess. But when she wanted to replace the bandage he stopped her.

'I'm getting up,' he said. 'I've had enough of bed. I'm coming down to dinner, and I don't want to be swathed in bandages. I hate being stared at. Just stick a bit of plaster over the punctures.'

She protested volubly. His mother would never forgive her, she declared, if she allowed him to do anything so foolish. But Toby was firm.

'Has Mrs Tait returned yet?' he asked her. 'She borrowed the Riley for this afternoon.'

'I haven't seen her since tea.'

Toby nodded, trying to seem unconcerned. Mrs Buell eyed him speculatively. He recognized the look; he had seen it in his mother's eyes whenever a girl-friend was under discussion. He got rid of Mrs Buell quickly, before she had time to lead up to that 'Is there anything in it?' question which he knew she was dying to ask.

He did not feel so good when he got downstairs. After he had patiently but unwillingly given each guest in turn a fictitious account of his accident he felt even worse. But he wasn't going to admit it to Mrs Buell, and he went in to dinner with the others.

There was still no sign of Crossetta. 'She didn't *say* she'd be out,' Mrs Buell told him, 'but young people nowadays are so haphazard about meals.'

That's the second time this evening she's used that adjective about Crossetta, he thought. Doesn't she approve of her?

He had steamed sole for dinner. Toby disliked fish unless it was fried; but the other guests were eating boiled beef, and he appreciated that Mrs Buell had cooked the sole especially for him, so he made an effort to finish it. But he wasn't hungry, and his head ached, and he was worried about the girl. Why wasn't she there?

He nearly choked over the last mouthful, as an unpleasant and disturbing possibility occurred to him. He remembered the look on her face — a smug I-bet-I-could-get-away-with-it kind of look — when she had told him of Watson's parties and of the man's partiality for young and pretty women.

Could she have been fool enough . . .

But no, she wasn't *that* crazy.

The meal was nearly over when he heard the Riley draw up outside, and a few moments later she almost danced into the dining-room.

Her eyes widened when she saw him. 'I didn't think you'd be up,' she said gaily. 'How's the head?'

'Fair. What have you been up to?'

She glanced quickly at the other diners, then leant towards him conspiratorially. 'Something's cooking up at you-know-where,' she whispered.

'What?'

'I don't know. But I mean to find out. I'm going to dash back again as soon as I've had something to eat. At least — '

She frowned, biting her lower lip. 'That's what I'd planned. Do you mind?'

'That depends. Tell me more.'

The maid slapped a plateful of boiled beef and vegetables in front of her. Crossetta grimaced, picked up her knife and fork, and began to eat ravenously.

'Gosh, but I'm hungry!' she said. 'I ought not to have come back, I suppose, but the old tum insisted.' She glanced up at the clock. 'Still, nothing is likely to happen before half-past eight, I imagine. That gives me half an hour.'

'How the heck can you know when something is likely to happen?'

'One of Mr Watson's friends told me,' she said calmly. 'Or perhaps he was a servant. He didn't say.'

Toby stared at her. He was temporarily speechless, his lips framing words he seemed unable to utter. Crossetta finished the last morsel on her plate, wiped her lips delicately, and signalled to the maid.

'I think,' he said at last, watching her start on the stewed fruit, 'that you'd best tell me what you've been doing this evening. In detail. Let's have the lot.'

'I was going to. The first part is pretty dull — I just went for a spin. Then I thought I'd have a look at Cardiff Street. I parked the car where we parked it the other night, and walked down the alley, and — what do you think? The doors were open. Or one of them was.'

'Could you see inside?'

'Yes. It's just an ordinary garage, as far

as I could tell. And there were two men there, and they were pushing a car out into the street as I arrived. They messed about under the bonnet for a while, and then one of them got in and drove it away.'

'Did you recognize either of them?'

'No. And I'm pretty sure neither of them could have been Landor. They weren't a bit like his description.'

'What happened then?'

She laughed. 'I tried to do my stuff. The man who was left started to lock up, so I skipped across the road and asked him where the nearest garage was. I gave him my most seductive smile, hoping he'd fall for it and try to get matey. But not him. He closed the door and locked it before he'd condescend even to speak to me. Then he told me where to find a garage and walked off. I was furious.'

He grinned at her. 'Go on.'

'Well, after that I drove over to Watson's place. As I passed the house I noticed a man standing on the other side of the road. I got the impression that he was watching the house, so I went on, waited for a few minutes, and drove back. And he was still there.'

'He wasn't one of the guys from the garage?'

'Oh, no. He was about thirty, I suppose; fair-haired, and quite nice-looking. He kept walking up and down and staring at Watson's house. If it hadn't been for his expression I'd have thought he might be a detective, or something like that. But he looked angry and unhappy, and his lips kept moving as though he were talking to himself.'

'You seem to have observed him pretty closely,' Toby said.

'Well, I went up and down the road several times. I kept hoping he'd go away, you see, so that I could park the car and watch the house myself for a while. But he never budged.

'Then I had a brainwave. I decided he must know that Watson wasn't at home — perhaps he'd already called at the house — and was waiting for him to return. So I went to a call-box, found Watson's number in the directory, and rang him up. As I expected, he was out.

But the man who answered the phone said he was expecting him back at eight-thirty or a little after.' She laughed. 'He must have thought I was one of the girl-friends.'

'It's eight-twenty now,' Toby said.

'Yes. I'll have to dash. You don't mind, do you?'

'I'm all in favour. In fact, I'm coming with you.'

She looked at him dubiously. 'Do you think you ought to?'

'Never mind that. I'm coming.'

He let her drive. He had hoped that he would feel better once they were in the car, but his head still ached abominably. But he temporarily forgot the pain as they turned into the tree-lined avenue and Crossetta said quickly, 'Look! He's still there.'

Toby took a good look at the man as they drove slowly past. He was much as the girl had described him. As their headlights lit the avenue he had turned eagerly, shading his eyes. Then, as they drew abreast of him and he could see the Riley properly, he plunged his hands into his trouser-pockets and turned his back on them.

'Take that turning on the right,' Toby said.

They were in the middle of the road and about to turn when a car came down the avenue towards them. Only its sidelights were on. As it swept past its sole occupant showed momentarily in the gleam of their dipped headlights.

'Watson!' said Toby. 'Quick! Pull over and let me out.'

This time he would make his own reconnaissance.

He ran down the road towards the house, his head thudding with every tread. The car turned in at the drive, and as he approached Toby saw the fair-haired man hurry across the road and disappear through the gates. By the time Toby himself had reached them the man was talking to Watson on the front porch.

'Looks like they're having quite an argument,' whispered Crossetta.

Toby jumped at the sound of her voice. He had not heard her come up behind him. 'Watson seems to be at the receiving end,' he said, with some satisfaction. 'I guess his visitor's temper hasn't improved with keeping.'

The man's voice was loud and angry, but they could not hear what he was saying. Watson kept shaking his head, obviously trying to pacify him. Then the front door was opened, and the two men, still arguing, disappeared inside the house. A light came on in one of the ground-floor rooms.

'Now what?' Toby said.

'We could creep up under that window, as I did last time,' she suggested.

He hesitated. Had he felt better he might have risked it. But he was in no shape for a scrap, and he knew it.

'Not to-night,' he said. 'I don't think Watson saw us, but if he did he may have a reception committee ready for us. You get the car. We'll stick around for a while and see what happens.'

Crossetta thought they were letting slip a golden opportunity, but she did not argue. She sped away into the darkness, and Toby waited by the gates for her return.

She stopped the Riley a few yards short of the drive. It was a silly place to park, he thought; they should be farther away on the other side of the road, and facing in the opposite direction. He walked back to tell her so. But the lights dazzled him, and as he reached the car he slipped on the kerb. He felt his ankle give, and threw out an arm to save himself. His right hand touched the wing and slid down it, and he pitched forward, his forehead crashing against the door-handle.

Dazed and hurt, he lay half on the running-board and half in the gutter. Then, painfully, his head throbbing and blood trickling into his eyes from the cut, he started to lever himself up. But Crossetta had already slipped out of the car on the far side, and was there to help him.

He sat on the running-board, only half conscious, dabbing at his forehead with a bloodstained handkerchief. Crossetta knelt on the pavement beside him, watching him anxiously.

'What on earth happened?' she asked.

'Nothing much. I slipped, that's all. I'll

be okay in a moment.'

She helped him to his feet. His ankle did not hurt much, but his head throbbed abominably. He hobbled round the front of the car and climbed into the passenger seat, sighing with relief as he relaxed against it.

Crossetta slipped in behind the wheel and pressed the starter. As the car began to move forward he said petulantly, 'Where are you going?'

'Back to the hotel. The sooner you have that cut attended to the better.'

'But we'll miss the fellow when he leaves,' he protested. 'I was hoping he might take us to Landor. Let's stick around for a while, Crossetta. I'll be okay.'

She did not even look at him. They were in top gear now, and gathering speed. 'You're going back to the hotel,' she said firmly. 'Landor can wait, but that cut can't.'

He felt too weak to protest further. But he was worried about the missing Landor. The days were passing, and they were still no nearer to knowing what had become of him. No doubt the police were doing all they could; but they did not know about Cardiff Street, and without that knowledge they must be severely handicapped. For somehow, somewhere, there *had* to be a connexion between Landor and Watson. It was up to him to find it. And the fair-haired stranger might have provided the missing link.

You darned fool, he told himself angrily; why the heck can't you look where you're going? Aloud he said, 'It won't take long to fix me up. Maybe he'll still be there when we get back.'

The girl shook her head, but made no spoken comment on this optimistic statement.

Mrs Buell was talking to one of the guests in the hall when they arrived. She exclaimed in horror when she saw Toby's blood-streaked face; but, being a sensible woman, she wasted no time in asking questions. 'Come along to my sitting-room,' she said briskly. 'I'll fetch some hot water.'

The cut was long, but not deep. The blood had stopped flowing. Crossetta watched the older woman as she bathed and cleaned it and put on a dressing. 'It's not pretty,' Mrs Buell said, as she stepped back to inspect her handiwork, 'but it'll do for to-night. And for goodness' sake don't bang it against anything else. You're not giving it a chance to heal.'

'I didn't do it on purpose,' he protested.

'Well, off to bed with you. I'll bring you up some hot milk. That and a couple of aspirins will help you to get some sleep. It must be very painful.'

He thanked her, but his eyes were on the girl. A multiplicity of hammers seemed to be banging around inside his head; the very thought of climbing into the Riley made him feel sick. Yet if they were going back they must go now.

'Well?' he said, when Mrs Buell had left them. 'How about it?'

She shook her head. 'We'd better call it off, Toby. You're not up to it.'

He was reluctant to admit defeat. 'It may be our last chance to investigate the blond guy,' he said. 'I hate to pass it up.'

'I know.' She hesitated. 'Er — you

wouldn't let me go alone, I suppose? Or is it mean of me to suggest it?'

'Not mean, no. But I can't say I like the idea. It isn't safe for you to play around with those thugs on your own.'

'I wasn't intending to play around with them. I need not even get out of the car if you don't want me to. I'll just sit in it until he comes out, and then follow him. I suppose he'll take a bus, unless Watson runs him home. The main thing is to find out where he lives, isn't it? Then we can keep an eye on him to-morrow.'

He was tempted to agree. Had he felt more sure of her he would have done so without further demur, for much might depend on it. But he knew Crossetta.

'You're so darned impulsive,' he told her. 'I don't trust you. You'll sit in the car for a while, maybe; but then if the blond guy doesn't show up you'll go peeping through windows again.'

'I won't, Toby. I promise I won't.' Something in his look told her he was weakening, and she leaned towards him, her lips parted. 'Please, Toby. And when I get back I'll come up to your room and tell you everything that's happened. How would you like that?'

'I'd like it fine. But Mrs Buell would be shocked, I guess.'

'Never mind about her. She need not know. Is it a deal?'

She was too lovely, too vital, for a young man as susceptible as Toby to resist. Despite the pain in his head, he once more experienced a strong desire to take her in his arms and kiss her. Her eyes seemed to be inviting him to do so. But because she was Crossetta, and because of that other evening when she had shrunk away from him in the car, he restrained the impulse. I'll get around to it soon, he promised himself; she can't keep me at arm's length much longer. This just isn't the right opportunity.

'Okay,' he sighed. 'You win. But no tricks, mind, or I never trust you again.'

Instantly she abandoned seduction. It had served its purpose. She gave his arm a squeeze, thanked him and told him he was a dear, danced a few steps out of sheer high spirits, and made for the door.

There she paused. 'What about when I

get back? Do I come up and see you, or don't I? I will if you like. But perhaps you would rather I kept the news until the morning? I don't want to spoil your night's rest.'

'You come up and see me to-night,' he told her. 'I shan't sleep until I know you're back. And for the Lord's sake be careful.'

She laughed. 'Why? Is it my reputation or yours that you're worried about?'

'Neither. I wasn't referring to reputations, and you know it.'

She blew him a kiss and disappeared. A few moments later he heard the Riley's engine spring to life, and then the rapid crescendo of acceleration. I hope she'll be okay, he thought anxiously. She should be — if she keeps her promise to stay in the car.

But Crossetta had no intention of keeping her promise. It had been given as a means to an end, and she was not going to spoil what might turn out to be a first-rate adventure through mawkish sentiment. She also had no intention of walking starry-eyed into the lion's den. If it should prove necessary to reconnoitre the enemy's stronghold she would do so. But she would make quite certain that this time she was not caught unprepared.

Delighting in the Riley's ancient but still virile engine, she hummed contentedly to herself as she drove, as fast as traffic would permit, northward through Hove. As she turned once more into the now familiar avenue she slowed and switched off her headlights, driving past the house in low gear so that she might glance quickly up the drive before deciding on her plan of campaign. The Sunbeam still stood in front of the house. But now a light showed in the hall, and not in the room.

She turned the car and came back, stopping on the opposite side of the road. Then she slipped out of the driving-seat and went across to the gates. As she reached them light flooded out from the now open front door, and she shrank back, uncertain if she were visible. A few moments later she heard voices. Peering cautiously forward, she saw Watson and the fair-haired man at the top of the steps. They were still arguing, apparently, but less heatedly. No doubt some of the steam has evaporated by now, she thought. They must have had quite a session.

She hesitated, uncertain of her next move. If, as seemed possible, the two men were about to drive away in the Sunbeam, they could not fail to see her if she stayed by the gates. In any case they would notice the Riley, parked so conspicuously opposite the house. Did Watson know the Riley? She wasn't sure.

She ran across the road, climbed into the car and, revving the engine as little as possible, drove away from the house and down the next turning. She turned the car round and, leaving the engine ticking over, ran back to the corner. As she reached it the headlights of the Sunbeam shone out from the drive and swung towards her.

She was back in the driving-seat and sliding the lever into bottom gear as the car passed the turning. There were two men in it. She waited a few seconds, and then eased back the clutch pedal and went in pursuit. The tail-light of the Sunbeam seemed to wink at her, as if in conspiracy. Her spirits soared with the prospect of adventure ahead, and she smiled to herself. Don't let to-night fizzle out like a damp squib, she prayed to an unknown god. Please, *please* let something happen!

★　★　★

It was nearly eleven-thirty when she tapped softly on Toby's door. He was sitting up in bed reading, making little headway with the book perched on his knees. During the past hour he had become increasingly concerned for her safety, and in imagination had reviewed in ever sharper forms the possible fates that might have befallen her.

'Thank the Lord you're back!' he said fervently. 'Where did the guy live? Glasgow?'

'Don't be peevish.' She planted herself daintily at the foot of the bed and smoothed the coverlet with a slim hand. 'I haven't been that long, have I?'

She did not look at him, and he thought he detected guilt in her demeanour. She's been up to some mischief, he thought. Probably snooping at windows again, despite her promise. But he was so pleased to see her that he could not bring himself to scold.

'Very nearly,' he said lightly. 'Far too long for my peace of mind, anyway. Come on, give. Let me know the worst.'

She shook her head.

'There isn't much to give, unfortunately. I bungled it.'

She went on to tell him how she had seen Watson and the stranger leave the house, and how she had followed them. 'I didn't want him to suspect he was being followed — and I thought he might recognize the Riley — so I had to keep my distance. And then we came to some traffic lights . . . and he accelerated just as they turned to amber . . . and I got left. I was *wild*. In fact I was so hopping mad that I'd have disregarded the lights and gone after him if there hadn't been a policeman standing on the corner. I only just spotted him in time.'

'Thank the Lord you did!' Toby said fervently. 'We're in enough trouble with the police already. Or we could be if they ever get wise to us. Whereabouts were those traffic lights?'

'I'm not sure. But I seemed to recognize the road. I think it was the one we took last night when we followed the Sunbeam. So I thought Watson might be making for Cardiff Street. And that's where I went.'

'What then?'

'Nothing. The place was deserted. No car, no Watson, no anybody. I hung around for a while, but nothing happened. So eventually I just packed up and came home. And here I am.'

'Have you parked the car?'

'Yes.' She sat up straight and looked at him sorrowfully. 'I made a mess of it, didn't I? I shouldn't have let the Sunbeam get so far ahead.'

'Nonsense.' Her dejection was a spur to his gallantry. 'I guess you just didn't get the breaks; being baulked by the traffic lights was plain unlucky. But I'm kind of surprised that you didn't try the barn

233

after drawing a blank at Cardiff Street. Knowing you, I should have said that was inevitable.' He paused, and then said slowly, 'You *didn't* go to the barn, I suppose?'

'No. I might have done so if I'd thought of it, but I didn't.' She stood up. 'Well, that's that. Now we may never know who he was, or where he lives.'

'We may,' Toby said cheerfully. 'But I guess it isn't so important at that. We're way off the ball, Crossetta. We're getting no place, and you know it. Maybe you're having a lot of fun; so am I, I guess — though I'm also having more bumps and bruises than seem strictly necessary for amusement. But I didn't start this for fun; I wanted to get Landor. Well, I haven't got him, and I guess I never will. So I'm handing over to the police.'

'Really, Toby, you're impossible,' she said indignantly. 'Talk about blowing hot and cold! I've never known such a man. You said all this last night, you know. But did you tell the police when you saw them this morning? Of course you didn't! And I don't suppose you'll tell them to-morrow, either. So why keep talking about it?'

Toby flushed. He was not a little ashamed of his vacillation, and he knew that her taunt was justified. It hurt the more because of that.

'We won't discuss it to-night,' he said. 'It's too late. But to-morrow — well, you'll see.'

Crossetta shrugged her shoulders.

'Don't expect me to visit you when you're in prison,' she said. 'If you insist on getting yourself gaoled you won't get any sympathy from me. Besides, I hate the very thought of prison. I wouldn't go near one.'

'Say!' He was startled by the vehemence in her voice. 'You'll be telling me next you've been inside one.'

'Not in the sense you mean. But there are other prisons besides those made of stone,' she said cryptically. 'Good night.'

10

Detective-Superintendent Herrod had slept badly. It was not the fault of the bed; nor, he believed, of his digestive organs. The latter did not always work as they should; but exercise did them good, and during the past few days he had been getting around more than usual. No. The cause of his insomnia, he decided, was due to mental fatigue. The case was getting him worried. He had taken it to bed with him, and it had proved a wakeful bedfellow.

The creases at the corners of his eyes were deeper and more numerous that morning, the eyes themselves less vivid in their blueness; but these were the only visible signs that he had not slept well. He had risen at his normal hour, he looked as spruce and his step was as brisk as ever as he strode down West Street and turned in at the police station. He gave the constable on duty at the reception desk his normal cheerful greeting, and was about to disappear down the passage when the man checked him.

'The Divisional Superintendent asked if you would see him as soon as you came in, sir,' he said.

Herrod stared at him, nodded, and walked on. It might mean news of the inquiry that was being conducted along the Polegate road, although he had not expected such an early result. Well, I hope it's concrete, he thought. This case needs more solidity in its foundations. At present it's mostly theory.

It was certainly concrete.

'Another murder,' the Divisional Superintendent said laconically. 'At Peacehaven. I thought you'd like to know. It may have nothing to do with your present inquiries, of course. But then again — it may.'

'And why may it?'

'Because the man was shot. In the back.'

This is the sort of thing that happens to one on a morning when one is not at one's best, thought Herrod. As if I hadn't enough on my plate without this! He had no doubt in his mind that it would be his to deal with, that the murder weapon would prove to be the gun that had killed Catherine Wilkes.

'Who's the victim?' he asked.

'Unidentified at present. Kane went down there about half an hour ago. I'll let you have any information he sends through.'

'It couldn't be Landor himself, I suppose?'

The other shook his head. 'Unlikely, I should say. No mention of a missing digit in the report. And by now every policeman in the division could quote you Landor's description. No, it wouldn't be him.'

'I don't think I'll wait for Kane's report,' Herrod said wearily. 'I'll go down there pronto. If it *does* turn out to be my pigeon — and I've a nasty suspicion that it will — the sooner I'm on the spot the better.'

He and Sergeant Wood had little to say on the journey down to Peacehaven. With no knowledge of the victim's identity speculation was profitless. Instead Herrod leaned back in his seat and closed his eyes; not to doze, but to re-examine in his mind the theory he had put forward the previous evening. Both his listeners had admitted the plausibility of his assumptions, had even been prepared to work on them. So far, so good. But it still remained only a theory, it needed definite evidence to turn it into fact. And without facts he had no case.

Perhaps this latest murder would provide the evidence. Perhaps on this occasion the killer had left some tangible clue to his identity, so that they might go after him as they had gone after Landor. Though with more success, I hope, thought Herrod glumly.

At Peacehaven police station they found that news of their expected arrival had preceded them; a constable was waiting to take them to the scene of the crime. It lay inland, on the very outskirts of the town, at the corner of an unmade road which, flanked on either side by a straggling and untidy hedge, led to where workmen were busy on the foundations of a row of new houses. The usual screens had been erected round the body; police were keeping curious spectators at a distance.

As Herrod stepped out of the car Inspector Kane came forward to greet him. 'I'm glad you're here, sir,' he said. 'I sent you a message at Lewes, but they told me you had already left.'

'It's one of ours, is it?' Herrod, who had been pounding a beat in London at the outbreak of the Second World War and had seen much — too much — of the blitz, thought how odd his words sounded now. And yet — how reminiscent of death.

'I think so, sir.'

The body lay on its back on the grass verge, staring sightlessly at the little white clouds lazily drifting across the sky. As Herrod and Wood walked round behind the canvas screens Inspector Kane watched them expectantly.

His expectancy was rewarded. Herrod's back stiffened, his left hand flew to an ear and pulled at the lobe. (Perhaps that's why they stick out so, thought Kane.) He looked at the impassive Wood, who contented himself with a brief nod.

There was no doubt in the mind of any of the three officers that this was, as Herrod had said, one of theirs. For the body that lay at their feet was that of Geoffrey Taylor, joint proprietor of the 'Dayanite' Café.

The Superintendent turned abruptly to Kane. 'Let's have the details, Inspector,' he said.

Taylor's body, said Kane, had been found by one of the builder's men on his way to work that morning. The man had paused to light a cigarette, and had then seen the body in the ditch. It had been partially concealed by the nettles and brambles through which it had fallen. 'I've questioned the occupants of most of the near-by houses' — and he pointed to the several modern-looking buildings that fringed the area — 'and two of them recall hearing last night what may have been the shot. Both of them put the time at around eleven o'clock — which agrees with the doctor's rough estimate of the time of death.'

'And I suppose neither of these two

ple took the trouble to investigate?'

'No, sir. They both claim to have heard a car — accelerating, one of them said, and going in the direction of the town — and thought it had back-fired.'

'Modern cars don't back-fire,' the Superintendent said testily. He looked with distaste at the eager spectators, whose ranks were rapidly increasing. 'Why can't people show a little natural curiosity at the right time?'

The photographer stood apart, his work done; but the rest of the normal routine investigation which takes place at the scene of a crime went steadily forward. Ditches, hedges, and ground were searched methodically by men trained to miss nothing. There had been no rain for days, and the ground was hard; there were tracks and footprints in plenty, but none had been freshly made. Herrod spoke to the man who had found the body, and to the two residents who claimed to have heard the shot. But he learned nothing new. He sent Wood off to make inquiries farther afield and, after dealing politely but firmly with reporters and local correspondents eager for information, turned his attention once more to the dead man himself.

The arrival of the Chief Constable, accompanied by Superintendent Baker, was preceded by an undertaker's van by some minutes. The Chief Constable looked a worried man. Murder was not a commonplace in his parish. This sudden spate of death was becoming a nightmare.

He listened quietly as Herrod told him the little there was to tell, and watched the removal of the body, which was followed by a rapid dwindling of the spectators. Then, after a talk with Inspector Kane, the three senior officers walked across to the parked cars.

'What do you make of it, Mr Herrod?' asked the Chief Constable.

'Something I don't like,' Herrod said grimly. 'Something I wasn't prepared for. Remember that fine theory of mine that I plugged last night at dinner, sir? Well, you can forget it. It was all so much poppy-cock.'

'Eh?' The Chief Constable was startled. 'How's that? You've dropped it fairly tly, haven't you?'

'It's dropped me, sir.' Herrod pointed to the grassy corner on which the dead body of Geoff Taylor had so recently lain. 'Why do you suppose that poor fellow was shot?'

'I don't know. But presumably because he got mixed up with Landor and the girl. Isn't that so?'

'It is. It must be. Yet Taylor's only connexion with the previous crimes is that Landor and Catherine Wilkes stopped at his café the night Caseman was killed. Which, to my mind, makes it a certainty that Landor killed him. Taylor didn't see the girl — and anyway she's dead, it couldn't be her. But Landor . . . ' He paused, and then said slowly, 'As far as we know, sir, Taylor was the only man in Sussex who knew Landor by sight.'

'Yes, I suppose he was.' The Chief Constable looked thoughtful. 'You think the two men met last night — by accident, presumably — and recognized each other?'

'Yes. And that Landor also recognized the danger Taylor represented. That's why he shot him. They wouldn't have met here, of course. Some place else — and Landor brought him here to dispose of him. In a stolen car, I imagine.'

'Knowing who Landor was, Taylor must have been out of his mind if he got into a car with him,' Baker said.

'He may have had no choice. The important point, to my mind, is that Landor has the gun. He shot this poor chap, he shot the girl — and he probably shot Caseman too. I was all wrong. Past record or no past record, it was Landor, not Catherine Wilkes, who was the killer. And still is.'

'Always assuming that Taylor was shot with the same two-five,' Baker said. 'That isn't yet certain.'

'No. But I bet he was. I may have been right up to a point; the gun may have belonged to the girl originally, she may even have used it to kill Caseman. Perhaps that put ideas into Landor's head.' Herrod kicked moodily at a tuft of grass. 'But after that — well, wherever they went they went together. They didn't separate, as I supposed.'

'But they *did* separate,' said the Chief Constable. 'Catherine Wilkes was with Mrs Kermode in the pub that night. But not Landor. And *he* didn't get a lift in Waide's car. So how and where did they meet later?'

'Some prearranged spot, no doubt,' Baker said. 'They may have decided it was safer not to be seen together during the day. Perhaps she even picked him up in Waide's car after she'd pinched it.'

Herrod nodded. It was a reasonable assumption.

'Well, this is where I start again,' he said. 'And the first thing is to trace Taylor's movement's last night. His wife may know what he was up to — if he has a wife. He had no keys, no wallet, and no papers on him; Landor took those, no doubt. There was some loose change in his trouser-pockets, and that's all. Where did he live? Hailsham?'

'Inspector Bostrell would know,' said the Chief Constable.

'Polegate, sir,' said Sergeant Wood, who had joined them. 'It was on his statement.'

'I'll ring Bostrell and get the exact address,' said the Chief Constable.

'Thanks. Ask him to meet me there in half an hour, will you?'

In the car Herrod sat moodily in his corner. It had been such an excellent theory; he had had such complete faith in it. It was a jolt to his self-esteem to find that he could reason so sensibly and be so wrong. He looked across at Wood. Wood had the right idea; he stuck to simple arithmetic, he put two and two together before he made four. He didn't juggle with symbols and probabilities.

The Taylors' house was a small red-brick villa on the outskirts of Polegate, one of a cluster of similar houses in a road that still retained something of the character of a country lane. Inspector Bostrell, tall and soldierly, was awaiting their arrival. With him was the local police sergeant.

'Anyone at home?' Herrod asked. He spoke briskly. With the prospect of action his moodiness had disappeared.

'I don't know, sir. We've seen no one since we got here, but we haven't called at the house. The Chief Constable said to wait for you.'

'H'm! Well, you and I had better do that now, Inspector. You've heard about Taylor?'

'Yes, sir. I'm sorry. He seemed a decent chap.'

They left the two Sergeants in the lane and walked slowly up the narrow concrete path. 'We get some unpleasant tasks,' Herrod said, pausing for a moment before the cream-painted front door, 'but this is the one I hate most. Well, let's get it over.'

He lifted the iron knocker and gave a double knock. Then they waited, both men a little apprehensive. A minute passed, and the Superintendent knocked again, louder this time. But there was no sound of movement within the house, no hurrying feet.

'Let's take a look round the back,' Herrod said.

Outside the back door stood a pint-sized milk-bottle, full — a mute answer to their search. Through the ground-floor windows they could see dirty crockery stacked on the draining-board in the kitchen; in the living-room the ash-trays were full, newspapers and periodicals littered the chairs and the floor, a tea-cup sat in its saucer on the mantelpiece.

'Doesn't look as though there's a woman around,' Herrod said. 'What has happened to Mrs T, I wonder? Perhaps the neighbours can tell us something.'

'They usually can,' said Bostrell.

Mrs Moss, the Taylors' immediate neighbour, was a plump little woman who showed alarm at the Inspector's uniform — alarm which was presently tempered by satisfaction at her own perspicacity. She had known, she said, that something was wrong.

'He went off yesterday afternoon,' she told them. 'About two o'clock, it'd be. Asked me to take a small white for him when the baker called — which I did. But he never came to collect it, and when my husband took it round before he went to the pub he couldn't get no answer. Nor I haven't seen him this morning, either.' Her round face was a ball of curiosity. 'And his van's been in the garage, so he couldn't have gone to work last night.

And I see the milk's not been took in this morning. I said to Bert (that's my husband), 'Geoff Taylor's had an accident,' I said. 'Why else would he have stayed away from home?'' She put the question that had been in her mind all the time she had been talking. 'What's happened, sir? Has he been run over?'

'Not run over,' Herrod said. 'But an accident, yes. That was why we wanted to see his wife.'

'She's away. Been away some days now.' She spoke hurriedly, anxious for further information. 'Is he bad?'

'Yes. Any idea where I can find his wife?'

'No. They might know where she works.'

'And where is that?'

'In Eastbourne somewhere,' said the woman. 'She never told me the name of the firm. Mrs Taylor's not one for talking about herself.'

There was a faint note of resentment in her voice that had not been there when she spoke of the man.

'When did she leave home?' Herrod asked.

'Thursday night.' The answer came

promptly. 'Leastways, it was Friday morning Geoff told me she'd gone.' She said, her voice hesitant and tinged with fear, 'He — he's not dead, is he?'

Herrod nodded. There was nothing to be gained in concealing the truth, and he told her what had happened. Her face lost its colour as she listened, and her eyes filled with tears. When they left she stood at the door and watched them until they were out in the road, dabbing at her eyes and occasionally shaking her head with a quick, nervous movement.

'Nice old thing,' Herrod said. 'Genuinely fond of Taylor, I should say, but dislikes his wife. Well — what now?'

'We might try the café,' Bostrell suggested. 'Taylor had a partner — a man named Ellis. He should know something.'

The Superintendent disliked Charlie Ellis on sight. Ellis was tall and thin, with carroty hair and restless eyes and a neat little moustache. His voice was unctuous, aping an educated accent that was obviously foreign to it and occasionally came unstuck. And he oozed good-fellowship and affability.

251

But he wasn't feeling affable about Geoff Taylor. Taylor, he said, had let him down badly. He didn't know where Geoff had gone or what he'd been up to, but he *did* know that he'd failed to turn up for the night shift. 'Perhaps you gentlemen can tell me why,' he said gravely. 'But it'll have to be something pretty serious to excuse his behaviour. I don't like a chap that lets his pals down.'

'Taylor has been murdered,' Herrod said. He waited for the other to recover from this broadside (I hope he considers murder serious enough, he thought grimly), and listened rather impatiently to the oily, conventional expressions of sorrow and regret that followed. But when Ellis embarked on what were intended to be a few well-chosen words in memoriam of his late partner the Superintendent cut him short.

'I understand Mrs Taylor is away,' he said. 'Can you help us to get in touch with her?'

No, Ellis said, he could not. Geoff had told him his wife was away — on business, he had said, and hadn't seemed

252

too pleased about it. But where — no, he couldn't help them there. Nor did he know when she would be back.

'Who are her employers in East-bourne?'

Ellis couldn't tell them that either. 'She worked in an office, I believe, not a shop. And it was near the station. I remember driving her to work once — ' his eyes flickered oddly, and he moistened his lips with his tongue — 'and she asked me to drop her by the station.'

The Superintendent looked at him, not liking what he saw. When he asked for a description of Mrs Taylor Ellis gave it in great detail, describing her charms with obvious relish. But it did not help greatly. It was a description that could have been fitted to most attractive young women of the same build and colouring.

On the journey back to Lewes Wood said, 'Did you watch Ellis's face while he was talking about Mrs Taylor? I fancy he won't be shedding any tears over her husband's death.'

The Superintendent grunted. The Ser-geant's remarks hinted at a new theory for Taylor's murder; he would not voice it himself, but he was prepared to give his senior a lead. But Herrod was not biting. After his last setback he found theory indigestible fare.

On reaching Lewes he went at once to county headquarters.

'We must find Mrs Taylor, sir,' he told the Chief Constable. 'If the Eastbourne police can locate her employers it's possible that we may be able to trace her through them. But Ellis could be wrong; she may not be away on business. Her employers may be as much in the dark as we are.'

'There's the Press,' the Chief Constable suggested.

'Yes. But how do we use it? We have to discover two things: how Taylor spent yesterday afternoon and evening, and where his wife is. And that means mentioning Taylor by name.'

'H'm! I don't like that. It's not the most sympathetic way in which to inform a woman that her husband has been murdered. It might do serious harm, Mr Herrod.'

'I know that, sir. But what else can we do?'

'How about two separate statements? 'An unknown man' etcetera — and, elsewhere, an appeal to Mrs Taylor to come forward. Wouldn't that do the trick?'

'It might. But suppose Mrs Taylor is somewhere she shouldn't be — with another man, say. Will she come forward immediately if she is unaware of the urgency? The necessity for secrecy may outweigh her curiosity.'

'Urgency can be stressed without mention of murder,' the Chief Constable said. 'And isn't curiosity supposed to be strong in women?'

Back at divisional headquarters Herrod telephoned Superintendent Farrar at Eastbourne. Farrar promised his help. 'We'll try the employment exchange first,' he said. 'If that doesn't work I'll have inquiries made near the station. Anything else?'

Herrod said there was nothing else, and asked after Mrs Kermode. But Farrar had nothing worth while to report. Mrs

Kermode, he said, had stuck mostly to her home; her only outing had been to the shops, her only visitor her sister.

'Did she make a phone-call while she was out, or post a letter?'

'No. But I suppose her sister could have done that for her.'

As Herrod replaced the receiver the Divisional Superintendent walked into his office. 'You will have heard about the bullet, I suppose,' he said.

'That it was a two-five? Yes. And I don't need any ballistics expert to tell me that it was fired from the gun that killed Caseman and Catherine Wilkes. To my mind that's a foregone conclusion. But it will have to be checked, of course,' he added hastily, aware that he was once more jumping in the dark.

'Well, here's something you *don't* know, I fancy. Your hunch has paid off.'

Herrod stared at him. 'Hunch? What hunch?'

'About the Polegate road. We've had a positive response.'

The stare became fixed. Then an expression of bewilderment spread over the detective's face.

'But that — that's old stuff!' he exclaimed. 'That was just an idea I had before we knew of Taylor's death. If I hadn't forgotten all about it I'd have called it off. It's out. It doesn't fit.'

The other shrugged.

'It may not fit; I wouldn't know about that. But it certainly isn't out. The car was seen. Not just any car — but Waide's Austin.'

Herrod took a deep breath. 'This gets madder and madder,' he said. 'If I wasn't involved in the darned thing I wouldn't believe it. Go on — let's have it.'

A certain John Ford, said the Divisional Superintendent, who lived near Wilmington and whose house stood only a few feet from the road, had been lying awake in bed on the Thursday night when he had heard a car approach from the direction of Polegate. A few yards short of his house it had stopped, and it had sounded to Ford as though the engine had cut out some distance before that. Since there were no other houses in the vicinity, he had decided that either the stop was involuntary or that here was a visitor for him. He had got out of bed and gone to the window; but the driver had forgotten to switch off his headlights, so that Ford's vision was blinded. Then he had heard footsteps running down the road. They came from behind the car — and presently there were voices, one of which he was certain was a woman's. Then the car doors banged, there was some heavy work on the self-starter, the engine eventually started, and the car drove off. Ford watched it pass under his window, and saw enough to recognize it as an Austin.

'And what is more,' the Divisional Superintendent concluded, 'he saw and remembered the rear number. That is to say, he remembered enough of it to pick Waide's number out of a prepared list that was shown to him.'

Herrod leaned back in his chair and half closed his eyes, trying to force his puzzled brain to absorb and correctly pigeon-hole this further item of conflicting information. But he did not try to bend it into a theory. For the present theories were out.

'Thanks,' he said. 'Sounds like a pick-up, certainly. Well, that was what I wanted. The devil of it is, I don't want it now. The woman's voice — that would be Catherine Wilkes, of course.'

'I — yes, I suppose so.' It was hesitantly said, so that Herrod looked at the other keenly. 'But this chap Ford — well, he's a blunt, dogmatic sort of chap from all accounts, and I fancy any statement he made would take some shaking. And it seems he is absolutely positive that the running footsteps were those of a woman. Which means, you see, that unless *two* women were involved Catherine Wilkes was *receiving* the lift, not giving it.'

11

Toby Vanne had spent an uncomfortable day. Apart from the damage to his forehead, which was still painful, Crossetta had been decidedly sulky. There had been no open quarrel — Toby had seen to that; he had not wanted to ruin what he romantically imagined might blossom into a beautiful friendship — but they had argued long and heatedly. Or Crossetta had. He himself had said little beyond assuring her, at regular intervals, that it was too late for argument. He had made up his mind, and nothing she could say would change it. This time he *would* go to the police.

'When?' she had asked.

'To-morrow.'

But he fancied that she did not believe him. Perhaps the 'to-morrow' was responsible for that; why not to-day? she would ask herself. He did not think it necessary to mention that twice that morning he had telephoned to Lewes police station, and that on each occasion Superintendent Herrod had been out. Nor did he tell her that he had left a message to say he would be over to see Herrod in the morning. It was better that she should not know that. He had given her the truth. If she refused to believe it so much the better; it made the argument more academic than real.

That evening they went to a cinema in Brighton. It was not, Toby thought, the best method of entertainment for a man with an aching head. But Crossetta had seemed restless after dinner, and he did not want her to go off on her own. He knew where that might lead her. The cinema also put a temporary and welcome end to the argument.

He bought an evening paper when they came out, and they walked in silence to the car. She had seemed to enjoy the performance, but he suspected she still bore him some resentment for his refusal to capitulate. And his head throbbed too violently for him to want to talk.

He let her drive, hoping to please her,

and she thanked him politely; but with the feel of the steering-wheel in her hands her ill humour soon began to evaporate. The lights were bright along the front; people crowded the pavements and spilled over on to the road. It was a gay, cheerful scene, and Crossetta responded to it.

She began to hum a tune. It was one Toby did not know, but as the same phrases were repeated again and again it soon formed a pattern in his brain.

'What's that you're humming?' he asked.

'I don't know what it's called.' She braked suddenly and skilfully as the car in front slowed and swerved to avoid a hurrying pedestrian. 'But I've often heard my — '

She did not complete the sentence. Toby guessed she had been thinking of her dead husband, and wondered why she would never talk of him. It could not be that her memories were sad ones, for on the rare occasions when he was obviously in her thoughts there seemed to be no curb on her high spirits.

They were nearing the hotel. 'Let's have a drink,' she said. 'It's too early for bed.'

He did not want a drink, but also he did not wish to check her good humour. 'Okay. But I must collect a letter from the hotel first. I forgot to post it, and it's urgent.'

'And I'll get a woolly,' she said. 'It's turning chilly.'

He collected the letter and waited for her in the hall, idly scanning the front page of the evening paper. Crossetta was kept talking outside her room by one of the guests, but presently she came running down the stairs, still humming. As soon as she saw his face she knew that something was wrong.

'What's happened?' she asked. 'You look as if you've just seen a ghost.'

'I've read about one, I think.' He handed her the paper, pointing to a paragraph on the front page. 'What do you make of that?'

'Another murder, eh?' she said, noting the headline. She read the paragraph quickly. 'Well, if it's supposed to ring a bell I'm afraid it doesn't. I don't know anyone at Peacehaven. Do you? Where is it, anyway?'

'Between here and Newhaven. But that's not the point. Don't you see, Crossetta, that this description fits the fair-haired guy we saw outside Watson's house last night?'

'Oh, does it?' She looked again at the paper. 'Yes, I suppose it does. But you're not seriously suggesting that it *is* him, are you? There must be hundreds of men who fit that description. Why pick on this one?'

'Why not? Damn it, we saw him arguing with Watson, didn't we? And when you went back later, weren't they still arguing? So they certainly weren't on friendly terms that evening. And then Watson took him off in the car — going east. But they didn't go to Cardiff Street, you say. Okay, then — where *did* they go?'

'How should I know? Watson may have offered to run him home.'

'Too true.' Toby sounded triumphant. He took the paper from her. 'And it says here that this guy came from near Eastbourne — and Peacehaven is on the coast road to Eastbourne.'

'But people don't go around shooting everyone they have an argument with. That's silly, Toby.'

'Not ordinary people, no. But Watson isn't ordinary, he's a crook. And he and his pals are accustomed to using a gun. I should know that, shouldn't I? Besides, it says the man was killed about eleven o'clock last night. What time did he and Watson leave the house?'

'I don't know exactly. Somewhere around ten, I suppose.'

'You see? It fits perfectly.'

'Yes, perhaps it does.' She sounded impatient. 'And if this man is the one we saw with Watson, then you'd have some reason to suspect that Watson killed him. But I say he isn't. You're just jumping to conclusions.'

Two of the guests came out of the lounge, switching off the lights as they did so. Impatiently Toby endured their chatter, discussing the weather and the film he and Crossetta had seen that evening, and assuring them that he was feeling a 'lot better, thank you.'

As soon as the couple had disappeared upstairs he dragged the girl into the empty room.

'If I'm jumping to conclusions at least they're sound conclusions,' he said earnestly. 'You can argue till you're beat, but I'm darned sure Watson killed that guy.'

She shrugged her shoulders lightly.

'In that case I'll save my breath. What do you propose to do about it? Tell the police?'

'Of course.'

'And Cardiff Street? Will you tell them about that too?'

'Yes. There's no alternative. I've been telling you all day that that's what I must do, only you wouldn't believe me. But you can see now that this clinches it.'

'I can see nothing of the sort,' she said evenly. 'But I hope you realize what it will involve.'

'I'll say I do! The Superintendent will play hell with me. But it's my own fault for being such a darned fool in the first place. If they clap me into gaol I shall have only myself to blame.'

'True. But what about me? Who am I to blame?'

'Me, I guess.' He was all contrition. 'And that worries me more than somewhat. I was a heel to let you get involved in this business, Crossetta. I should have kept you out of it.'

Rather to his surprise (had she not begged him to take her into partnership?) she did not dispute this. 'It worries me too,' she said. 'I'd rather kill myself than go to prison. And I mean that.'

She spoke with such heat that Toby was shocked. Once more he regretted her dislike of physical contact. It would have been so much easier to discuss this with an arm about her waist.

'You shouldn't talk that way,' he said. 'It's all wrong. Besides, there's no danger of your going to prison. In fact, I don't see why I shouldn't try to keep you out of it altogether.' He paused, considering this. 'Yes, that's quite an idea. It might be a little tricky, but it's worth trying. And even if it doesn't succeed I can say you only came along with me for the ride, that you had no idea what I was up to. I could even say that it was you who insisted, when you found out what was going on, that I should tell the police. Okay?'

'Thank you, Toby.' Her voice was warmer, more friendly. 'You must think me an awful coward. But it's funny — I simply adore excitement and adventure, and I don't mind how much danger is attached to it — yet I'd be absolutely petrified if the police wanted to question me.'

He laughed. 'Not you. You'd have them tamed and eating out of your hand in next to no time.'

Her smile was uncertain, and faded quickly. 'I hope it never comes to that,' she said. 'You — I suppose there's nothing I can say or do to make you change your mind?'

'Absolutely nothing. In fact, I couldn't if I wanted to. I've already committed myself. I'm to be at Lewes police station at ten o'clock tomorrow morning. I fixed that long before I knew about this guy being murdered. So you see — '

'Yes, I see.' She spoke quietly, with little inflection in her voice. 'Why didn't you tell me?'

'I figured it would merely increase the existing friction. And I didn't want that. You must know by now, Crossetta, how much — ' He saw her eyes narrow, and checked himself. 'Well, I guess it's too late for a drink now. The pubs will be closing in a few minutes. I'll put the car away, and then I'd best sit myself down and try to figure out how to break the ugly news to the Superintendent to-morrow.' He shivered. 'Ugh! Am I dreading it!'

'Do you want me to come with you?'

He was touched and pleased at the tentative offer.

'Only if you want to. Not otherwise. I've brought enough trouble on you without dragging you out on a jaunt like this.'

'I was thinking of your head,' she said. 'Will you feel fit enough to drive?'

'Good Lord, yes! It's still sore; but I guess I'd have had a headache anyway with this little lot on my mind. I'll be okay in the morning. Don't you worry about that.'

'Well, I'll see. I may come — it'll depend on how I feel to-morrow morning. And if you like I'll put the car away for you now. It's late. If you want to rehearse your speech for the police you'd better get started.'

Toby thanked her. As she reached the door he said, 'Switch off the light, will you? My one-cylinder brain ticks over more smoothly in the dark.'

But it was not ticking over smoothly that evening, he found. He settled himself in an armchair by the window, determined to bring order to the thoughts that jostled each other in his mind. But he still had a headache, and although he knew what he had to say he could not find the right words in which to say it. Maybe they'll come to me later, he thought; although even if they do I may never get a chance to use them. I guess the Superintendent will have his own ideas on how to run the interview.

His thoughts drifted from Herrod to the girl. Her fear of the police surprised and faintly troubled him. Most Britishers, he had found, admired their police, looked on them as friends. Not the crooks, maybe. But then Crossetta wasn't a crook.

Was her fear psychological, perhaps?

He shifted restlessly. Hell! he thought, why should I worry what's behind it? She's pretty and gay and attractive, and that's good enough for me. I don't aim to marry the girl, do I?

That was what he told himself. But because he was Toby, and because each beautiful girl he fell for became in turn the most beautiful girl in the world (with most of the other superlatives thrown in for good measure), his answer did not entirely satisfy him.

He was still in the armchair, thinking about her, when Crossetta returned. She did not switch on the light, but came over to the window and stood beside him. When he made to get up she pushed him back.

'How's it going?' she asked. 'Rehearsal over?'

'I'm afraid it's a wash-out. I seem unable to get started.' He thought she sounded breathless, and there had been a tenseness in her voice that he had not heard before. 'What's the matter? You sound as though you've been running. Some wolf been chasing you?'

'No.' He had spoken lightly on purpose, but she did not respond to his banter. 'Are you going to sit up all night? Personally, I'm for bed.'

'Good idea. I can continue the unequal struggle there.'

He heaved himself out of the armchair. She was very close to him, and the street lamp across the road threw just enough light through the uncurtained windows to show him the pale beauty of her face. He hesitated, and then turned abruptly away.

One of these days, he told himself, I'm going to lose my self-control and take her in my arms and kiss her. I guess I'll get my face slapped, but it ought to be worth it.

Then he stiffened, romance and the girl temporarily forgotten. A man stood under the street lamp — and he was staring fixedly at the hotel.

'Good Lord!' Toby said. He heard Crossetta give a faint gasp as her eyes followed his pointing finger, but she said nothing. 'Know who that is? No — no, you wouldn't, of course. Well, I'll tell you. It's Mr Nathaniel Wilkes, the brother of the girl who was murdered.' Still she did not speak. After a few moments of puzzled thought he went on, 'But what the heck is Wilkes doing here? He can't know anyone in the place except myself. And what would he want with me?'

'I don't know.' The tension was back in her voice, and she withdrew farther into the room, so that her face was no longer visible. 'Toby, you — you remember you said I was breathless when I came in. As though I'd been running. Well, I had.'

'Why?' And then, understanding, 'You mean to tell me the fellow was chasing you?'

'Not exactly. But he was there in the carpark, and as I was leaving he went over to the Riley and had a look at it. Then he came after me and asked me whom it belonged to. He was quite polite, but — well, he's rather frightening to look at, isn't he? I thought he might be one of Watson's men. And I didn't want to land

273

you in any more trouble, so I just said that it belonged to a friend of mine, and walked off.'

'And he followed you?'

'He must have done. I didn't actually see him, but I kept hearing footsteps behind me. They never seemed to get any nearer, but they were always there. And after a bit they got on my nerves and I — well, I panicked. I just ran.'

Although puzzled and worried by Wilkes's apparent interest in him, Toby could not repress a slight feeling of relief that Crossetta had nerves, and could panic like any other girl. Despite her beauty and her gaiety, she had hitherto seemed to him somewhat inhuman in her disregard for personal safety.

'I ought not to have let you go alone,' he said, all contrition. 'Even in daylight Wilkes isn't exactly a joyous sight. I'm not surprised that you panicked. Shall I go out and tell him to beat it? Mind you, I don't suppose he *meant* to scare you. It's me he's after; he knows the Riley, he saw it when I met him and the Inspector at the barn that afternoon. But what can he want? And why does he just stand there? Why doesn't he come in?'

'He's gone,' the girl said.

It was true. The street was empty.

They went upstairs silently. Once in his room Toby threw himself on the bed, and lay staring gloomily at the ceiling. Life was already sufficiently complicated without Wilkes complicating it further. He didn't want to puzzle over Wilkes's odd behaviour, he wanted to give his whole attention to the problem of what he should say to the Superintendent on the morrow. Yet Wilkes . . .

What the heck was the man playing at?

A little later he sat up with a jerk. A tiny seed of fear had germinated in his heart. He began to sweat.

Did Wilkes believe that he, Toby Vanne, had murdered his sister?

★ ★ ★

He slept little that night. When he came down to breakfast Crossetta, who seemed to have recovered her good spirits, took him to task.

'You look awful,' she told him. 'You'll have to pull yourself together, my lad; if the police see you looking like that they'll probably decide you've committed a murder yourself.' Toby winced, recalling the unhappy thought that had come to him the previous night. If Wilkes believed that, might not the police believe it also? 'And eat a good breakfast. It may be your last decent meal before you start tucking in to prison fare.'

If she were trying to jolly him into a brighter mood the effort failed. Toby saw no humour in her remarks.

'Are you coming with me?' he asked.

'No. I couldn't face it. But I'll come part of the way. You can drop me off in Brighton. If I am to be put on trial for whatever crime it is that you and I are supposed to have committed I intend to look my best in court. I'm going to buy myself a new frock. *And* a new hat. There's no point now in being thrifty. One can't spend money in gaol, can one?'

'You're not going to gaol,' he said. 'You know that. It's just an excuse to go shopping. However, if it makes you feel better — well, good luck to you.'

Suddenly she was serious.

'It's you who'll need the good luck, I imagine. Oh, I do so wish you'd change your mind and not go. It's still not too late.'

'I guess it is.'

Crossetta sighed. 'Well, I hope they aren't too hard on you. Will you tell them about last night? About Wilkes being here?'

'I haven't made up my mind.' If he did he certainly would not give his own interpretation of Wilkes's interest in him. There was no sense in putting ideas like that into their heads. 'I'll decide when the time comes.'

They left after breakfast, and he dropped her off at Hannington's. It was with a sense of loss that he saw her disappear into the shop; he had hoped that once she was in the car she would decide to accompany him to Lewes. He could have done with some moral support.

The Riley was running well. It romped

up the hill to Falmer, seemingly more anxious to reach its destination than was its owner. Near the top a slow-moving van baulked him, and he swung out to overtake. The move nearly proved fatal. Accelerating fiercely, he flung the wheel sharply over, scraping the front of the van and avoiding by inches a fast oncoming car.

A stream of abuse came faintly to his ears.

Darned fool! he reproved himself. You may be heading for an unpleasant interview, but that's no reason for attempting suicide *en route*. Take it easy.

On the far side of Falmer the road runs downhill in a long straight stretch, with a right-hand bend at the bottom. Toby took it gently, recovering from the shock of his narrow escape. He had always prided himself on his driving. It was a blow to his self-esteem to discover that under stress he could commit the sins he had so often deplored in others.

He was half-way down the hill when he realized that something was wrong. The steering-wheel felt odd; there was, as it were, no weight to it. The car was moving out towards the crown of the road, and even as he spun the wheel he knew that it was useless, that the car was out of control.

The steering had gone.

What happened next happened quickly. Perhaps the brakes were imperfectly adjusted, or the front wheels hit a bump in the road; but as he trod hard on the brake pedal the Riley swung in towards the kerb. There was a bump as it mounted the footpath and topped the grass bank, a sickening lurch as its front wheels dropped almost instantly into the ditch on the other side; and then, with a jarring crash that shook most of the breath from his body, the car hit a tree and was precariously at rest.

Dazed, Toby sat for a few moments in the driving-seat. The Riley was tilted at an acute angle, and he clung tightly to the steering-wheel. Then he slid down the seat, clambered awkwardly over the jammed door, and stumbled into the ditch.

Leaning against the bank, he put a hand to his forehead, and was surprised to find that no blood was flowing. Slowly he moved arms and legs and twisted his body, anticipating the excruciating pain that would announce a fracture. But there was no pain.

Good Lord! he thought. I'm not even scratched!

He became aware of cars stopping on the road, doors slamming, of people hastening to his aid and of their excited, anxious voices. He turned his back on them, self-conscious in his lucky escape. They would expect a little blood at least.

Faces peered down at him. Eager, fearful, curious faces.

'Is he badly hurt?'

'What happened? Did you see?'

'He looks all right. But you can't tell, of course.'

'He's very pale. Must have hit his head against something — there's a nasty bruise on his forehead.'

'I hope they won't try to move him until they've made certain there are no bones broken.'

'What happened? Did you see?'

'Is he badly hurt?'

They were the voices of a crowd, impersonal, disembodied. Reluctantly Toby turned to face them. Above him stooped a man with a straggling red beard and kindly grey eyes.

'Are you all right, old chap?' asked the man.

'I think so,' Toby said. 'If you could give me a hand out of the ditch . . . '

Hands under his armpits, tugging gently, a little fearfully, afraid of aggravating a hidden injury. Then he was standing among them, smiling ruefully, self-consciously aware of their inquisitive eyes.

'Thanks,' he said. 'I'm okay now.'

'He ought to sit down,' came a woman's voice from the back of the little bunch of people. 'Delayed shock, you know.'

'The steering went,' Toby said, feeling he owed them an explanation.

A man was down in the ditch, examining the Riley. 'Looks as though the chassis is twisted,' he announced cheerfully. 'And the radiator's had it. Leaking like a sieve.'

The bearded man took control. 'Where were you making for?' he asked. 'I could run you back to Brighton if you like. You'll want some one to collect the car, won't you?'

Toby nodded. Inwardly he was fighting a moral battle. Here was a chance to escape the ordeal that awaited him in Lewes. No one could blame him if he returned to Brighton now and, after making arrangements for the collection and repair of the Riley, stayed there. After such an ordeal he could hardly be expected deliberately to seek another. But then there was always to-morrow. And, if necessary, the day after to-morrow. And the excuse could not be made to last indefinitely.

'I have an appointment in Lewes,' he said. 'But I'd be mighty grateful if you would call in at Caffyn's for me and tell them what's happened. They'll deal with it.'

'I'm going to Lewes,' a man's voice said quietly. 'I'll give you a lift.'

'Thanks,' Toby said, turning to face him. 'That would — ' He paused. ' — be good of you,' he finished slowly.

He was looking into the ugly, sallow

face of Nat Wilkes!

'I was right behind you, Lieutenant,' Wilkes said, seemingly oblivious of the staring eyes that now switched their attention from Toby to him. 'I could see you were going to crash, but there was nothing I could do to prevent it.'

'No, of course not,' Toby said. He wondered if Wilkes had been following him.

'I gather you know this gentleman,' the bearded man said. 'That's fine. And leave me to see about the car. If you'll let me have your name and address . . . '

The crowd had been growing; now it began to disperse. The show was over. The line of cars halted by the roadside moved off slowly. The bearded man wrote in a little notebook, wished Toby luck, and walked away to his car.

Toby was alone with Wilkes. Passing cars slowed as they caught sight of the Riley, and then, realizing that they had come too late on the scene, accelerated away. One or two drivers leaned from their windows to ask if they could be of help. Wilkes shook his head. But Toby scarcely saw or heard them. All his attention was concentrated on his companion.

'We'll get going, shall we?' Wilkes said.

The Buick was big and roomy. Toby sat apart from the driver, apprehensive — yet telling himself he was foolish to feel that way. Whatever Wilkes suspected, whatever he had it in his mind to do, there could be no immediate danger. He had not escaped Scylla to be overwhelmed by Charybdis. It was a bright, sunny morning, they were travelling along a main road, and Lewes was only a few miles away.

'Enjoying your leave, Lieutenant?' Wilkes asked, his eyes on the road ahead.

'I was until this happened.'

'Yes. Most unfortunate for you. You say the steering went suddenly? That sounds as though a nut must have worked loose on the drag-link. Probably a sheered split-pin.'

'Probably,' Toby agreed. The other's quietly conversational tone emboldened him to ask a question. 'Are you staying in Brighton?'

'For a day or so, yes. I have some

284

unfinished business to attend to. I'm looking for some one.'

Landor — or himself? wondered Toby. 'I hope you find him,' he said.

'I'll find him,' came the reply.

Toby shifted uncomfortably. The conversation had suddenly switched from conventionalities to a more menacing form. Was Wilkes about to tax him with murder? And after that — what? Determined not to be intimidated, Toby decided to attack.

'I saw you last night, Mr Wilkes,' he said. 'Outside my hotel. What were you doing there? If you wanted to speak to me why didn't you come in?'

The other took some time to answer.

'I'm afraid your very natural curiosity must go unsatisfied,' he said eventually. 'Sorry.'

Toby waited for him to say more. But Wilkes was silent. Perhaps he thought he had already said too much. And as they climbed the long, steep hill into Lewes Toby's annoyance left him, to be replaced by a feeling of sympathy. After all, the poor fellow's sister had been murdered.

And if he thought Toby had killed her, hadn't he a right to keep an eye on him, to harass him until he knew the truth? Toby wondered whether he should protest his innocence. Yet to do so might be taken as proof of his guilt. Better to express his sympathy, to offer his help.

'I'm terribly sorry about your sister,' he said, uncomfortably aware of how banal the words sounded. 'I guess I'll never forget the way she looked; so beautiful, so — so alone. How could any man come to kill a girl like that?' He winced as he caught sight of the prison; there, perhaps, stood his future home. 'The papers hinted it was this fellow Landor who did it, and I've been keeping my eyes skinned for him. You'll have been doing the same, I guess.' His companion gave a slight nod, but made no comment. 'I'll be staying in Hove for at least another week, and if there's anything I can do to help I sure hope you'll call on me. You — er — you know where I'm staying.'

'Thank you. I'll bear your offer in mind.' They were well into the town now. 'Where shall I drop you?'

'Any place here will do fine.'

Toby knew that the other did not believe him, that his words had done nothing to allay suspicion. He felt aggrieved.

Wilkes brought the big Buick to a stop outside the Town Hall. Then he turned to look at Toby.

'May I give you a word of advice, Lieutenant?' he said.

'Depends what it is.'

'I suggest you *don't* spend another week in Hove. I suggest you go back to your unit. Today, for preference.'

'Why?' Toby was bewildered. He had not expected that.

'Because if you stay here much longer you may never go back at all. Not unless you express a wish to be buried there.'

He made this outrageous statement almost casually. Toby, angry now, sat up sharply.

'Say, are you threatening me?' he demanded.

'I'm giving you advice. You don't have to take it.'

He returned Toby's angry glare with a

blank, expressionless face. Then, as the young man made no move to leave the car, he leaned across him and opened the door.

Toby got out, closing the door behind him. Then he poked his head through the open window.

'You can't scare me, Wilkes,' he said. 'I'm staying. If you're out to get me — well, just try, that's all.'

Wilkes nodded, unperturbed.

'Suit yourself. But have a look at that draglink when you get back to Brighton. It may make you change your mind.'

12

Shortly after 9.30 that morning the Eastbourne police located the office where Claire Taylor was employed. It was that of the Lester Trading Company, Superintendent Farrar told Herrod over the phone; it employed only a small staff, of which Mrs Taylor was the head. She had not been to the office since the previous Thursday, but had left a note in the letter-box to the effect that she would be away until the Monday. The staff had had no communication from her since then.

'And it's now Wednesday,' Herrod commented. 'Did they seem surprised or worried at her continued absence?'

'I gather not,' Farrar said. 'But I haven't been up there myself. I thought I'd get in touch with you first. Are you coming over?'

'I'll send Wood. How's Anna?'

'Definitely subdued. Doesn't leave the

289

house except for a spot of shopping in the mornings.'

Taylor had been killed on Monday night; Herrod wondered whether his death might have any connexion with his wife's absence. And was Ellis involved? Both of these were possibilities, but neither explained how Taylor came to be shot by a bullet from the same .25 as had been used to kill Caseman and Catherine Wilkes. Unless Landor had parted with the gun, he alone could have had a hand in all three murders.

A bare-headed constable knocked, entered, and stood smartly at attention. 'A Lieutenant Vanne to see you, sir. American. Says he has an appointment.'

'Vanne?' Herrod said absently. 'Oh, yes — Vanne. All right, I'll see him.'

Toby was nervous. The accident and the clash with Wilkes had unsettled him. He mumbled an apology for his lateness, his eyes anxiously searching the Superintendent's face. Was the fellow in a good mood or a bad?

'The Brighton air seems to have inflated your ego,' Herrod said, smiling faintly. But the smile vanished as his visitor gazed at him uncomprehendingly. He shrugged his shoulders. 'Sorry. That was meant as a joke; I was referring to your swollen head. But forget it. What can I do for you, Lieutenant? You haven't found another body, I suppose? They seem fairly plentiful in these parts.'

'No. I — I have a confession to make.'

'A confession? About what?'

'About the girl. Miss Wilkes. You won't like it, I guess. In fact, I reckon you'll be mad as hell.'

'Don't let's worry about whether I like it or not, sir. What is it?'

Toby was right. Herrod did not like it. His expression hardened as he learned of the piece of paper which Toby had found by the dead girl's body and had concealed from the police.

'One moment, sir,' he interrupted. 'You realize, I suppose, that this is a very serious admission? One that may result in an indictment? If you wish — '

'I understand that,' Toby said. 'Are you going to warn me? That's usual over here, isn't it?' Now that he had made a start,

291

had confessed what was to his mind the only item he had to confess (there was nothing culpable, surely, in his later actions?), he felt much better. 'Though I guess it'll make no difference. I've made up my mind to get this off my chest, and get it off I will. And if you like to have one of your fellows write it down, that'll be okay by me,' he added generously.

Slightly taken aback, the Superintendent warned him. With a stenographer in attendance, Toby began again. He described how he had found the piece of paper in his pocket, his visit to Cardiff Street, and his meeting with Watson. He told how he had explored the upper storey of No. 17 the next evening, of the shot fired at him and of his subsequent escape. So far he had made no mention of Crossetta. But as he warmed to his recital he grew careless. He was describing the third visit to Cardiff Street when the fatal 'we' slipped out.

Herrod pounced on it.

' 'We'? Who are 'we', Lieutenant?'

Toby hedged. 'I thought I said 'I'.'

'You said 'we,' and you meant 'we,'' the

Superintendent said sternly. 'Who was your companion?'

'Just a girl who is staying in the hotel. We got friendly, and I told her about this, and — well, she came with me.'

'What's her name?'

'Crossetta Tait. She's a widow. Her husband was killed in an air crash.'

But Herrod hardly heard the last two sentences. '*What* was that first name?' he asked, puzzled. 'Crossetta?'

'Yes.' Toby spelt it for him. It had become so much a part of his daily life that it no longer sounded strange to his ear. But he realized that the Superintendent had not had that advantage, and proceeded to explain its origin. 'Little cross — Crossetta,' he concluded. 'Cute, isn't it?'

'Very,' Herrod said drily. 'And was this Mrs Tait with you on your previous excursions to Cardiff Street?'

'Not the first. The second, yes.'

'Scrub that, will you?' Herrod instructed the stenographer. Then he turned to Toby, voice and expression distinctly angry.

'You delayed five whole days, sir, before

293

revealing what may prove to be vital evidence. Five days! And now, as if that were not sufficient delay, you come here and make a statement that is deliberately misleading.' He thumped the table with his fist. 'Damn it, man — if you're going to tell the truth, tell it! But don't muck about with it!'

Toby flushed, feeling like a small boy under the stern eye of his headmaster. 'It was my fault she became involved,' he excused himself. 'I figured it was up to me to keep her name out of it.'

Herrod leaned forward.

'I'm not interested in chivalry at the moment, Lieutenant. It doesn't go with murder. Now! Do I get the truth — or don't I?'

He got it.

Having been forced to commit Crossetta (and, after all, she really had nothing to worry about, he told himself. The police might want to check his statement with her, but there couldn't be more to it than that), Toby gave full measure. He omitted nothing. And when he concluded with the accident to the Riley and his subsequent conversation with Nat Wilkes he thought he had made a fairly good job of it.

He looked hopefully at the Superintendent. But what Herrod thought was not apparent on his face. The creases round his eyes multiplied as he sat hunched up in his chair — left elbow on the table, left hand supporting his chin — sliding a pencil up and down between the thumb and first finger of his right hand.

'It occurs to me, sir, that Wilkes was giving you sound advice when he suggested that you should quit Brighton,' he said, his voice once more low-pitched and measured. 'If one includes your lady friend's attempt to crown you with a brick you have had three narrow escapes from death. You may not be so lucky the fourth time.'

'The brick was an accident,' Toby said. 'And, unless Wilkes has inside information, so was the smash-up this morning. Anyhow, I'm not going. I intend to stay and see this through.'

'I hope not,' Herrod said. 'Stay if you must, but leave the seeing-it-through part to us, will you?'

'Yes, sure.' Toby was abashed. 'Er — what happens now? To me, I mean. Do you charge me and lock me up? Or do I just walk out?'

'I'm not charging you, sir. Not yet, anyway. And for the present you can wait downstairs until I'm ready. I'll have your statement typed; you can sign it later, if you will.'

Herrod left his office to visit the Divisional Superintendent.

'This place Edburton,' he said, pointing it out on the map. 'Is it in your area?'

'No. West Sussex. You'll have to liaise with them. Is Watson's house in Hove?'

'Vanne seemed to think so. Why?'

'It's rather tricky there. Hove comes under East Sussex, but it's sandwiched between West Sussex and Brighton Borough. However, Inspector Dainsford at Hove will see that you don't go treading on anyone's toes. I'll warn him to expect you.'

Back in his own office Herrod got busy on the telephone. He rang the Chief Constable first. Finding him out, he got through to Superintendent Baker, told him the news, and asked him to pass it on to the Chief Constable when the latter returned. He contacted the Brighton Borough police, and the headquarters of the West Sussex Constabulary at Chichester. He was still speaking to the latter when Sergeant Wood returned from Eastbourne.

'Any luck?' he asked, as he replaced the receiver.

Wood didn't think so. The Lester Trading Company's offices, he said, consisted of one room in a private house; the staff, in Mrs Taylor's absence, of an elderly woman and a pimply youth. Both the youth and the woman professed to know nothing of Mrs Taylor's absence beyond the fact that on the Friday morning they had found a note from her in the letter-box to the effect that she would be away on business until the following Monday. As this had happened before, it did not surprise them. The boss had rung up later that morning and had asked to speak to Mrs Taylor, but had made no comment when told she was away. He had called in on the Saturday, however, and had asked to see the note. Then he had torn it up and left — again without comment.

'An accommodating boss,' Herrod said. 'Who is he?'

'A man named Mike Watson. Lives in Brighton.'

'Hove.' Herrod's eyes gleamed. 'You mustn't confuse the two.' Noting his subordinate's astonished expression, he added, 'I've been hearing a lot about Mr Watson this morning. I think he would well repay a visit. What does the Lester Trading Company trade in?'

Wood said he thought it was phoney. The two employees either would not or could not give any details. 'General dealers, the woman said. I gather they have several warehouses dotted around Sussex, but I couldn't discover where.'

'I could probably find two of them,' Herrod told him.

Inspector Kane joined them. 'This has just been handed in, sir,' he said, handing the Superintendent a leather wallet. 'A small boy found it this morning on the beach near Telscombe Cliffs. Looks like it belonged to Taylor.' As Herrod took it eagerly he went on, 'It was handled by the whole family in turn, so we're unlikely to find any useful prints on it.'

The contents of the wallet were few. A half-crown book of stamps the return half of a day return ticket, dated the 16th, from Eastbourne to Brighton; a driving licence; a wireless licence; a football pool coupon; sundry receipts and bills; and a pencilled note signed 'Claire'.

A small bunch of keys was attached to the wallet by a thin chain.

It was the note that attracted most of Herrod's interest:

Sorry, darling, but Mike Watson came over from Brighton and asked me to go to Birmingham for him this evening. He ran me home to pack a few things and to say good-bye, but you had already left for the café. I suppose we were late.

Must dash now. Mike's waiting to take me to the station, and there isn't much time. I'll be away about three days — back Monday morning, I hope.

Be seeing you. Look after yourself.
Love,
CLAIRE

He handed the note to Wood without comment, and took up the railway ticket.

'Monday, eh? The day Vanne said he saw Taylor — or the man he thinks was Taylor — at Watson's house.' He remembered that the Sergeant knew nothing of the young man's visit. 'I'll explain about that later. Right now I want to make sure that it *was* Taylor.'

Once more they went down to the mortuary. In twenty-five years I never saw a dead body, Toby thought, as he watched the Sergeant unlock the door; and now I am about to see my second corpse within a week.

He did not look long at the dead man; not because the sight upset him (as it did), but because he had no need.

'Yes, that's him,' he said. 'That's the fellow we saw at Watson's place on Monday evening.'

They left for Brighton as soon as Toby had read and signed the typed copy of his statement; the three detectives in one car, with Toby and a uniformed constable in another. Herrod wanted to be able to talk to his subordinates without the circumspection which the young man's presence would have imposed.

'We'll pick up Inspector Dainsford at Hove,' he said, after giving them the gist of the American's statement, 'and then pay a call on this chap Watson. It should prove an interesting visit.'

'I don't get it,' said Wood, puzzled. 'If Mrs Taylor's note to her husband was genuine, then Watson knew she was going away. So why did he try to telephone her at the office the next morning, and even call in there the day after that to read her note? Was he putting on an act of some sort?'

'Perhaps. But that is only one of the many things I hope he'll explain,' Herrod said. 'Another is, why was that note written at all? If what she wrote to her husband was the truth Mrs Taylor knew before she left the office that she was going to Birmingham. She could have told the staff then, presumably.'

'There were no currency notes in Taylor's wallet,' Kane said, 'and only a little silver in his pockets. He could have been murdered for the cash he had on him.'

'He could, of course. But it's more likely that pinching the money was an after-thought. Intended to mislead us, perhaps. Or it could have been taken by the people who found the wallet. That doesn't neces-sarily mean the boy or his family. Some one else could have found it before them, stolen the money, and left the wallet.'

'This Mrs Tait,' Kane said thoughtfully. 'What did you say her first name is, sir?'

'Crossetta.'

'H'm. Unusual, isn't it? And the initials — C.T. Do you think — '

'No,' said Herrod, 'I don't. I had that idea myself, but I discarded it. I agree it's a coincidence that Crossetta Tait should appear in Brighton — I beg its pardon, Hove — the morning after Claire Taylor vanishes from Polegate; but I believe it's no more than a coincidence. Mrs Tait seems to have assisted Vanne wholeheart-edly in spying on Watson, and that doesn't make sense if she is really Claire Taylor. Watson is Claire Taylor's boss, and apparently the two are on very good terms. We'll get some one who knows her — Ellis, or that neighbour of hers — to have a look at this girl. But I think you'll find I'm right.'

'A pity,' Kane said. 'How about Wilkes, sir? Was Vanne mistaken, or is Wilkes really gunning for him? What with him and Landor and Watson on the job, the Sussex air isn't so healthy these days.'

The Superintendent admitted that he was uneasy about Wilkes. 'He's so damned mysterious and reticent,' he said, with some irritation. 'I've no doubt he's a wrong 'un, as the Croydon police suggested. But what is he hanging around for? What keeps him here now that the inquest and the funeral are over? He may have doted on his sister, but surely he wouldn't be such a damned fool as to rub Vanne out just because the wretched man happened to find the girl? There must be more to it than that. The question is — what?'

As they went up the hill to Falmer they passed the Riley. A breakdown lorry had it in tow, and it looked surprisingly whole. Herrod made a mental note to check with the garage about the cause of the accident. If Vanne had reported Wilkes correctly it would appear that the crash was no accident, but a deliberate attempt to get rid of that young man. Some one was finding him a nuisance. And that, thought Herrod, I can well believe.

They were on the outskirts of Brighton when Sergeant Wood, who had not spoken for some time, said, 'Watson could have killed Wilkes's sister, Mr Herrod. It seems fairly certain that the note Mrs Taylor left for her husband was a phoney; if she went away on business it was her own business, not the firm's. All the same, Watson could have been in Eastbourne that evening, and have picked up Catherine Wilkes on the way home. That would explain Ford's evidence — that it was a woman, not a man, whom he heard running after the car. He takes her up that track and starts making advances to her — and she pulls out that gun of hers. Perhaps there was a struggle — the gun goes off accidentally — '

'There was no sign of a struggle,' Kane said. 'And she was shot in the back.'

'Okay. So there wasn't a struggle. But somehow he gets the gun from her and kills her. And on Monday, when Mrs Taylor fails to return home, Taylor goes over to Brighton, shows Watson her note, and demands to be told where she is. Watson doesn't know, and says so. The note's a phoney, he says. Taylor doesn't believe him — nor would I — and tells Watson that if he doesn't come clean he'll blab to the police about Watson's racket, whatever that may be. That puts Watson in a spot; with a murder on his hands police inquiries would be more than usually unwelcome. So he has to get rid of Taylor before Taylor can talk. He offers to run him home, and uses the girl's gun to bump him off *en route*.'

'He'd go via Lewes, not Peacehaven,' Kane objected. 'More direct.'

'Is it?' Wood considered this. 'Well, perhaps he chose Peacehaven for that very reason. It would appear less obvious that Taylor was killed on his way home from Brighton.'

Sergeant Wood's flights of fancy were so rare that Herrod never liked to condemn them out of hand; and this particular flight certainly had possibilities, as he at once conceded. 'But it doesn't explain how the girl's finger-prints came to be on the steering-wheel of Waide's car,' he pointed out.

'Watson might have pinched it,' the Sergeant said promptly. 'That could be his racket.'

Somewhat doubtfully, Herrod admitted the possibility of this.

Before they reached Hove he had changed his plans. 'I want to speak to your Mrs Tait,' he told Toby, as they left the cars at the police station. 'If Sergeant Wood runs you back to the hotel, do you think you can persuade her to come along here and answer a few questions?'

Toby looked dubious. 'She's not sold on policemen,' he said. 'I don't think she'll come.'

'I'll have to visit her there if she doesn't,' Herrod said. 'No doubt she would like that even less. And tell her I'm quite tame. Practically human, in fact.'

Toby promised to do his best.

Sergeant Wood waited outside in the car. Lunch at Coniston was nearly over — realizing the time, Toby suddenly felt hungry — and there was only Crossetta and another guest in the dining-room.

His sudden appearance obviously startled the girl. I must be looking a bit grim, he thought, and forced a smile. Unless he treated the matter airily she would dig in her toes.

'What happened?' she asked nervously. And then, responding to his smile, 'You didn't get a very heavy sentence, did you? Or are you out on bail?'

'They were pretty decent,' he told her. 'Nice guy, that Superintendent. He slammed into me, of course, but I reckon I'll get away with it. My main concern at the moment is the Riley. The steering went, and I ended up in the ditch.'

He felt gratified by the concern shown on her face. Maybe she isn't as indifferent to me as I thought, he told himself hopefully. When all this is over I must find out.

'You — you're not hurt?' she asked.

He reassured her, and went on to tell

her about Wilkes and of his talk with Herrod. Mrs Buell brought him lunch, but he regretfully refused it. There was no time, he said, thinking of the waiting Sergeant. He and Mrs Tait had to go out; he would get a sandwich later.

'I wish I knew what was going on,' Mrs Buell said, annoyed and upset. 'You're for ever dashing in and out of the place, the pair of you. And you with a lump on your head the size of an orange! Goodness knows what your poor mother would say if she knew. And what's that police car doing outside? What's happened to your own? You're not in trouble with the police, are you?'

'No, of course not. I had an accident, and they very kindly brought me back,' he said, inwardly cursing as he noticed the alarm on Crossetta's face. 'Don't worry, I'm not hurt.'

'And what are they waiting for now, I'd like to know?'

'I — well, I have to go to the police station to make a statement.'

'And what about me?' the girl asked, when Mrs Buell had eventually departed.

'Why am I going out?'

Her voice was hard, her defences were up. He gave her a watery smile.

'Honestly, Crossetta, I did my best to keep you out of it,' he said earnestly. 'It just wasn't possible, that's all. But I told them you didn't know what it was all about, that you only came with me for the fun of it. Only — well, naturally they have to check up on me, make sure I'm telling the truth. And you're the only person they can ask. But all you have to do is go along to the police station here and confirm what I said. No, wait a minute, please' — as she pushed back her chair and stood up — 'don't run out on me, Crossetta. There's nothing to be scared of, honestly there isn't. You'll like the Superintendent when you see him, he's a great guy. Oh, yes — he told me to tell you that he's quite tame and almost human. And it's true, he is.'

'I told you before, Toby, I'm not having anything to do with the police.' He had never seen her angry. It did not detract from her beauty, he thought. She looked magnificent, almost imperial. 'If you wanted to confess, that was your affair and I couldn't stop you. But you had absolutely no right to drag me into it.'

'Say, that's great!' He was nettled by the unfairness of the attack. 'Dragged you into it, did I? Why, I'd no sooner mentioned this guy Landor than you jumped into the chase with both feet and your eyes wide open. Don't get me wrong — I was real glad to have you with me. But don't tell me now that I dragged you into it.'

'I wasn't referring to Landor. I said you had no right to include me in your stupid confession.'

'I told you, I couldn't help it.' But a slanging match was no way to win her over, and he changed his tactics. 'Come off it, Crossetta. Do as the Superintendent asks — he won't keep you long. It's not like you to be scared.'

'I'm not scared, you idiot. I just don't want my name in the papers, and all the fuss and publicity.'

'There may not be any publicity.'

'Of course there will be. There always is.'

She walked over towards the window — far enough to see and yet not be seen — and stood for a while looking thoughtfully at the waiting police car. When she spoke again her voice was calmer. Toby sensed genuine curiosity when she asked, 'What happens if I refuse to go?'

'They'll come here. Would you prefer that?'

'No.' She turned to him, frowning. 'I suppose I'll have to do as I'm told, damn you! But Heaven help you, Toby, if I get dragged into this business. I'll never forgive you for it.'

It was a silent journey. They had nothing to say to each other in the presence of the police, and Sergeant Wood was his usual taciturn self. Toby hoped fervently that the Superintendent was a tactful man. If he handled Crossetta badly there'd be the devil to pay.

He was not present at the interview. He spent the time in another room, his ears strained to catch the first sound of the girl's voice raised in anger. But he heard nothing.

When Crossetta eventually returned with the Superintendent she was smiling. Toby stared at her in disbelief of his own eyes.

'Mrs Tait has been most helpful,' Herrod said, his voice a purr. 'Now I wonder if one of you would be kind enough to show us where this Mr Watson lives? You won't be confronted with him, of course. We'll keep you out of sight while we talk to him.'

'Sure,' Toby said with alacrity. Apart from a genuine wish to help, he hoped that in so doing he might expunge some of the black marks against him.

'I'll come too,' Crossetta said.

Bewildered, Toby looked at the Superintendent in open admiration.

They went in two cars. When Toby had pointed out Watson's house he and the girl were driven farther up the road to await the detectives' return. 'The driver will run you back to the hotel now if you wish,' Herrod had said. 'But if you're in no great hurry I'd like Mrs Tait to show me later where she lost Watson's car on Monday evening.'

They had declared, almost in unison, that they were perfectly willing to wait.

'I'm looking forward to this,' Herrod said, as he and Wood and Inspector Dainsford waited under the porch for an answer to their ring. 'This is the first chance we've had to get our teeth into something.'

13

A man opened the door to them. He was of medium height and wore a blue suit, and Herrod glanced quickly at his hand.

None of the fingers was missing.

'Mr Watson's out,' said the man. Alarm had been plain on his face when he saw the Inspector's uniform, but he was quick to recover. 'Care to leave a message?'

Herrod suspected he was lying. But without a warrant they could not force their way into the house. The alternative would be to keep it under observation. That meant delay; and to the Superintendent, now hot on the scent, delay was irksome.

'We are police officers, and it is important that we should contact Mr Watson immediately,' he said. 'Any idea where he is?'

'Search me,' said the man. 'Might be anywhere.'

'Right. Then we'll wait here until he turns up,' Herrod said.

The other hesitated, uncertain whether they expected to be invited into the house or were prepared to wait outside. This was as Herrod had anticipated. He stood close to the jamb. The man could not close the door without first asking him to move; and this, Herrod suspected, he lacked the nerve to do.

Voices came from the room to the left of the hall. Herrod saw his opportunity and took a chance.

'Mistaken, aren't you?' He stepped through the open doorway. Wood and Dainsford followed him. 'That sounds like Mr Watson's voice. Tell him we're here, will you?'

To the frightened man it seemed that he was surrounded by policemen. He had no stomach for further protest. Meekly he turned, and left them in possession of the hall.

Herrod grinned happily at his companions.

They were not kept waiting. A tall, good-looking man came out from the room on the left. Across the back of his right hand an ugly scar, not yet fully healed, glowed angrily. So that explains the bandage, Herrod thought. Looks like a knife-wound — and not come by honestly, I'll be bound.

'I'm Mike Watson. Sorry you fellows were fobbed off with that hoary old excuse. An excess of zeal on Harry's part — he knew I had another visitor.' He spoke genially, the words correct but the accent less so. 'Come in and have a drink, and tell me how I can help you.'

They followed him into a small study on the right of the hall, but declined the drink. Herrod introduced himself and the other officers.

'Scotland Yard, eh? Must be important. Well, let's have it.'

'We are inquiring into the murder, last Monday night, of a man named Geoffrey Taylor,' Herrod said. 'You knew him, didn't you?'

Watson's reaction — a blend of surprise, horror, and regret — was just right. If it was acting it was good acting. 'I only met him a few times,' he told them finally, 'but he seemed a very decent chap. Can't imagine why anyone should want to bump him off.'

'When did you last see him, sir?' Herrod asked.

Watson hesitated. Herrod thought he must be wondering how much they knew. But if he had considered a lie he did not risk it.

'If he was killed on Monday, then I must have been one of the last to see him alive,' he said. 'He was here that evening, and I ran him to the station later.'

'What time was that?'

'I'm not sure. But I dropped him at Brighton station in good time to catch the ten-something-or-other to Eastbourne.' In turn he looked at the three unrevealing faces before him. 'I don't want to seem unduly inquisitive, Superintendent, but where was Taylor killed? And how?'

'He was shot in the back, sir. His body was found near Peacehaven the next morning. So it doesn't look as though he caught that train, does it?'

'No.' Watson looked puzzled. 'But why not, I wonder?'

'So do I. Why did he come here to see you?'

Again the other hesitated.

'Do I have to answer that? It was on a personal matter.'

'You don't have to answer anything,' Herrod told him. 'But I'll put the question in another form. Had Taylor's visit to do with his wife's disappearance?'

'Oh! So you know about that, do you? Yes, it had.' And then, in a burst of apparent frankness, 'He seemed to think I was in some way responsible. It took me quite a while to convince him he was wrong.'

'But you did convince him?'

'I hope so.'

It was too much like sparring for the Superintendent. He wanted to get in close.

'I'll be frank with you, sir. We know that Mrs Taylor works for you in Eastbourne, and we have made some inquiries at the offices of the Lester Trading Company. That's yours, isn't it?' Watson nodded. 'We have also seen the note that Mrs Taylor left for her husband. Did Taylor show it to you?'

'He brought it with him Monday night.

It didn't make sense to me, and I told him so; but if I'd been in the poor chap's place I expect I'd have been as suspicious as he was. Yet I assure you, Superintendent, that whatever the business Mrs Taylor went on it certainly wasn't mine. I didn't know she was going, and I haven't a clue as to why she went or where she is. So why did she drag my name into it? Why make me the scapegoat for whatever it is she's up to? I wasn't even in Eastbourne that evening.'

Watching him closely, Herrod said, 'You rent or own premises in Brighton, don't you? In Cardiff Street?'

'Quite right, I do. I use them for a storage occasionally, though they're empty at present. But what has Cardiff Street to do with Mrs Taylor?'

'Last Friday, sir, a girl named Catherine Wilkes was found murdered near Lewes.' Herrod was looking at the man's hands, and it seemed to him that the knuckles suddenly showed whiter, as though the skin was being stretched more tightly over them. 'You may have read about it in the papers.'

'Yes. But I still don't see — '

Herrod produced the map that Toby had given him.

'Did you draw that, Mr Watson?' he asked briskly.

Watson's hands shook as he held the paper; there were beads of perspiration on his forehead. He was so long in replying that Herrod said, 'If you're in any doubt we could compare the handwriting.'

Watson shook his head.

'I've no doubt it's mine,' he said, a new hoarseness in his voice. 'I've drawn several like it. I must have given this to some one who doesn't know the place. A driver, most likely.'

'But you couldn't say who?'

'No.'

Since Herrod did not believe him, he did not press the point.

'It was found beside the body of Catherine Wilkes,' he said quietly. And, as Watson jumped to his feet, 'Perhaps I should also tell you that Miss Wilkes was killed by a bullet from the same gun as that used to murder Geoffrey Taylor. So now you see the connexion.'

Watson swayed on his feet, both hands resting on the table. He looked as though he needed its support.

'But I don't know the girl,' he almost shouted. 'I'd never even heard of her until I read her name in the papers. And I don't own a gun; never even used one. You're not trying to make out that I killed her, are you?'

Herrod shrugged.

'Can you explain how that piece of paper came to be where we found it?' he asked.

Watson poured himself a stiff brandy, added soda, and sat down. He sipped steadily, his brows furrowed in thought.

'I've no idea at all,' he said presently. 'What's more, I'm not answering any more questions until I've seen my solicitor. I didn't kill the girl, and I didn't kill Taylor; but maybe, when I've had time to think it over, I'll be able to let you in on one or two things that might help. Provided, of course, that my solicitor approves. I can't say fairer than that, can I?'

Herrod thought he could, and urged

him to telephone his solicitor at once. Time was precious. Watson, outwardly anxious to co-operate, picked up the receiver.

'No luck,' he said eventually. 'He's not in his office. But I'll get in touch with him later.'

Herrod grunted, fuming at the delay. He produced a document from his pocket.

'This is a warrant, Mr Watson, empowering us to search your premises in Cardiff Street. Do you wish to be present?'

The other shook his head.

'You don't need a warrant, Superintendent; I've got nothing to hide. The Lord knows what you expect to find there, but go ahead and search if you want to. I'll send Harry with you. No.' He produced a bunch of keys from his pocket, removed one from the ring, and threw it on the table. 'There you are — that's the key. Give me a receipt for it, and let me have it back when you've finished. I don't want your chaps forcing the lock.'

He led the way into the hall. His voice

had recovered its smooth geniality, and as he opened the front door for them, with Harry lurking nervously in the background, he said, 'There's something damned queer about all this, Superintendent. The girl was murdered last week, wasn't she? If you found that map near her body, how come you bloodhounds haven't been to see me before this?'

It was a reasonable question, but one which Herrod had no intention of answering. 'You'd better put a tail on that gentleman,' he said to Dainsford as they walked down the drive. 'I don't think he'll bolt, and I don't think he'll lead us anywhere he doesn't want us to go. He must know we'll be keeping an eye on him. But I'm taking no chances.'

Crossetta and Toby were still waiting. The girl was in high good humour, and had apparently lost her former dread of the police. She led them along the route over which she had followed Watson and Taylor on the Monday evening, and pointed out the traffic lights at which she had lost them.

'Could they have gone this way to the

station?' Herrod asked the Inspector.

'They could. Or to Peacehaven.'

There was a further wait at Brighton police station while Herrod collected the two police officers he had arranged to meet there. With the officers was a local firearms expert.

Then they went on to Cardiff Street.

As Watson had said, No. 17 was empty. And not only empty; it had recently been cleaned and swept, so that no traces of its former use or contents remained. 'The antics of Vanne and his girl friend must have put him on his guard,' Herrod said to Wood. 'I don't imagine their investigations were very discreetly conducted. Watson couldn't be sure they would confide in us; but it'd be the logical conclusion, and no doubt he couldn't afford to take chances. Let's hope the West Sussex chaps have better luck out at Edburton.'

Toby and Crossetta were fetched from the car, taken round to the back, and asked to reenact their movements on the night they first visited the building together. Afterwards Toby stood on the balcony and watched the detectives examine the heavy wooden beam that supported the guttering.

Crossetta remained by the gate.

It was one of the Brighton police who found the bullet. He dug it out of the wood and handed it to the expert.

The latter examined it. 'Almost certainly a .25,' he said.

Sergeant Wood's eyes gleamed.

'Looks like I was right about Watson, Mr Herrod. He killed Taylor and the girl, and took a shot at Vanne when he found him snooping up here. If we searched his house we might find the gun.'

Herrod shook his head.

'If he ever had it he'll have got rid of it by now. He knows he's in a tight spot.' He peered at the hole in the woodwork, and then down at the ground. 'Must have been fired almost vertically.'

They had forgotten Toby and the girl. Crossetta was too far away to hear their conversation. But Toby heard.

'The guy was down there at the foot of the steps,' he said, pointing. 'I saw the flash as he fired. Er — do we have to go on with this playacting, Superintendent? In the next scene I jump down on to the roof of that shed, and it comes a bit hard on the ankles. Couldn't we leave it out?'

Herrod said he thought they could. He was now anxious to be rid of the two young people. The death of Geoffrey Taylor had weakened his taste for theory, but it had not killed it. Already a new and even more fantastic theory was forming in his fertile brain.

But there was one more piece of information to be got from them first.

'How dark was it that night?' he asked, frowning. 'Could you see the gate from up here?'

'I could see through the entrance,' Toby said, remembering. 'I mean, I could see the road, because of the street lamp on the corner. But inside the yard itself it was pitch-dark. I couldn't even see Mrs Tait; she was in the shadow of the wall. It was only when she called out to warn me that I knew she was still there.'

The frown deepened.

'You didn't see the man who fired at you? If he was at the foot of the steps he would be considerably nearer than the gate.'

'I didn't see a darned thing. Only the flash as he fired.'

'But if he came through that gateway you'd have seen him then, wouldn't you? He'd have been silhouetted against the light in the street.'

Toby shook his head. 'He could only have slipped into the yard while Mrs Tait was on the steps,' he said. 'And at that time I was inside the building.'

'Ah, yes,' Herrod said thoughtfully. 'So you were.'

Inspector Dainsford took Toby and the girl back to Hove police station, where Crossetta signed the statement she had previously made. An elderly woman, short and plump and with greying hair, was talking to a uniformed Inspector as they went in. She eyed them curiously.

The woman was still there when they came out. Inspector Dainsford dispatched them to their hotel in a police car, and then hurried back into the building.

'Well?' he asked, mindful of what Herrod had told him.

Inspector Bostrell shook his head.

'This is Mrs Moss,' he said, indicating the elderly woman. 'She lives next door to the Taylors. She says the girl who left with you just now is a complete stranger to her.'

'Never set eyes on her before,' Mrs Moss declared.

★   ★   ★

The West Sussex Constabulary had better luck than Herrod. Their men arrived at the barn near Edburton just as a lorry laden with cigarettes — the final load, according to the driver — was leaving for a destination in the Midlands. The cigarettes had certainly been stolen — although not, the police thought, from local firms. Probably the barn was used as a store for a fairly widespread organization.

But so far there was nothing to connect this organization with Watson — a connexion which to Herrod had seemed all-important. Apart from the missing Landor, Watson appeared to be the only certain link between the murders of Taylor and the girl. Although he had denied complicity, he had hinted at knowledge. The difficulty was to get him to talk. The murders might be linked with his other criminal activities, so that to discuss one would be to disclose the other; and if he was a crook he'd most likely have a crook lawyer, who would advise him to keep his mouth shut. Herrod had hoped that by charging him with being in possession of stolen property the necessity to keep his mouth shut would be eliminated. Provided, of course, that he was not directly implicated in the murders.

But that hope did not now look like being realized. In addition to the lorry-driver and his mate the police had arrested the caretaker, who lived in an adjacent farmhouse (probably Vanne's friend, thought Herrod). The three men had denied all knowledge of the goods they were handling (the cigarettes had been transferred from their cartons into stout wooden boxes), and seemed indignant at having been imposed on. They had talked willingly, but to little purpose.

The men on the lorry were employed by a transport firm in the Midlands; it was their first visit to the barn, they said. The caretaker had insisted that he did not know the name of his actual employer, but said he was instructed and paid by a man called Sparks. He had no idea where Sparks lived, but had given the police a description of the man.

The Superintendent pursed his lips. The description was vague, but as far as it went it fitted Watson's friend Harry. Well, that was a possible channel to be explored. But not by him; the men on the spot could handle that. He had a still more urgent investigation to make — one which, if his new-born theory were right, made Watson's probable evidence (and he had a shrewd idea of what that might be) of secondary importance.

To his surprise the Chief Constable agreed with him.

'It's a long shot, Superintendent, but it may be a winner. What help do you need from me?'

'Quite a lot, sir. We'll have to comb the whole area between Upper Dicker and

Jevington. Well, not all of it, perhaps; your fellows will know the more likely places. And if we're not successful there it means searching the Downs between Jevington and Eastbourne.'

The Chief Constable whistled softly.

'That's a tall order. It'll take a lot of men and a lot of time. Well, I'll manage the men — but there's only a few hours of daylight left. Wouldn't it be wiser to make the arrest now, and hope for the evidence to-morrow?'

Herrod shook his head.

'I've been wrong twice on this case. I may be wrong now.'

'I was thinking of Vanne,' said the other. 'That accident — '

'I know. I was thinking of Vanne too. But, if we've achieved nothing else to-day, at least we have ensured his safety. For the time being, anyway. His death is no longer essential, the way I see it. Unless he sticks his neck out again.'

The Chief Constable got briskly to his feet. Once a decision had been taken he liked the action to follow swiftly. 'Bostrell's the chap,' he said. 'He knows the district well. I'll take what men I can from here, and tell the Bexhill division to send out every man they can spare.'

'Are you going yourself, sir?'

'Of course,' said the other, surprised. 'Aren't you?'

'No. I'm going to Polegate first. I want to have a look inside Taylor's house; I've got his keys. I'm not expecting to find direct evidence — there can't be any there — but I may be able to prove that we're on the right track.'

'Do you want me to hold up the search?'

'No. Even if I'm wrong the search isn't. We should have organized it before.'

'What about Wilkes?'

'Yes,' Herrod said. 'It would be too bad if Mr Wilkes disappeared before we were ready for him. But I don't think he will; Sergeant Wood is keeping an eye on him.' He frowned. 'Unless Wilkes got away before Wood could pick him up. No reason why he should, though.'

'If you're right there is every reason why he shouldn't,' the other said cheerfully. 'He hasn't accomplished what he came for.'

'We hope!' Herrod said fervently.

The Taylors' villa at Polegate still appeared to be deserted, but the Superintendent waited a few moments before trying the keys in the lock. The Chief Constable's ready cooperation had bolstered up his sagging belief in himself, but he could not quieten the small voice inside him which kept insisting on how far-fetched was his present notion. Another knock . . . and feet might come hurrying, the door might open . . . and bang would go yet another theory.

The feet came hurrying, but not from inside the house. Up the path trotted Mrs Moss, a startling black and yellow hat perched on top of her grey hair.

'I've only this minute got back,' she said, wheezing a little. And then, noting the keys, 'Are you going in?'

Herrod nodded.

'Oh! Well, she hasn't been back since you was here Tuesday. No one's been near the place.' Her voice dropped to a conspiratorial whisper, although there was none to overhear. 'That girl in the police station at Hove. That wasn't her.'

'So I understand. I'm sorry we had to trouble you.'

He began to try the keys in the lock.

'Oh, I didn't mind. It was a nice ride, and the young man was ever so pleasant.' She hesitated. 'I saw about Geoff Taylor in the papers. That *was* him, wasn't it? At Peacehaven?'

He nodded. A key turned in the lock. 'Would you mind coming round with me?' he asked her. 'Just to ensure I don't pinch the silver.'

She accepted eagerly.

He went quickly through the rooms on the ground floor, with Mrs Moss in close attendance. Everything was as it had been when he had peered through the windows on his previous visit. There was a little more dust; that was the only difference. But he did not see what he was seeking, and he went upstairs and into the main bedroom, with Mrs Moss chattering doggedly at his heels. The bed was unmade, male clothing was piled untidily on a chair, a newspaper lay on the floor. On the mantelpiece numerous photographs, unframed and unmounted, stood propped among the ornaments.

Herrod picked one up.

'That was taken just after their wedding,' said Mrs Moss. 'Nice, isn't it?'

★   ★   ★

Inspector Bostrell considered the problem and the map. The map was for the benefit of the Chief Constable and the Inspector from Bexhill; he himself knew the area too well to need its aid. He preferred to visualize it, lane by lane and track by track, with his mind's eye.

'I'd try Hailsham Common first, sir,' he said. 'There's plenty of cover there, both north and south of the road. And here' — he pointed to the map, tracing a line with his pencil — 'that's a wire fence enclosing the wood. It reaches the Wilmington road a few hundred yards south of the road junction. About there. A chap could lie hid inside that wood for months.'

Outside the police station the road was lined with cars, each car laden with policemen. On the opposite pavement the people of Hailsham were gathering, curious and a little awed at this unusual police activity. A Southdown bus went by, its occupants craning their necks at the crowd and the cars.

The Chief Constable frowned.

'Not inside the wire,' he said. 'Too difficult. It should be easily get-at-able by car, I think. No — we'll try the common.'

He strode impatiently from the Inspector's inner sanctum, the others following. It had taken longer than he had expected to assemble the necessary men, and all too soon it would be dark. 'We'll discuss the next move if and when this one fails,' he threw at them over his shoulder.

As they stepped out into the shadowed street a car came swiftly towards them from the south. It pulled up against the opposite kerb, and Superintendent Herrod leapt nimbly out, almost running across the road in his eagerness.

The Chief Constable went to meet him. Triumphantly, his blue eyes sparkling, Herrod handed him a photograph. 'I think that clinches it,' he said gaily. 'There can't be any doubt now. Look, sir. The third from the left.'

For a brief moment the Chief Constable studied the photograph. Then he looked up and smiled. The Superintendent's exuberance was infectious.

'No doubt at all, Mr Herrod,' he agreed. There was relief in his voice, a new vitality. 'Congratulations. And now let's get cracking. We've been led by the nose long enough; it'll be a pleasant change to do a bit of leading ourselves. You may be wrong about Landor, but I'm damned sure you're right about the rest.'

'I'm right about Landor too,' Herrod said. 'I know it.'

He said it with such absolute conviction that the Chief Constable was startled. Then he grinned.

'Fey, eh? Well, let's go and see what the fairies can find in the woods.'

'I must phone Dainsford first,' Herrod said. 'I want him to pick up those two young people and take them into custody.'

'What — both of them? On what charge?'

'The charge doesn't matter. 'Obstructing the police' will be sufficient. The main thing is to get them safely under lock and key.'

They drove through Hailsham and over the railway bridge. They crossed the main Eastbourne road, heading west. The common spread away on either side of them, but Inspector Bostrell did not stop. 'The other end would be the most likely, sir,' he said. 'If they came from Upper Dicker they'd go south, not east.'

They turned on to the Wilmington road, and stopped when they came to the wire. As the men left the cars and began to line up the Superintendent said doubtfully, 'We're a bit thin on the ground, aren't we? It's a wide stretch to sweep, and heavy going in places by the look of it.'

'It narrows quickly,' Bostrell told him. 'The road runs due east and the wire north-east.'

Herrod nodded, and pointed to a rutted track just outside the wire that led, through bushes and brambles, to the dark interior of a copse. 'How about that? Right on their route, and a handy spot in which to hide the car. I'll try that myself.'

He waited for the men to spread out, and then, at the given signal, began to advance along the track. The Chief Constable went with him. On their right a constable picked his way with difficulty along the humped bank that bordered the wire. On their left they could hear, and occasionally see, men battling their way through the thick undergrowth and brambles that caught and pulled at their uniforms.

'Tough on those fellows,' Herrod said, his eyes searching avidly.

'Don't look now,' the Chief Constable warned him, 'but it's going to be tough on us too. This is a dead end.'

It was true. Scraps of paper, cigarette packets, and rusting tins showed where a succession of picnickers had rested briefly and untidily. Beyond them the tree-studded ground sloped gently upward to a knoll obscuring the wire. And beyond the knoll were the brambles.

'Gloomy spot for a picnic,' Herrod said,

mounting the slope. 'Some people — '

The constable on his right shouted excitedly, bent to peer down into the hollow between the bank and the wire, and then straightened. As he turned to face them he put a whistle to his lips and blew shrilly.

The two officers hurried towards him. Behind them another whistle shrilled. There was the sound of men crashing through the bushes, pain and discomfort disregarded in the anticipation of success.

Silently they clustered on the bank, gazing down at the remains of what had once been a man. The dead lips were parted in a snarl; dirt filled eyes and mouth and nostrils. The blue suit was crumpled and stained, the brown shoes no longer held a polish. His hair was matted, entwined with twigs and snippets of bramble. On his left hand was a dirty chamois glove.

And from the uncovered right hand the middle finger was missing.

'Landor!' Herrod said. His voice conveyed neither surprise nor triumph. 'Landor!'

A few idlers had gathered on the road. Drivers of passing cars stopped, inquired of the watchers what was toward, and then, either from lack of interest or the need for haste, went on their way. An amateur photographer was busy with his camera, snapping police, the track, even the bystanders. 'Editors pay big money for news pictures,' he told them. 'This may be quite a scoop.'

A big Buick came down the road from the south. The driver's foot was pressing on the brake as the car rounded the slight bend, his hand was already at the gear lever. Then he saw the line of cars by the roadside, the numerous blue-clad figures, the patient, watchful spectators. His foot moved from the brake to the accelerator. As he passed the track he glanced quickly down it; but the light was beginning to fade, and the track was merged in the shadows.

'So they've got around to it at last, have they?' he muttered to himself, a grim expression on his ugly, misshapen face. 'A few more hours and I'd have made it, blast them! Now — well, it's going to depend on how fast a policeman can think. I hope to hell this one's slow!'

14

'What next?' asked Crossetta. 'I'm not going to sit drinking all the evening. I want to *do* something.'

'It's pleasant here,' Toby said. They had already done enough for one day, he thought. 'Don't rush me.'

They were sitting in the saloon bar of the Palmeira Hotel in Hove. It was a pleasant place in which to relax, thought Toby, sipping his third whisky; snug and comfortable, with a warm, friendly atmosphere. A pity Crossetta was in a restless mood. For his part he would have been happy to stay there until closing time.

It had been an eventful day, he reflected. Lewes and the accident to the Riley in the morning, the visits to Watson's house and Cardiff Street in the afternoon. And even then Crossetta had not let him rest. They had gone to Caffyn's Garage after tea to have a look at the Riley; after which, much to his surprise, Crossetta had insisted they should go for a walk. Not along the front, since the wind bothered her, but up the hill towards the Dyke golf-course. Toby had never loved his Riley so dearly as then, when he had to do without it; he was not a happy walker. It had been a relief to turn and come downhill, and a still greater relief to accept the welcome that the Palmeira had offered.

They had sat there for nearly two hours now, and night was already closing down on the city. They had eaten their way steadily through a pile of freshly cut sandwiches. Toby, after quenching his thirst with beer, had switched to whisky; Crossetta, as usual, had drunk little. It bothered him that she should be so abstemious. A little more gin, he thought, might soften her heart towards him. It wasn't fair that some one so lovely should be so cold.

'Let's have one for the road,' he said hopefully, seizing her glass. 'Then we'll go.'

'Not for me.' She put out a hand to

stop him. 'And not for you either. You've had quite enough for one evening. Sit down and make a suggestion.'

The suggestion he would like to make, Toby thought, would earn him a slap on the face. He put it regretfully from his mind. 'How about the movies?' he said. In the cinema there would be proximity. And darkness.

'No. I don't want to sit and watch. I told you, I want to *do* something.'

'Well, how about a nice walk? That would make a pleasant change.'

She laughed. 'Careful! I might take you up on that.'

'Or a dance?' he said hastily.

She considered this.

'Yes, that's an idea. Though I warn you I'm a rotten dancer.'

That surprised him. She was slim and agile, and all her movements were graceful. 'I bet you dance like an angel,' he said, leaning towards her.

She looked at him doubtfully. 'You're not tight, are you? You've had a lot to drink.'

Was he? A little, perhaps. 'Me? Good heavens, no!'

'All right, then. Where do we dance?'

'The Regent, I guess.' A vision of the dance-floor, of music and soft lighting, came to him, and suddenly he was filled with a desire to be there, holding Crossetta in his arms. Why hadn't he thought of it before? He stood up, gulping down his drink. 'Come on, let's go.'

As he helped her into her coat his fingers brushed the soft skin at the nape of her neck, and he shivered ecstatically. Perhaps it's the whisky, he thought, or maybe I've been working up to this ever since I met her; but I've a hunch that to-night's the night. And I figure she owes it to me, too.

He pondered on the dark interior of a taxi. Then he had a better idea. His knowledge of the town should be put to use.

'We'll cut down through St Anns Well to Western Road,' he told her, as they left the hotel. 'We can take a bus from there.'

He did not mention that they could more easily have caught a bus outside the Palmeira.

He made no attempt to take her arm.

As they walked down Somerhill Road Crossetta chattered gaily, but Toby spoke only when he had to. His conscience was fighting a losing battle with desire.

It annoyed him that there should be this battle. Isn't it perfectly natural, Desire said to Conscience, that a man should take a pretty girl in his arms and kiss her? Perfectly natural, Conscience agreed, provided the girl does not object; otherwise he's behaving like a heel. That's all very well, said Desire; but how is he to know unless he tries? Sometimes he can't, Conscience admitted, but this time he can. He knows darned well she'll object.

Okay, Toby told himself. Just for once I'll be a heel. I've made up my mind to kiss her, and kiss her I will. A girl as pretty as Crossetta just *has* to be kissed.

St Anns Well has tennis courts and a pavilion at the northern end. For the rest it is mainly grass, hilly and tree-studded, and intersected by winding paths. As Toby took her arm and steered her through the wide gates the girl looked up at him and then away.

'It's a short cut,' he said, and wondered

if his voice sounded as odd to her as it did to him.

They walked down the path without speaking. At the pavilion it divided, and Toby took the right fork. It was darker there, with the trees on their right and the pavilion shielding them from the lights of Nizells Avenue. Toby's mouth was dry. A pulse throbbed madly in his forehead, his heart beat so loudly that he thought she must hear it.

His grip on her arm tightened suddenly.

Crossetta turned to look at him. Her face was a white gleam of enchantment, picked out by a stray beam of light filtering through the trees. Without a word he swung her towards him, his arms went round her, and he bent to kiss her lips.

Caught off her guard, for a too brief moment Crossetta stayed passive in his embrace. Then she strained away from him, and every fibre and muscle in her slim body went into action as she struggled to free herself.

'Crossetta!' he murmured, as she

moved her head from side to side to avoid his kisses. 'Crossetta, honey. Please!'

A hissing sound escaped her clenched teeth, but she did not speak. Her arms were pinioned, and with an effort she swung her handbag upward to hit him on the back of the head. The bag flew open, scattering its contents on the path.

The blow did not hurt, but it brought him to his senses. Fearful that she might run away from him, he did not let her go; but his grip loosened. Ashamed, he looked anxiously down at her.

'I — I'm sorry,' he stammered. 'You were right, I must have had too — much — to — drink; I — '

He had spoken hurriedly at first, anxious to placate her. But the end of the sentence came haltingly; his voice faded to a whisper and finally died. He was staring wide-eyed at something that lay on the ground, something that gleamed wickedly where the light found it. It must have fallen from her handbag. But what —

'Good God!' His hands moved from her waist to grip her arms. 'Crossetta, you — '

The girl's knee came up sharply, viciously. It caught him in the groin, and he fell away from her, his body doubled up in agony.

Vaguely, as from a great distance, he heard her voice. What she said he did not know; nor, even when the pain began to ease, did he greatly care. Horror had assaulted his brain even more forcibly than his body had been assaulted.

Slowly he straightened.

Crossetta stood a few feet away from him. The light flickered on her face as the wind moved the branches of the trees; grotesque and shadowy patterns chased each other across the whiteness of her coat.

She stood very still. Only the slight tremor of the gun held in her right hand betrayed her agitation.

★　★　★

'Yes,' Watson said. 'Yes, that's Claire.'

Herrod took the photograph from him and tucked it away in his pocket. It was strange, he thought, how, after a week of disappointments and vain searching, success should suddenly be heaped on success. It was only that morning that Vanne had come to him with his confession — and how much had been achieved since! His own long-odds fancy had proved a winner, they had found Landor, and now Watson was talking. For the local police force had caught up with Sparks . . . and Sparks, as Herrod had hopefully anticipated, had proved to be Harry . . . and Harry had shown no fight at all. Like the small-time crook he obviously was, he had sold Watson all down the line.

And Watson knew it, knew there was no way out, knew he could save nothing from the wreck. Harry had proved himself a competent Judas. When the time came, Watson thought grimly, he would reckon with Harry. What mattered now was to clear himself of the charge of murder. At least they shouldn't pin that on him.

'I did think it might be her,' he said. 'Just at first. But then the papers said it was this other girl, and I couldn't see — '

'We won't go into that again,' Herrod said brusquely.

Despite the success that now seemed to be crowning his efforts, there was an undercurrent of unease in the Superintendent's triumph. His instructions to Inspector Dainsford had been given too late; Vanne and the girl had already left the hotel. And now it was nearly nine o'clock — and still no news of them.

And Wilkes. Wilkes too was missing. Since he had dropped Vanne in Lewes that morning Wilkes had vanished completely. Where was he? What was he up to? Herrod would have given much to know.

But he couldn't know. Not until one or other of the three swam into the vision of a policeman and was snatched up in the net that had been spread in and around the town. Until that happened he could only wait. There was nothing else.

Except Watson. Herrod thought he knew most of what Watson had to tell him, but it was as well to be sure.

The other caught his eye. 'All right, all right,' he said. 'But what is it you want? I said I was ready to talk, didn't I?'

'I want to know about Claire Taylor,' Herrod said. 'I'm not interested in your various criminal activities except where they concern her. The local police will deal with you on the other counts. Was it on your instructions that Mrs Taylor pinched that car?'

'No. She suggested it herself. She and the woman Anna had worked it once before. Anna took the man back to her flat for the night, and Claire brought the car over here.'

'Why? Was she in love with you, or was it all in the way of business?'

'She wanted the money,' Watson said. 'She was always wanting money. When we went away together it cost me a packet.'

'A gold-digger, eh?'

'I suppose so. Though she never made any bones about it, she told me straight she was on the make.' He sighed. 'But I didn't care. She was a lovely girl.'

Herrod was unaffected by the sigh. A crook's illicit desire for his gold-digging paramour was no cause for sentiment, he thought.

'Let's hear what happened that Thursday night,' he said curtly. 'Or what you expected to happen.'

Bit by bit he got the story. A fortnight ago, Watson said, Claire had suggested that she and Anna should lift another car when the opportunity offered. He had agreed, but had told her not to take the car to his house, as she had done on the previous occasion, but direct to Cardiff Street. Since she did not know the district he had given her a map, so that she might find her way there without asking.

At about eleven-thirty on the previous Thursday night Claire had telephoned to say that she had the car and was on her way over. Why not stay the night? he had said. Why not stay several nights? Till the Monday, say. They might spend a few days in London, as they had done before. She could leave a note for her husband and at the office to say she would be away on business.

Claire had agreed, and he had gone to Cardiff Street to meet her.

'But she never turned up,' Watson said, spreading his arms in a gesture of despair. 'I waited hours, but she never turned up.'

'What then?' asked Herrod.

'It had me worried. I didn't know

354

whether she'd been pinched, or done the dirty on me, or what. Next morning I phoned the office, and they told me about the note. That didn't make the situation any clearer. I even thought of contacting her husband. But I hadn't the nerve.

'Then I read in the papers about this girl who had been murdered.'

'And you thought it was Mrs Taylor, eh?' said Herrod.

'Well, I did and I didn't. It would explain why she never turned up, of course, but I couldn't understand the jersey and trousers. Claire would never dress like that. She was going away for a gay week-end, and Claire was fussy about clothes. She could afford to be, too, on the money she wheedled out of me.'

'So you sat on the fence.'

'More or less,' Watson agreed cheerfully. He had been sullen and angry when they had first brought him to Hove police station, but talking seemed to have restored his geniality. 'I went over to Eastbourne Saturday morning, but there was nothing new at the office. And I couldn't go to the police, could I? Not the way things were.' He grinned at the detective, unabashed. 'I wasn't half relieved when I read in the papers that the dead girl had been identified as some one else.'

'But you still didn't know what had happened to Mrs Taylor.'

'Well, I knew she wasn't dead. Or I thought I knew. That was something. Got a cigarette on you, Superintendent? I've run out.'

Herrod handed him a packet.

'What about Anna Kermode?' he asked. 'Didn't she get in touch with you? She knew the dead girl was Mrs Taylor. She saw the body.'

'Anna didn't know about me. We'd never met. She and Claire fixed it between them.'

'Didn't you pay her?'

'Claire saw to that out of what I gave her. It was nothing to do with me.'

The hands of the clock were creeping round towards nine-thirty. What the hell's happening? wondered the Superintendent, his irritation growing. Why haven't any of them been picked up yet? Where have they got to, damn them?

'Monday,' he said sharply. 'What happened that evening?'

'You mean Taylor, eh?' Watson grimaced. 'Yes, that was a bit awkward. I imagined he'd come over with news of Claire. It shook me no end when he showed me the note she'd left for him — the one I'd told her to write — and demanded to know where she was.'

'Had he no suspicions of what you and Mrs Taylor had been up to?'

'Well, Claire always said he hadn't. He trusted her implicitly, she said. But he wasn't in a very trusting mood that evening, I can tell you. Threatened me with the police if I didn't produce her.'

'I appreciate your predicament,' Herrod said politely.

Watson grinned. 'Tricky, wasn't it? I couldn't afford to have you fellows poking your noses into my business. On the other hand, I couldn't oblige him by producing his wife. So what was I to do?'

'Drive him over to Peacehaven and put a bullet in him,' Herrod said evenly.

The grin vanished abruptly.

'That's a damned lie!' Watson leaned forward, gripping the seat of his chair. 'I took him to the station, as I told you this morning. I didn't kill Taylor, Superintendent, and you know it. What's more, I can prove it. Harry — '

He stopped abruptly.

'Yes?' prompted Herrod. 'What about Harry?'

'Nothing.' Harry wouldn't help him to prove anything. Harry would say only what the police wanted him to say.

'And how,' asked Herrod, 'did you persuade Taylor to depart so meekly?'

'I told him he could search the house — which he did. I told him I was as worried as he was about his wife's disappearance, that I'd do everything I could to help him find her. I laid it on good and thick. In the end I think he believed me. And why shouldn't he? I was telling the truth, wasn't I?'

'Half the truth,' Herrod said. 'You didn't tell him — '

A knock on the door, and Inspector Dainsford hurried into the room.

'Excuse me, sir. Sergeant Wood is here.'

Herrod's eyes gleamed. 'Alone?'
'No, sir. Wilkes is with him.'

★ ★ ★

'You won't do that again,' said Crossetta.

If her body was steady her voice was not. There was fury in it, and a fierce contempt. The words came jerkily from her lips, as though her breathing was not yet under control.

Toby did not answer at once. He had almost forgotten the reason for her anger. His eyes were mesmerized by the gun, so small and yet so menacing. And he was trying desperately to think, to understand. With the first glimpse of the gun there had flashed into his mind the memory of the girl he had found lying dead among the corn; Wilkes's sister. And the shopkeeper. And the man whose body had been found at Peacehaven, the fair-haired man they had seen outside Watson's house. He had thought —

No. No, that was Landor's work. The police thought so, they were still looking for him. Yet why had Crossetta —

The gun moved slightly.

'No,' he said huskily. 'No, I won't do it again.'

He could watch her hand, but he would not be able to see her finger tighten on the trigger. There would be no warning. His eyes sought her face, searching it hopefully.

The girl met his look with a hard, unwavering stare.

'Put that gun away, Crossetta,' he pleaded. 'I guess I behaved badly, but there's no need for this dramatic gesture. I've already apologized, and it won't happen again. You don't have to threaten me with that.'

A slight sound came from her lips. It might have been a laugh. Yet could anyone laugh under such circumstances?

'This isn't a gesture,' she said. 'I don't carry a gun for fun. I use it.'

She moved a pace towards him. The sweat started on his forehead, his legs felt incapable of supporting his weight. There was a sickness in his stomach.

For what seemed to Toby an eternity they faced each other. Then anger seized him, momentarily swamping fear.

'Damn it, woman, you can't shoot a man just because he tries to kiss you!' he said indignantly.

'Can't I? I've done it before.'

He believed her. He knew too that it was Crossetta the police should be hunting, not Landor. Or both, maybe. She had killed those people. He did not know why or how, and his mind was too full of his own danger to ponder on it. But he knew it had happened.

All about them were the sounds of the city. The whines and rumblings of the cars and the buses. Music came faintly from a distant radio, and only a few yards away people were walking and talking. And living. But he, Toby Vanne, was about to die.

Or — was he? Hadn't he still got a chance? If he were to rush her, how swift would be her reaction, how sure her aim? Even if she had time to fire, the bullet might not kill.

Not, perhaps, the first bullet. But there would be others.

Well, what the hell? he thought

defiantly. I'm a dead duck for sure. What have I got to lose?

The gun moved again, and he flinched. But he needed time in which to nerve himself for the final spring, and he said hurriedly, 'Say, I thought we were friends, you and I. Remember Cardiff Street that first evening? You saved my life then. Why bump me off now?'

He was pleased at the firmness with which he had spoken. At least she should not have the satisfaction of knowing he was afraid.

Crossetta laughed. There was no doubting it this time.

'I tried to kill you, you mean.'

'You did?' His incredulity was real. 'I don't believe it.'

'Why not? There was no one else in the yard.'

'But you were at the gate! The shot came from the steps.'

'I called out from the gate. That was a precaution in case I missed, and also to make you pause,' she said. There was no hurry to be done, as there had been on those other occasions. They were alone in

362

a lonely place, and for both of them time was standing still. She had no feeling for him except aversion, disgust at the memory of his embrace. But it pleased her that he should know the truth before he died. 'I ran to the steps and fired, and then got back to the gate. You didn't hear me; I was wearing plimsolls.'

'But you seemed kind of upset afterwards. I thought — '

'You thought I was upset because I had exposed you to danger? You're too simple, Toby. No. I was furious with myself at having missed. It was such a wonderful opportunity to get rid of you. No one knew we were together, no one would have suspected me.'

'But why? Why the heck did you *want* to get rid of me? I hadn't harmed you in any way, had I?'

'No. But you were a threat, you had that piece of paper with the map on it. I didn't want you to show it to the police.'

He still did not understand fully. But now he was no longer trying to understand. For the first time since eternity had beckoned him he saw a faint gleam of hope. The gun was no longer pointing at his middle; it had dropped. Was that because her arm was tiring? Or was her purpose weakening?

'I'm sorry,' he said, his eyes on the gun. 'I thought you kind of liked me. Quite a sucker, wasn't I?'

'You're no worse than most men,' said Crossetta.

Her voice fanned the flickering hope. It was calmly conversational. Was she actually enjoying this macabre introduction to death? Or was there now a tiny seed of doubt in her mind?

He said, trying to sound interested — although all that interested him now was her purpose — 'And when you knocked me out with the brick that afternoon at the barn — you weren't trying to hit the other guy, were you? It was me you aimed at?'

'Of course. I should have said it was an accident. And the man wouldn't have called the police, he'd have let his boss deal with it.' She shrugged, and the gun dropped further. 'I was safe enough.'

You're wrong there, he thought. You

wouldn't have been *that* safe. Even if Watson's men had played ball — and they might not, at that — how would you have explained my non-return to Mrs Buell? *She* wouldn't have let you get away with it. She'd have gone to the police.

But to argue, to cast doubt on the sanity of her reasoning, might anger her. It was wiser to agree.

'I guess you're right,' he said docilely.

Should he rush her now, or should he wait? Better to wait, perhaps, to try first to talk her out of it. Precipitate action might startle her into firing, even though her intention to do so were now less firm.

'It was you loosened that nut on the Riley, I suppose,' he said. 'When you parked it last night. You didn't want me to talk to the Superintendent. It wasn't Wilkes, as I'd figured. It was you.'

'No, it wasn't Wilkes,' she said. 'I told you, didn't I, that I was a good mechanic? I hoped you'd break your stupid neck; but you didn't, you were lucky, you — ' Her voice had hardened, and he tensed himself for action. 'You've had quite a lot of luck, haven't you? But not any more. I shan't miss this time.'

He knew he had lost his chance. As the gun came up he flung himself sideways, so that he collided with a tree and nearly fell. There was a crack, a sharp, searing pain in his left arm. Then he was up and running through the shadowy dark, making for the blessed safety of the lighted streets.

Crossetta fired again.

★ ★ ★

Nat Wilkes's face was as expressionless as ever. But his voice, the tautness of the skin over the knuckles of his clenched fists, the way he squared his shoulders as though anticipating trouble, betrayed the strain under which he was labouring. His eyes were bloodshot from lack of sleep.

'You've got nothing against me,' he said hoarsely. 'Why have I been brought here?'

Herrod looked at him.

'False identification will do for a start,' he said mildly. Now that Wilkes was actually there in front of him he felt happier. 'You have also connived at murder, haven't you? Four murders. Caseman, Landor, Claire Taylor, Geoffrey Taylor.' His voice hardened as he ticked them off on his fingers. 'That's a lot of murders for one man to have on his conscience, Wilkes.'

'Who's Taylor?' asked Wilkes. 'The girl's husband?'

'I'm putting the questions,' Herrod snapped at him. 'Why did you identify that girl as your sister?'

Wilkes glared at him without answering. Through the windows of the police station came the sound of traffic in Church Road, the occasional sharp patter of feet on the pavement, snatches of unintelligible conversation.

Herrod closed the window. 'Why did you do it?' he asked again. And then, as the other still remained silent, 'Oh, don't be a bloody fool, man! You can't help your sister now. Half the police in the district are looking for her. We've searched her room at the hotel; we've got enough evidence to convict her four times over.' Wilkes started, clenching his fists. 'I'm sorry if that hits you on the raw; but

it's the truth, and the sooner you appreciate it the better. Don't kid yourself that
you'll be allowed to walk out of here to-night,
that there's still a chance you may find her
and smuggle her away. You'll not leave this
building until that precious sister of yours
is safely under lock and key. We don't take
chances on murder, Wilkes.'

He paused for breath and to cool his
temper. Wilkes said nothing, but his body
sagged slightly.

'We'll try again,' said Herrod. 'Why did
you identify that girl as your sister?'

'Mind if I sit down?' asked the other.

He almost slumped into the chair that
Wood placed for him. He's cracking,
thought Herrod, noting the drooping
shoulders, the lines that seemed suddenly
to criss-cross the man's face. He waited
expectantly for the other to speak. But
Wilkes did not speak. He was content to
sit.

'Playing dumb, eh?' Herrod said,
keeping his anger in check. 'All right. I'll
tell *you* what happened, shall I?'

Wilkes shrugged. 'Please yourself. I
can't stop you.'

'You're damned right you can't. You're not much good at stopping anyone, are you?' Since the man was unresponsive to reason, perhaps he could be goaded into losing his temper, into making the unguarded retort that would reveal some fraction of the truth. 'You let that precious sister of yours prance round the countryside with a gun, shooting at will. And when some one gets killed — what do you do? Help us to ensure that it doesn't happen again? No. You cover up for her, encourage her to indulge in a little more human target practice. You identified that girl as your sister because you knew we would lay off her and concentrate on Landor. Isn't that so?'

'It worked, didn't it?' said Wilkes.

'Oh, yes, it worked. You gave her a few more days of liberty. She made the most of it, too. If you hadn't told that lie Taylor would be alive to-day. Doesn't that trouble your conscience?'

'Don't worry about my conscience. It can look after itself.'

'I dare say. No doubt it's had plenty of practice. Now — would you like to take over? Or shall I continue?'

'Go to hell!'

'I'd rather not,' Herrod said equably. 'There'd be too many of the Wilkes family present for my liking. But we'll drop personalities, shall we? Let's get down to facts.

'We'll start with the Forest Row murder. Landor and your sister broke into the shop, and when the old man appeared she shot him. Not in self-defence, mind you; she wasn't inside the shop, she was by the door. Perhaps she didn't like the colour of his eyes, or maybe she had an itching finger. Anyway, she shot him.

'They went south. Landor had the wind up — he hadn't reckoned on a trigger-happy Amazon for a companion. He wanted to get as far from Forest Row as quickly as he could. But not your sister. She was hungry. A little thing like killing a defenceless old man couldn't spoil *her* appetite. She made Landor stop at a café.

'They moved on when another car approached. They turned off the main road, and when they came to a likely spot they parked. There may have been an interlude for romance (I say 'romance' out of delicacy. There are other words), but at some time during the night they started to divide the spoils. And that was Landor's undoing, poor devil. Miss Wilkes wasn't going to be satisfied with part of the loot, she wanted the whole damned lot. No half-measures for that young lady.

'So she shot him. Just like that.'

'That's a bloody lie!' Wilkes leapt to his feet, fists clenched, eyes glaring. His twisted upper lip was drawn back over the blackened teeth; there were specks of foam at his mouth. 'She shot him because the filthy rat tried to get fresh with her.'

'Did she tell you that?' asked the Superintendent, concealing his elation.

'Yes, she told me. But she didn't have to, I'd have known it anyway. Cathie loathes anything to do with sex. It — well, it's because of something that happened when she was a kid. Joe Landor wasn't the first to kick his guts out because he couldn't keep his hands off her. She drilled a guy once before, only the police never got wise to her. I saw to that.'

They stared at him, aghast. Herrod broke into a cold sweat. Somewhere in the city Vanne and the girl were together. And Vanne was obviously infatuated. I hope to God the young fool keeps his hands to himself, he thought, fervently.

'Holy mackerel! What sort of a ruddy monster is she?' said Wood, unable to restrain himself.

Herrod frowned at the interruption, forcing his eyes away from the clock. Time was not important. There was no deadline in time to the anxiety that plagued him.

'And yet, knowing that, you still let her have a gun to play with?' he demanded.

'It wasn't hers, it was mine,' Wilkes said sullenly. 'She took it from my room. I didn't know she had it.'

'H'm. Later we may want to see your certificate for it. But let's get on. Shall I tell you, or will you tell me?'

'You tell me,' said Wilkes. 'It's your story, I wouldn't want to spoil it for you.'

He sat down and stared intently at the

floor. His arms rested loosely on his thighs.

'All right, I will. She dragged Landor's body into a ditch, and then drove down to Jevington. She ran out of petrol there; so she abandoned the car and walked over the Downs to Eastbourne. She had packed a frock in her suitcase (That's not guesswork. We found it when we searched her room this evening), and somewhere on the way she put it on. Perhaps that's why she wasn't spotted by the Eastbourne police. That — and the fact that she'd got rid of Landor.

'With plenty of money and no conscience she probably spent quite an enjoyable day by the sea. But something urged her to move on. Maybe she felt that travel broadens the mind; and she had a few cartridges left, she wouldn't want to waste them. She had deposited a perfectly good corpse a few miles north of Eastbourne; why shouldn't Brighton have one too? She might even put in a little practice at Lewes on the way. So — '

'Shut up!' Wilkes gripped the arms of his chair, his face contorted with rage. Or was it agony, agony of mind? wondered Herrod. 'Shut your damned mouth before I shut it for you.'

Herrod leaned forward.

'If you don't like the way I'm telling it,' he said calmly, 'you have an alternative. You can tell it yourself.'

'You and your bloody sneers!' stormed Wilkes, unheeding. 'You think you know everything, don't you? Well, you don't know Cathie. You wouldn't understand her in a million years. She's not like that, she's — oh, *damn* you!'

He slumped forward, his head moving desperately from side to side. For a few moments Herrod watched him. Then he went over to stand in front of him.

'Well?' he asked quietly. 'What is she?'

Slowly Wilkes sat up. He stared at Herrod, tears glistening in his bloodshot eyes. The Superintendent wondered whether the man's tormented mind had been able to absorb the question.

'Tell me about your sister,' he said.

Wilkes closed his eyes.

'You wouldn't understand,' he said again, his voice a groan. 'I don't always understand myself. It's something inside her that makes her do it. She's impulsive . . . she gets involved in things . . . she — '

'Other people get involved in things,' Herrod said. 'But they don't resort to murder.'

'I know. But Cathie's different. She — she doesn't hold life important. Every one has to die, she says, so why does it matter when?' He blinked away the tears. 'Oh, what's the use! You've never met anyone like Cathie. You just wouldn't understand.'

'It's difficult,' Herrod agreed. 'But I'm trying.'

'She didn't set out to kill those people,' Wilkes said. He was staring hard at Herrod now, pleading with eyes and voice. All his rage and sullen defiance had gone. 'She fired at the man in the shop because she was excited and keyed up — she didn't really know what she was doing. The gun was in her hand, and she pulled the trigger. It — it was just an accident.'

Does he really believe that? Herrod wondered, recalling the girl's later actions. Or is he trying to kid himself as well as me? But he did not argue the statement. Now that he had at last broken down the other's resistance he did not want to antagonize him further.

'All right,' he said. 'And Landor — well, I think I understand about him. But there's still the girl.'

'She *had* to kill her, Mr Herrod. It was the girl or her. I can see that.'

'Suppose you tell me about it,' Herrod said. 'I'd like to see it too.'

'She left Eastbourne because she thought the police would be looking for her there. In case they were watching the station she took a bus out of the town and started walking along the Brighton road, hoping for a lift. Presently a car passed her, slowing down. It stopped up the road, and when she caught up with it a girl was leaning over the bonnet. There wasn't much wrong, Cathie said; a lead shorting across the engine. She put it right, and the girl agreed to give her a lift.

'Cathie got in the back. She was tired, she wanted to sleep. But she didn't sleep. Not when she saw the girl's expensive-looking suitcase and the clothes she was wearing.' He sighed. 'Cathie is crazy about clothes. Maybe if I could afford more — '

'She killed the girl for her clothes?' Herrod asked.

'No!' Wilkes said earnestly. 'Oh, no. She put the gun against the girl's back and made her turn off the road. You know where. Then she told her to get out and strip, and gave her the trousers and jersey to put on instead.

'It was when the girl had changed that Cathie realized the danger she was in. As soon as she had gone the girl would phone the police; Cathie wouldn't have a chance. She *had* to kill her.'

Herrod shuddered, recalling how he had warmed to Cathie Wilkes's beauty and vitality and charm. How incongruous, how appallingly wrong, that they should cloak such a vile monstrosity. And Wilkes? What sort of a creature was he? 'She *had* to kill her.' Did he really believe that?

Wilkes was droning on, anxious to be done. He was very tired. He knew now that he could do no more for Cathie, that this was the end.

'She put the girl's clothes in the suitcase, had a look inside the handbag' — Watson's map must have fallen out then, Herrod thought, the detective in him alert despite his repugnance — 'and drove away. She spent the night in the car, and went on to Brighton the next morning. When she got a room at the Coniston she registered as Mrs Tait because of the girl's initials. They were on the bag and the suitcase.'

Wilkes paused. It seemed that he had finished, and Herrod said sharply, 'How about Taylor?'

Wilkes had been staring at the floor. Now he looked up.

'Who's Taylor?' he asked, as he had at the beginning. He did not sound greatly interested.

Herrod told him.

'That wouldn't be Cathie's doing,' Wilkes said. 'She'd have told me. Unless she forgot.'

The Superintendent tried to envisage some one who could commit a murder and forget it two days later. Even for

Cathie Wilkes that seemed impossible. Yet if the girl had not killed Taylor, who had? Watson? Watson had been infatuated with Taylor's wife, had been partly responsible for her disappearance. Or thought he had. And Taylor had confronted him with an impossible dilemma by threatening to go to the police.

Yes, Watson had had more reason than the girl to kill Taylor. She, to his knowledge, had had no reason at all. But what significance was there in that? Over-excitement, a man getting fresh with her, envy of another girl's clothes; were those reasons for murder?

'You spoke to your sister last night?' he said. 'It was then she told you about Landor and the others?'

'Yes.'

The quiet monosyllable caused Herrod to explode.

'And you did nothing? Good God, man, you're as much a murderer as she is!'

His wrath was infectious. 'What the hell could I do?' Wilkes said heatedly. 'She wouldn't come away with me; she was having too good a time, she said. I couldn't carry her off by force, could I?'

'Be damned to that! You should have informed the police.'

'And what then? They'd have said she was insane, they'd have shut her up for life. Do you think I'd do that to Cathie? No ruddy fear.' His voice rose hysterically. 'Why, I'd rather shoot her myself.'

Herrod turned away in disgust. The fellow's as crazy as his damned sister, he thought. Then, remembering, he wheeled sharply.

'Did you engineer Vanne's accident this morning?'

'No, I did not.'

'Another of your sister's little pranks, eh?'

'Perhaps. She didn't say.'

'Too insignificant, I suppose,' Herrod said. 'But if you didn't know the car had been tampered with why were you following it? Where were you going?'

'To look for Landor's body,' Wilkes said harshly. 'If I could bury it in some unlikely spot before you or anyone else found it I knew Cathie would still have a chance. But her directions were too vague. You got there first.'

The room was hot and stuffy. Herrod nodded to Wood and the Inspector and walked out. He needed fresh air to clear his head, a cool breeze to blow away some of the filth that Watson and Wilkes seemed to have brought with them into the station. There was no more to be done in there. No more — until they found Catherine Wilkes. Or Vanne.

He opened the heavy door and went out to stand in Norton Street. The breeze was there, it blew up Fourth Avenue from the sea. Down there the lights were twinkling on Kingsway, couples were strolling along the front or down on the beach.

Were Vanne and the girl among them? Or were they in some more secret place?

The heavy door opened again, and Wood came to stand beside him.

'It's been quite a day,' said the Sergeant. 'I shan't be sorry when they pick those two up.'

'No use getting impatient,' Herrod said, ignoring his own impatience. 'If they're out for the evening, and if young Vanne doesn't do anything his mother wouldn't like him to do, we may have to wait some hours yet.'

'I hope not. What put you wise to the girl, Mr Herrod? I've been so busy chasing Wilkes all afternoon and evening that I haven't had a chance to ask you before.'

'Well, I suppose it was really Vanne's account of their visit to Cardiff Street. You remember they said that the girl was at the gate until Vanne had disappeared inside the building. Then, she said, she left her post to climb the steps, but was back at the gate in time to warn Vanne when he reappeared on the balcony.

'There was a flaw there; I wonder Vanne wasn't alive to it. Since they were positive that no one had entered the yard while Vanne was on view, how could this supposed gunman have known he was there? And if he didn't know Vanne had gone into the building why should he be waiting for him to come out?

'Another thing. Why only one shot? If it had been Landor or one of Watson's gang he'd have gone on banging away until he got him. Or until Vanne escaped. A second shot while Vanne was on the balcony, perhaps, another as he hit the shed roof, another as he went through the gate.

'But the girl dare not risk that. She couldn't be sure what Vanne would do. A two-five is not normally a lethal weapon except at close range and in the hands of an expert. If she went on firing and missing Vanne would reach the gate before her. That meant he would rumble her for certain.

'I couldn't be sure, of course. Not then. But when I found that photograph of Mrs Taylor in her bedroom, and knew that Wilkes had been lying — '

'Mr Herrod, sir!'

The two detectives turned quickly. It was the station sergeant.

'A call has just come through from Brighton, sir. A man has been shot up at St Anns Well.'

15

'No, I don't hate her,' Toby said. 'Even when — when it happened I don't think I hated her. I guess I was too terrified to feel any other emotion.' He looked at Wilkes's haggard, unhappy face. 'I — I sure am sorry. For you, I mean,' he said awkwardly.

They stood beside one of the several police cars that ringed St Anns Well. All down Nizells Avenue and Somerhill Road, as far as they could see, were policemen. Toby supposed there were other cars and other policemen on the far side of the garden, on Furze Hill.

Outside the cordon of police spectators stood in groups, some silent, some talkative, their numbers growing as the news spread. One such group had gathered on the pavement behind Toby and Wilkes; with every newcomer came the same questions, the same answers, the same excited speculation. Toby knew himself to be the cynosure of many pairs of eyes, and was duly embarrassed. He was glad that so far no one seemed to have probed Wilkes's identity.

He scarcely felt the wound in his arm, where the bullet had nicked the flesh; the second shot had missed. At the sound of the shooting people had come running to his aid, but none had ventured inside the garden. A woman from one of the houses opposite had deftly bandaged his arm; her husband had telephoned for the police. They had wanted to send for an ambulance, but Toby would not let them. He wanted to be there when the police arrived — to see, not to be told, the end of the affair.

The police had come almost before the woman had finished attending to his arm. Superintendent Herrod had not been one of the first; but when he did come he had asked Toby a few crisp questions, and had then left him with Wilkes. A couple of large policemen stood beside them. Toby supposed they were there to keep an eye on Wilkes, not on himself.

Wilkes seemed oblivious to all that

went on around him. He had spoken freely to Toby, telling him of his sister in short, jerky sentences. But all the time his eyes never left the dark interior of the garden. Was she still there? wondered Toby. Quick as the police had been, might there not have been time for her to escape?

That, he supposed, was what Wilkes was praying for — if a man such as Wilkes knew how to pray. Toby found himself adding his own prayer. He did not want her to be caught. Despite the death he had so narrowly escaped, he could not bear to think of her within the cold, narrow confines of a prison cell. Later, perhaps, he might think differently. All he knew now was that he wanted her to be free.

'I still can't believe it,' he said. 'She was so sure of herself, so — so real in the part she was playing. She *was* Crossetta Tait. Even the name . . . ' He told Wilkes the explanation the girl had given him. 'Could she have invented that on the spur of the moment? The way she said it, it sounded so convincing.'

'She loved to dramatize herself,' Wilkes said, still staring at the dark trees. Toby wondered at the past tense. Did the man think of her as already dead? 'That would be why she chose the rôle of a widow. Did she wear a wedding ring?'

'Yes.'

'She must have taken it from the dead girl.'

He showed no emotion in referring to his sister's victim. Toby's sympathy began to wane.

Superintendent Herrod came up to them, walking briskly, other police officers with him. 'I'm taking a loud-speaker car through the gates,' he said to Wilkes. 'I'm going to appeal to your sister to give herself up. If she's still in there she can't hope to get away. But she may listen to you where she won't listen to me. I want you to come with me.'

Wilkes nodded.

'We're going now,' Herrod said. 'Come.'

Toby watched the police car nose its way through the entrance, another following. They reached the pavilion and then stopped, parking obliquely, so that the headlights probed the darkness of the tree-studded garden.

He strained his eyes, endeavouring to see even beyond the light.

A crackling sound came from the loudspeaker on the leading car. The watching crowd was suddenly silent, tense with the expectation of drama (or would it be tragedy?) about to unfold before them.

Herrod's voice blared out into the night.

'Catherine Wilkes, this is Superintendent Herrod speaking. I want you to put down your gun and come out here with your arms above your head. You cannot escape from the garden; the whole area is surrounded. Do as I tell you and no one will harm you.'

The voice ceased. The silence was uncanny. Hundreds of pairs of eyes were fixed intently on the area of light, their owners scarce daring to breathe lest they should miss an instant glimpse of the hunted girl.

But no voice answered, no slim figure showed itself in the light. Gradually, at first in whispers and then more loudly, talk began again — only to die away as once more the loud-speaker challenged the night.

It was Wilkes's voice.

'Cathie, this is Nat. I want you to do as the Superintendent has told you. If there were any chance of escape I'd tell you to take it — and be damned to the police. But there isn't, Cathie. There's no way out but this.

'Come out, Cathie dear. Put down the gun and come out into the light where I can see you. I'm here, in the first car; I'll see that no one hurts you. You trust me, don't you?

'Please, Cathie! For my sake.'

The harsh voice ceased. But through the harshness the anguish and despair had been poignantly evident to the waiting crowd, and they were slow to break the silence.

Then, like a small breeze that suddenly blows up from nowhere on a still summer's day, a sibilant whisper rippled along the pavement, growing in volume as it went. A woman screamed.

389

Cathie Wilkes, gun in hand, walked slowly into the fringe of light. Her voice came faintly to those in Somerhill Road. Only the men inside the garden could catch the words.

'I want to talk to Nat,' she said. 'If anyone else comes near me I'll shoot.'

For a few seconds she stood there. Then she was lost in the shadows.

Inside the leading car Herrod looked doubtfully at Wilkes.

'Better let me go,' Wilkes said. 'I'll be safe enough.'

The Superintendent hesitated. This was a job for the police. They could rush her. In the darkness they could close in on her with little risk to themselves. She might have time to fire once, perhaps twice, before they got her. And it would be wild, haphazard shooting. She would probably miss.

But she might not. Had he the right to risk men's lives if an alternative offered?

'Very well,' he said curtly. 'Go ahead. If you can persuade her to hand over the gun, put it on the ground where we can see it. But no funny business, Wilkes. One false move and we'll rush the pair of you. And if we do that — well, some one is liable to get hurt.'

Without a word Nat Wilkes left the car and walked slowly over the grass to where Cathie had stood. As he got nearer he could see her waiting for him in the shadows. She still held the gun.

He stopped a few feet away, beckoning her into the light.

'Cathie!' he said. 'You little fool! Why did you do it?'

'Shoot Toby, you mean?' Her voice was untroubled. 'He tried to make love to me. It — it was disgusting.'

She frowned at the recollection.

'But why did you stay here?' he asked desperately. 'Why didn't you go before the police came?'

'I got confused. It was dark, and there seemed to be so many paths.' She looked past him to the waiting cars. 'Do they know everything, Nat? The others as well as Toby?'

'They know about Landor and the girl,' he told her. 'And the man at Forest Row. They say you killed the girl's husband too. Did you, Cathie?'

'Yes.'

'Why didn't you tell me?'

'I don't know. I suppose I forgot.'

'Will you tell me now?'

He did not really want to know. What could it matter to him how Taylor died? But now that he was with her he wanted to keep her there, to watch her and listen to her voice, to delay — for ever, if possible — the dread moment of return.

'It was on the Monday, I think,' she said, wrinkling her brows. 'Watson took him to the station, and I followed in Toby's car. Watson didn't wait to see him off, so I thought I'd find out which train he took. It was all part of the adventure, you see. I stood next to him at the bookstall. He didn't take any notice of me until he saw the handbag. This one.' She held it up, and the gilt initials glinted in the light. 'Then he grabbed my arm and accused me of stealing it. He said it belonged to his wife.

'People were watching us. I told him I could explain, and took him out to the car. I said his wife was a friend of mine,

392

that she had lent me the bag. He got very excited, and wanted me to take him to her. So I said I would.

'I drove along the front. I didn't know where we were going, and when we came to a town I drove through it until we came to a quiet place. Then I stopped the car and told him that was where his wife was staying.

'I shot him as he got out of the car. I took his wallet — I thought that might hamper the police — and pushed him into a ditch. I threw the wallet over the cliff on my way back.'

He had listened to her — and yet he had not listened. He had been hearing her voice, watching her face, imprinting her on his memory as though he were seeing her for the last time.

She sighed. 'Nat — what will they do to me?'

'Nothing, Cathie.' The hint of fear in her voice was like a dagger in his heart. 'I won't let them hurt you.'

'I don't mean now. But after? Will they put me in prison?'

'Yes. For a little while. But I shall be

allowed to see you.'

'And — after that?'

He did not answer. He could not bear to think of 'after that'.

'I don't mind dying,' she said. 'It doesn't hurt, it doesn't mean anything. One's just — dead. But I'm frightened, Nat. They'll say I'm mad, they'll shut me up in prison, in an asylum. I'll be there for ever.'

He tried to comfort her, but she would not be comforted. She was not crying, but she came to him and gripped his arm, and he could feel her body trembling.

'I tried to shoot myself, Nat. But I couldn't. Isn't that funny?' She gave a little hysterical laugh that was half a sob. 'That was why I wanted to see you. I want you to do it for me. Will you, Nat?'

'Cathie! I'm not a murderer!'

Instantly he regretted the words. But there was no bitterness in her voice as she said, 'Aren't you? I am.'

'But you're my sister, Cathie.'

'Yes. That's why I thought you would do it for me. No one else would.'

'Cathie, I can't. You don't know what

394

you're asking, I — '

'Please, Nat.'

To kill her — and have to go on living. How could she ask that of him? It would be like taking his own life, robbing himself of everything that was dear. Yet she was right — they might say she was insane, they might put her away for life. That would be a cruelty he could not bear to contemplate.

He shuddered. Was he thinking of himself — or of her? He had never had to ask himself that question before.

The girl's eyes were on his face, watching him, reading the struggle in his mind. And suddenly he could bear it no longer, and he smiled at her. All his love was in the smile, so that for a moment his ugly, misshapen face became transfigured.

'Give me the gun, Cathie dear,' he said quietly. 'We'll go together. We've always been together. They shan't part us now.'

She moved closer and handed it to him. He put an arm round her and bent to kiss her cheek. It was cold against his lips.

'Quickly, Nat,' she said. 'They're coming.'

He could hear the Superintendent's voice calling his name. Steadily his finger squeezed the trigger. The gun barked, there was the smell of cordite. Cathie gasped and shuddered. Her eyes closed, her slim body slid away from him.

Gently he laid her on the grass. Her eyelids trembled as though she were trying desperately to open them.

'Good-bye, Nat.' The words came faintly and very slowly. 'I'm sorry you can't come with me. That was the last bullet. That — was — why — '

He felt her body tremble. She sighed, a small, tremulous sigh. And then she died.

★ ★ ★

Gently he withdrew his arm from under her.

'Good-bye, Cathie,' he said.

For a moment he watched her, the tears running down his cheeks. Then he turned and walked unsteadily into the light towards the dark, advancing figures silhouetted against it.

We do hope that you have enjoyed reading this large print book.

Did you know that all of our titles are available for purchase?

We publish a wide range of high quality large print books including:
Romances, Mysteries, Classics
General Fiction
Non Fiction and Westerns

Special interest titles available in large print are:
The Little Oxford Dictionary
Music Book, Song Book
Hymn Book, Service Book

Also available from us courtesy of Oxford University Press:
Young Readers' Dictionary
(large print edition)
Young Readers' Thesaurus
(large print edition)

For further information or a free brochure, please contact us at:
Ulverscroft Large Print Books Ltd.,
The Green, Bradgate Road, Anstey,
Leicester, LE7 7FU, England.
Tel: (00 44) **0116 236 4325**
Fax: (00 44) **0116 234 0205**

Other titles in the
Linford Mystery Library:

THE FROZEN LIMIT

John Russell Fearn

Defying the edict of the Medical Council, Dr. Robert Cranston, helped by Dr. Campbell, carries out an unauthorised medical experiment with a 'deep freeze' system of suspended animation. The volunteer is Claire Baxter, an attractive film stunt-girl. But when Claire undergoes deep freeze unconsciousness, the two doctors discover that they cannot restore the girl. She is barely alive. Despite every endeavour to revive the girl, nothing happens, and Cranston and Campbell find themselves charged with murder . . .

THE SPACE-BORN

E. C. Tubb

Jay West was a killer — he had to be. No human kindness could swerve him from duty, because the ironclad law of the Space Ship was that no one — *no one* — ever must live past forty! But how could he fulfil his next assignment — the murder of his sweetheart's father? Yet, how could he *not* do it? The old had to make way for the new generations. There was no air, no food, and no room for the old . . .

THE SECRET POLICEMAN

Rafe McGregor

When a superintendent in the Security Branch is murdered, top detective Jack Forrester is assigned to the case. Realising his new colleagues are keeping vital information from him, Jack Forrester sets out to catch the killer on his own. But Forrester soon becomes ensnared in a web of drug traffickers, Moslem vigilantes, and international terrorists. As he delves deeper into the superintendent's past, he realises he must make an arrest quickly — before he becomes the next police casualty . . .